For Your Sins

Richard Pitman is a former champion jump jockey. During the past 30-odd years he has also presented horseracing on Sky TV on a weekly basis, written for national newspapers, bred thorough-breds and run a successful pre-training stable for top licensed trainers. Besides writing with Joe McNally, Richard has written six non-fiction books including the racing biography of the Queen Mother. He lives near The Valley of The Racehorse – Lambourn and is now retired.

Ex-stable lad Joe McNally first took an interest in racing when he was 12 years old. He and Richard first met when they both worked for racing broadcaster Satellite Information Services and their fiction-writing partnership grew from there. Joe went on to become marketing manager at Aintree and later commercial director on the board of Tote Bookmakers. He is semi-retired and living in Scotland.

T0312504

By Richard Pitman & Joe McNally

Bet Your Life
For Your Sins (previously *Joseph's Mansions*)
Dead Ringer
The Third Degree
Running Scared
Blood Ties
Hunted
Warned Off

Richard Pitman and Joe McNally

For Your Sins

HARPER

This novel is entirely a work of fiction.
The names, characters and incidents portrayed in it are
the work of the author's imagination. Any resemblance to
actual persons, living or dead, events or localities is
entirely coincidental.

Harper
An imprint of HarperCollins*Publishers*
1 London Bridge Street
London SE1 9GF

www.harpercollins.co.uk

This revised paperback edition 2015
1

First published in Great Britain by
HarperCollins*Publishers* 2001

Previously entitled *Joseph's Mansions*

A catalogue record for this book is
available from the British Library

ISBN: 9780008138363

Dear Reader,

If you are following the Eddie Malloy series, Eddie does not appear in this book. *For Your Sins* is the first book featuring Frankie Houlihan. Eddie and Frankie are featured working together in *Bet Your Life*.

Please note, this book has been re-titled for this edition; it was first published in print with the title *Joseph's Mansions*.

Richard and Joe.

For Tilly, with love

1

A black Mercedes pulled away from the main gate of Leopardstown racecourse and headed for Dublin.

The car was driven by Brendan Gleeson, a gambler who was seldom lucky and often drunk. His rear-seat passengers were his boss Kelly Corell, a gangster at the top of his game, and a young English scientist, David Hewitt.

The windows of the Mercedes were tinted dark green. They were bulletproof. The underside of the car was reinforced against explosives. Mister Hewitt did not know this. Nor did he know that Kelly Corell's right hand, the one he was shaking as they said farewell at the airport, had dried blood lodged below the signet ring he wore. Corell had not been as thorough as he usually was when cleaning up after slitting the throat of rival John O'Rourke in Corell's cellar games room that morning.

Hewitt got out of the car and said, 'It's been a pleasure meeting you at last Mister Corell. I'm so excited about working on this project with you. Thanks for the opportunity.'

'Ah, you're very welcome Mister Hewitt. It's a privilege for an entrepreneur like me to be able to support you. You'd not even be ruling out a Nobel Prize if you pull this one off, I'd think, eh?'

Hewitt laughed nervously. 'I'll settle for the professional satisfaction Mister Corell. It will be long and difficult; I don't want to build your expectations too high.'

'Time is something we have plenty of, and money too. Let me know when you've found the ideal property and I'll get my lawyers onto it.'

'I will, I will. My current project won't be completed for six months. You're sure that's okay?'

'Don't be worrying now. I'm an investor that takes the longer view for the bigger return.'

'That's such a novel thing to hear these days Mister Corell. You're a breath of fresh air, indeed!'

'Good man. Good luck.' Corell closed the door and returned Hewitt's goodbye wave. He smiled as he nudged Gleeson. 'I'm a breath of fresh air, Brendan, d'ye hear that!'

Gleeson looked at his boss in the mirror, unsure how to respond. 'I did, Mister Corell.'

Corell sat back, laughing. 'A breath of fresh fuckin' air! Get me home before I piss meself.'

Gleeson checked his mirrors and pulled away.

2

At the same time as Corell's car was travelling through Dublin, a field of steeplechasers thundered down the Cheltenham hill toward the third last jump, an obstacle notorious for ending dreams and sometimes lives.

A beautiful and famous young journalist, Kathy Spencer had chosen this race to make her debut as an amateur jockey on a horse called Zuiderzie. As the black fence loomed closer, Miss Spencer was losing control of her mount. Here is how she described in her globally syndicated column what happened next.

> My arms had been tiring gradually since we'd jumped the fifth-last and my legs, God, my legs! My thighs felt like my stretch marks had been laced with acid. I'd been training for six months for this, riding a saddle-less bike up hills, doing innumerable boring squats in the gym, running across sand dunes with a heavy backpack, and now my legs were getting their own back on me. The ache spread to my knees and ankles. I'd been perched in these stirrups for around seven minutes wrestling with this big chestnut thoroughbred and I realized as we came to the fence that Zuiderzie was winning the bout.
>
> My weakening fingers let the reins slip through and he stretched his head further to take advantage. The hill

increased his momentum. They tell me we were travelling at about thirty miles an hour. It felt like seventy. No windscreen here to dull the screaming gale, no brakes or steering wheel. Just half a ton of hard-trained muscle, flaring nostrils sucking air, veins filled, head bobbing, mane flying, doing what he loved, what every gene in him had been bred to do over thousands of years. And twenty strides from the big black birch fence, so stiff and broad I could have walked along the top of it, I accepted that I'd lost control.

Everything I'd been taught about trying to 'see a stride' (pick your point of take-off) and getting him organized for it was useless to me. My exhausted muscles couldn't deliver. I was aware now of those around me, hard-faced, half-starved jockeys who risked their lives regularly. Victory at Cheltenham was very sweet to most of these guys and they seemed to crowd me now, surround me in this mass of colour and sound, breaking what remained of my concentration.

Then we hit.

Zuiderzie took off far too late and slammed into the fence. I felt for an instant as though I'd been frozen in time. Then the momentum caught up with me and I felt myself catapulted skywards. It seemed a long time before I crashed. My brain desperately recalled the lessons of the past six months. Don't land on your head. Tuck it in as you approach the ground. Try to land on rounded shoulder- blades and start rolling immediately into a ball. There'll be other horses jumping just behind you, make yourself as small a target for their hooves as possible...

It had all seemed so practical and achievable sitting sipping coffee at the kitchen table. Come the day, I simply didn't know which way up I was until my back thumped into the life-saving lush turf, pounding the air from my lungs and slamming my helmeted head so hard on the ground that I lost consciousness.

When I opened my eyes, a priest was leaning over me. Last Rites were my first thought and I thanked God I had no children or husband to grieve and rage at my selfishness. Then, in the sweetest Irish accent I've ever heard, the priest said, 'Are you alright?'

I nodded.

''Twas a purler of a fall,' he said.

I smiled. 'I haven't heard that word for ages,' I said.

He looked vaguely puzzled. 'Purler?'

'Purler.' I mimicked his accent. I saw from his face, framed against the sky, that neither of us was sure that I wasn't in the first stages of delirium. He blushed. I said, 'Do you like swaddling?'

'It's OK. Haven't done it for ages myself.'

'The word, I mean! It's one of my favourite parts of Christmas; you get to hear the word "swaddling".'

He nodded. 'I think you'll be needing some treatment, Miss.'

'I think you might be right,' I said.

The priest's name was Frankie Houlihan, a Dubliner, who'd caught the racing bug from his father. The sport was his sole pastime since he'd been moved to his parish in England.

When the first-aiders scooped her up in a stretcher, she asked Frankie to come with her in the ambulance.

'I'm fine, thanks,' he said. 'I'll walk back for the fresh air.'

Kathy turned her head, which now housed a jackhammer ache. 'I want to say thank you properly.' Frankie hesitated.

'In a vertical position …'

Frankie smiled now.

'…without a funny hat on.'

He shook his head slowly. The stretcher-bearers stood at the open door of the ambulance looking at Kathy, then at Frankie. She said to him, 'You're keeping these guys waiting.' Still smiling, he moved forward and followed them into the ambulance.

3

It was a week before Kathy Spencer saw Frankie Houlihan again. She had come to his church to hear him say morning mass. When everyone left she sat silently in her pale blue dress, willing him to come back out the door which led to the sacristy. And he did, he came out singing softly, a song she didn't recognize. He didn't look her way but genuflected and went up to clear the altar in readiness for evening mass.

Coming back down the red-carpeted steps, he saw her and stopped. And smiled. She felt she should walk up the centre aisle to him but she was suddenly uncertain, nervous, her confidence slipping away. Afterwards they'd laugh about the noise his shoes made as he'd walked toward her. He'd changed into old crepe-soled comfortable shoes immediately after mass and they peeled themselves pore by pore from each polished rubber tile, the sound echoing in the vastness.

She was close to the end of the pew. He stopped. 'Hello again.'

'Hello to you, Father Frankie.'

They looked at each other; Kathy's instincts that she wanted this man to love her grew stronger. Frankie was aware only that, as with the first time, he was completely comfortable with her. Although this feeling was new to him, he had no reason to suspect that it was one he should worry about. His height, his athlete's frame, dark hair and fine features had made him the target of many girls as a teenager but he had never felt strongly for anyone other than his family members.

Kathy said, 'You're looking down at me again. You're always doing that.'

Frankie smiled. 'How's your head?'

'Fine. They kept me in overnight for observation and -'

'And you were out next morning after a hearty breakfast at Cheltenham General.'

'You saw it in the papers?'

'I did. I recognized the smile, which was about all I could see of you last week under that hard hat.'

'Saved my life that hat did.'

'Ahh, I think that oul' head of yours might have survived without it.'

'This "oul' head" as you put it has only been on my shoulders for twenty-eight years, I'll have you know.'

Frankie feigned surprise. 'And where did you keep it before then?'

'You're very forward, Father, considering we've only met twice.'

'Now, I've never been accused of that before! '

The banter continued over tea in the chapel house, with Frankie too naive, maybe, to think that Kathy's surprise arrival meant anything more than she said it did; to say a proper thank you to him. He walked her to her car that day assuming that when he closed the door he would never see her again. Only as her BMW disappeared through the gates did the slight twinge of regret at her going give any warning of what lay ahead.

Come spring, they were seeing each other twice most weeks, always away from the church. He hadn't yet been to her home. Neither had said anything about their feelings. Kathy was happier than she had ever hoped to be, simply being with him. Although she wanted him to tell her how he felt, she recognized that it wasn't necessary.

That autumn, on a glorious October day by the banks of the South Oxford Canal, without breaking his stride or turning to look at her Frankie said, 'I'm thinking of leaving the priesthood.'

They walked another ten paces before she replied, quietly, 'It's a big step, Frankie.'

It had been almost a year they had been friends. Still they'd said nothing more intimate to each other than 'I enjoy your company' and 'You make me laugh'.

Frankie said, 'Tis. It's been in my mind for a while now.'

She knew the tortures he must have gone through and the thought of his pain hurt her. She longed to hold him and sympathize but she could not break their unspoken agreement. Whatever weight of argument Frankie had built to justify leaving or not leaving, she could not risk adding a single gram to it. The decision had to be his alone.

She prepared herself for what she knew he'd say next. They were still walking, hadn't broken stride. In the same even voice he said, 'I want to spend the next month praying every day for God's guidance.'

'That's OK. I have my winter project to prepare for.' She worried it had come out a little too pat, too hurried.

'I won't be able to see you,' he said.

She thought she detected a slight tremor in his voice. She said, 'I understand. I'll pray for you too.'

'Thanks.'

4

Frankie made his way through Dublin's streets on foot. He'd arrived by air an hour before. On past visits, he'd always hurried to his family. This time his first destination was Holy Cross College.

The archbishop's house, a square mansion of granite, was in the grounds of the College. In the final half-mile as he closed on the meeting place, Frankie kept up the rhythm of his step and had to resist the urge to swing his arms like a sergeant major. Marching on, head up, his way of steeling himself, of keeping his mood confident. He needed to speak to Archbishop Mahoney secure in the belief he'd now formed; it was vital, in his mind, to accomplish what he'd come for. There was no room in him for nerves, for self-doubt. He'd been all the way along that tortuous path, spent dark nights in his own Gethsemane.

Frankie turned off Clonliffe Road to go through the shiny black metal gate, beyond which the entry to the house lay. He fixed his eyes on the door and as he walked the rich brown block paving, the door opened and Archbishop Mahoney himself stood in the doorway dressed the same as Frankie, smiling and slowly raising both hands straight in front of him, tilting his small, almost bald head to the right, his eyes twinkling with genuine warmth and affection. He put his arms around the young priest he'd ordained eight years previously and said, 'Francis, Francis, welcome home!' and Frankie rested his head briefly on the old man's left shoulder, smelling the soap on his skin, battling his emotions, his sudden need to weep. The Garden of Gethsemane came to his mind once more. His image of himself this time was as Judas.

The archbishop led him along varnished floors of old knotted boards, past paintings of the saints hanging below ceilings of varying heights, in rooms whose difference in size would have been plain to a blind man listening to acoustic effects in the voices of the pair as they moved through the house. The room they sat down in had walls the colour of the reeds carried on Palm Sunday. The big pale green chairs that held them faced each other across a wide hearth backed by a tall marble mantelpiece, above which hung a life-size painting of Pope Pius XII.

The deep sills of two arched windows held fat pink vases filled with fresh flowers. Their scents perfumed the room. Dusk was falling. Six sets of candle-shaped lights burned around the walls, casting a glow, which Frankie thought made the old man look even more serene. The archbishop sat with his hands together in his lap, legs crossed at the ankles. His black shoes shone but Frankie noticed a tiny tear in the right one, just on the fold of the instep. He looked up slowly. All the small talk had been disposed of on the journey to this room. It was time to say the words he had rehearsed so often that he imagined the letters in them to be worn at the edges from the millions of times they had tumbled around inside his head.

He sat forward, elbows on knees, hands clasped loosely and said, 'Archbishop, I have news for you that you would not be expecting to hear. I have decided to give up my vocation. I have decided to leave the formal ministry.'

The old man's smile never changed. He nodded slowly. 'You used the word "decided" twice, Frankie. You are a man who's very definite about what he's going to do.'

'There is no need for me to explain to Your Grace how much thought and prayer I have given to this in the past months. Your Grace will know me well enough to be aware of that.'

'How many months?'

Frankie steepled his fingers then flattened them to join his hands. 'Almost nine, Archbishop.'

They sat looking at each other. The temptation came to Frankie, as he'd known it would, to fill the silence with heartfelt explanations and pleas for understanding and forgiveness, but saying nothing, maintaining the dignity, was what he had prepared so hard for. Any gushing now of the pain of all this, of his sorrow and deep sadness, would only serve his own selfishness. The archbishop would know everything Frankie had been through. He'd been eighteen when he'd first met the old man who sat across from him The archbishop knew him better than his own father had.

For half an hour, they talked. The archbishop asked her name, what she was like. He tried gently but firmly to get Frankie to reconsider, to seek counselling. Frankie held out against the pleas.

The old man gripped his shoulder. 'Human love changes, Frankie, as people get older. It can fade. God's love is constant.'

'I know, Your Grace,' Frankie said quietly.

He sighed. 'You know, but you won't change your mind?'

'No, Your Grace.'

The archbishop stood up and walked to the mantelpiece to look down at Frankie. 'You'll give them some time to find a replacement, Frankie?'

'Of course, Archbishop.'

'Three months?'

'Three months will be fine, Your Grace.'

There was a silence. For the first time Frankie looked away from the face of the older man. There was no relief in him, only sadness. The flower scents hung heavy. It was almost dark beyond the arched windows. The bare fireplace seemed as cold and empty as his heart. He felt a light touch on his forehead and looked up. The old man smiled and ruffled his hair. Frankie wept.

5

He made his way down O'Connell Street through the light rain, bypassing the taxi ranks. The walk to his mother's house in Infirmary Road was a long one, but Frankie needed the time it would take to marshal his thoughts. He went into a hardware shop and bought a black umbrella with a shiny wooden handle.

Turning south on Drumcondra Road, he tried to get back into the marching rhythm he'd adopted as he'd gone to the cathedral but his legs wouldn't obey. The dread in his heart at the prospect of telling his mother weighed heavy, making him almost drag his steps. His mother, who had raised him since he drew his first breath to be a priest. His mother who, as she clutched the hands of midwives and pushed him out into the world, had had the priest standing by to bless not just him but the hospital cot that was to be his first bed. His mother who had insisted that the blood and placenta remnants be washed from his howling body with nothing but holy water. His mother whose life had been stained by bitterness and bigotry. The only thing she had to boast about, the single source of pride in her existence was her son, Father Francis Houlihan. Involuntarily, he drew a huge breath and the sigh that carried it back out made the woman approaching him raise her head to look.

She was pulling a battered metal shopping trolley with squeaking wheels, on which balanced a suitcase. She looked up at Frankie as they passed each other, and he saw the tears on her cheeks and pain in her eyes. He stopped, forgetting his own troubles, and looked at her as she went away from him. 'Are you alright missus?' he called, surprising himself with the richness of his own accent.

She didn't turn round and he watched as she reached the junction and turned to go down O'Connell Street, Frankie flushed the rain from his umbrella, put it above his head once more and continued the journey to his mother's house.

Bridget Gleeson, the tearful woman with the suitcase, had heard the priest call her, but she had no faith in the Catholic Church anymore and little faith in anything else. It had been knocked out of her physically and emotionally, and she was now doing what she had long promised she would. Bridget was the mother of twelve-year-old Sean and the wife of alcoholic Brendan, chauffeur to gangster Kelly Corell. She had held on as long as she could, but a woman could only take so much when she was thirty-seven, her life withering further from every drunken beating and the happiness she'd always wished for looking beyond hope.

Leaving Brendan now, just after their fifteenth wedding anniversary, caused her no sadness. His years of losing money to bookmakers and casinos had condemned them to a life of poverty. And she had struggled on because there was always some love there for him and she hadn't wanted Sean to suffer from a break-up.

But a year previously Brendan had started drinking heavily too, and taking everything out on her. She'd sworn she'd stand for most things but not for being battered. She'd warned him. Now he'd wake up from his stupor on the floor by the gas fire (many times she'd been tempted to leave the gas on and unlit for she knew the first thing he did when coming round was light a cigarette) and see she'd finally gone.

She'd miss her son. Someday she'd come back for him or bring him to her. They had lived in St Joseph's Mansions all their married life and she recalled many good times there. Sean had loved it; the enclosed playground, the hordes of playmates. And she'd been happy there too in what had been a close and supportive community.

Then the drug-dealers had moved in, making junkies of the teenagers, then corpses of the junkies. It had spread like cancer through the Mansions, devouring the extremities first then moving with grim inevitability through the body until the heart of the community was barely beating. The Gleesons were one of only three families remaining and now, Bridget thought, there'd be one Gleeson less. St Joseph's Mansions was a ghetto, and living in a ghetto had never been in Bridget Gleeson's life-plan.

Sean wiped the cold wet windowpane with the corner of his bed sheet, the image of his mother slinking away in the November rain still strong in his mind. What made him saddest was the sight of those old canvas moccasins she wore, lest the click-clack of her street shoes woke his father.

She had begged him to go with her. 'I can't, Ma. I can't leave the ponies.' Sean was one of many boys in Dublin who raced ponies. Most of them did it for a laugh, for the crack, but Sean did it because he wanted to make a career of it; he wanted to become a proper jockey.

'Ma, you know Mister Cosgrave's looking for a new boy. They're all sayin' it and my name's been mentioned.'

She looked frustrated. 'Mister Cosgrave's a proper trainer; he's not interested in street races and kids like you. I'm sorry, Sean, I don't mean to hurt ye and I know how good a rider ye are, but Mister Cosgrave lives in a different world.'

'Well that's the world for me, Ma. It's not this one in the Mansions. I'll not be here forever. When I go over to England, 'twill be as a proper jockey to ride in the Cheltenham Gold Cup.'

He'd watched her pretty face crease in sorrow. He sensed that she wanted to reach and cuddle him. But he was too old for that now and it had been her choice anyway.

Her tears rose again. Sean said, 'Don't cry, Ma. We'll all be back together before you know it and me da'll be fine. I've a good strong feelin' it'll all work out.'

The second-storey flat Sean lived in was one of two hundred and eighty-six that made up St Joseph's Mansions. The drug-dealers and their customers had turned the block into a warren of squalor; a disease-ridden, graffiti-strewn monolith whose stairwells and flaking corridors stank of urine and faeces. Apart from the Gleesons, only two families remained, both determined not to give in to the criminals who still used the place for their night-time dealings.

The Gleesons refused to move partly because Sean had so many happy memories of growing up there and wanted to stay, but mostly because Brendan, Sean's father, had always plied his 'trade' in this area. For five years, he had worked for Dublin's richest and most successful criminal, Kelly Corell. Part of Gleeson's work was occasional drug dealing and this was where his market was. While his neighbours had battled to keep the dealers out, Brendan Gleeson had joined the enemy.

Corell knew that Gleeson's skills were limited but he did what he was told and the next job Corell wanted doing wasn't difficult. The main thing was that if something went wrong, Gleeson wouldn't be missed. He was the most expendable of Corell's men.

6

Brendan Gleeson could not remember being so nervous, so stressed as he felt on this drive. He was with his boss in south-west England. Corell was in the rear seat of a hired Mercedes and his temper was getting shorter. Gleeson couldn't find the house he was supposed to be taking Corell to and he was sweating, close to panic. Corell was a great guy to be with when he was in good form, but Gleeson knew how quickly his moods changed. He'd seen Corell's appetite for violence at first hand, having witnessed the man spreadeagling one of his criminal rivals on a snooker table and hammering six-inch nails through his screaming enemy's hands until they'd split the polished wood of the surround.

Gleeson had pulled into the side of the road near the top of a hill. He had lost count of the times he'd unfolded the fax. It was grubby and dog-eared and the interior light in the hire car wasn't bright. Gleeson screwed his eyes up as he tilted the paper under the weak, pinkish beam. 'About a mile and a half outside Lambourn on the B4001, near the top of the hill. Turn left along a road which goes through tall trees and drive to the big gates at the end then ring the bell.'

Corell watched him. 'Does it say anything different from the last ten times you looked at it, Brendan?'

Turning to face his solemn passenger Gleeson said, 'Mister Corell, this is the bloody B4001. I've been up and down it for the past half-hour and there's no road! Look!' He tried to give the sheet to Corell who kept his hands on his thighs.

'His number's on it,' Corell said. 'Call him and tell him you're sorry to drag him out on such a cold night, but you're such a shite driver that you can't get me there without help.'

Gleeson looked at him and decided not to argue.

Fifteen minutes later, he was driving behind David Hewitt's black Audi Quattro. He felt calmer. Hewitt had been decent to him, told him the turnoff was almost impossible to find in the dark. He said quite a few missed it in daylight too. Gleeson said he wouldn't mind having his maximum bet that the turn-off wasn't on this road at all. Hewitt had smiled and said, 'Follow me.' Corell left the Mercedes and travelled with Hewitt.

7

Hewitt drove fast but skilfully. Corell said, 'I don't suppose you're looking for a chauffeur's job?' Hewitt chuckled. 'You shouldn't be too harsh on your man, Mister Corell. You'll see when we get there; it isn't the easiest of roads to find. I should have remembered you might be travelling in the dark when I faxed the instructions.'

'You coulda rolled out a ball of string from here to Dublin and he still wouldn't've been able to follow it back.'

'That bad?'

Corell smiled, remembering that he needed Hewitt to have some trust in Gleeson's ability to set him up with a decent supplier. 'Nah, he's a good man, really. He's no genius, is Brendan, but he's smart enough and you can count on him to do what he's told. He'd walk off a cliff if I asked him to, so he would.'

'You must treat him well, if he shows that sort of respect.'

Corell resisted making a clever remark. He realized Hewitt believed what Corell had told him when they'd first met at Leopardstown, that he was simply a businessman. Most people in Corell's world could interpret the euphemism well enough, but he was conscious that Hewitt came from a completely different background.

Corell rarely set up deals personally; there was too much risk involved. But this one, if Hewitt managed to deliver, would be the biggest Corell would ever do. He replied to the scientist's question,

'I'd like to think I have the respect of all the people who work for me,'

'I'm sure that I too will find our association a pleasure,' Hewitt replied.

'And a profitable pleasure, too. That's what we all want,' Corell said as they approached the high black gates.

When they got through the entrance and parked, an animated Gleeson came quickly from his car. When Corell opened his door, Gleeson leaned forward, almost blocking his way, and said, 'Road! That was never a road! Jeez, they talk about Ireland being a backward country! That was a pig-track, Mister Corell!' He looked across at Hewitt. 'No offence to your directions there, Mister Hewitt, but Christopher bloody Columbus couldn't have found that turning!'

Hewitt smiled kindly at him. 'He only found America by mistake, so you're probably right.' Gleeson went round the car to cement the alliance and stayed close to Hewitt as they walked across the gravel, almost jostling him as he sought vindication, leaning over and looking up into the taller man's face. 'Ye couldn't blame anybody for missing that now, could ye? I mean, what chance've ye got when the directions says a road and it's no more a road than... well, it's like sayin' look out for a racehorse and what ye find's a bloody donkey, eh?'

As Hewitt used his thumb to key a four-figure code into a control panel to the right of the double door, Gleeson was uncrumpling the old fax once more; moving beside his boss again and pointing to the words he said, 'Look, road, road! Road my arse!'

Corell said, menacingly quiet, 'Give it a rest.'

Inside, seated in what seemed to Gleeson like a library, he declined the offer of a drink. He was dying for one, but he knew he had a drink problem and he didn't want Corell to get a sniff of that. If the man found out, Gleeson would be redundant. 'Ahh, a glass of lemonade would be fine,' he said, trying to look enthusiastic about it.

'There might be some in the kitchen,' Hewitt said. 'Bear with me.'

When he left the room, Corell turned to Gleeson; 'Drink the friggin' lemonade then tell him you've got to go to the car and make a few calls. Wait there until I'm done.'

Out in the cold, Gleeson watched through the window as Hewitt poured a big measure of whiskey from a decanter and handed the glass to Corell. Gleeson sighed and wandered toward the car.

Hewitt toasted Corell. 'To success.'

'Success.' Corell saluted with his glass and said, 'Would you bring me up to date, now, on how things are?'

'Sure.' Hewitt outlined the scope of the project with great enthusiasm. The young scientist didn't bullshit; he told Corell the timescales were completely unpredictable and that long-term resources would be necessary. 'No problem,' Corell told him. 'Now what about the raw materials?' He smiled.

'As I mentioned on the phone, I need to establish a regular supply of racehorses. I'd want each for twenty-four hours maximum. They don't have to be racing currently and there'd be no necessity for them to be completely sound, certainly not for this stage of the project.'

Corell nodded. 'I was thinking of setting up a deal with a fella in an abattoir. He brings you horses he's picked up for slaughter. You do what you need to then he collects them. We pay him two hundred and fifty pounds a time. How does that sound to you?'

'Would you be prepared to pay more if the horse has some talent?'

'If it helps you along with the project, no problem.' Corell smiled. 'Mister Gleeson will sort everything out for you within the next forty-eight hours.'

'Good. And you brought the cash?'

'It's in the car. A bloody big bag of it.'

'Sterling?'

"Tis.'

'Good.'

Corell drank what remained in his glass. Hewitt, looking serious, leant forward, elbows on knees and said, 'Just to be clear - Mister Gleeson's not aware of the actual project we're working on here?' Corell shook his head. 'He knows what he needs to. He won't ask questions.'

Hewitt nodded. He said, 'And you don't mind if I call you direct if I have a problem? I know you must be a busy man.'

Corell got to his feet. 'I don't mind at all. This is probably the most important project I've ever launched. I'll give you whatever help I can.'

Hewitt smiled warmly and reached to shake his hand. 'I'm sure we'll make a good team.'

8

Frankie returned to his parish and began preparing for his final three months. Although he longed to see her, to hear her voice, it didn't seem right to call Kathy on the first day back in England. He waited three days before ringing.

They met on a mellow mid-November afternoon in a park in Cheltenham. The sun was low, its weak, watery light just enough to cast shadows on the paths which were sticky with wet leaves. He watched her come toward him, the first time they'd met for more than six weeks. She wore a long dark coat, buttoned, with the collar turned up. A white cashmere scarf filled the V at the top, accentuating the rich shades of her olive skin. Frankie drew an involuntary breath; he'd forgotten how beautiful she was.

She smiled as she stopped in front of him and the temptation to throw his arms around her and hold her was the strongest impulse by far he had ever experienced. But he resisted. 'Hello Kathy,' he said and held out his hand awkwardly.

'Hello Frankie.' She shook his hand, careful not to hold on a second longer than might seem proper. 'It's good to see you.'

'Good to see you too.' A smile found its way through the frown that had seemed almost constant these past weeks. 'Do you want to walk, or would you like to go and have a drink somewhere?'

'Let's walk,' she said and they ambled off, settling deeper into that comfortable companionship with each stride. A lone mallard glided on a leaf-strewn pond.

'My last day in the formal ministry is January thirty-first.'

She nodded slowly. They walked ten paces before she spoke. 'Does that mean it's your last day as a priest?'

'Once a priest, always a priest. That's what we were taught. There's no renouncing of the vows, only the breaking of them. But I suppose that is what it means, my last day as a priest.'

They walked on for a while in silence, then Kathy said, 'Are you OK?'

'I'll be fine. There are some practical things to sort out and I might need to ask your advice on some of the stuff I need to plan for, sort of post-ministry, if you know what I mean.'

'Sure, I'll help in any way I can. How did your mother take the news?'

He sighed. 'As though she'd just found out there was no God after all. 'Twas like the end of the world, Judgement Day, and she was stood there waiting for the Lord to appear and tell all the good people that the day of reward was here only to have the Devil himself come out on stage and say, "Surprise, surprise."'

Kathy smiled gently and watched her suede-booted feet step in time with Frankie's black brogues. Frankie said, 'I thought we were going to have to call the doctor out to sedate her.'

'Is she alright, though?'

'She's well enough to write me letters cursing me to eternity. There are holes in the pages of them where her rage has forced the nib through. And she's well enough to have warned the family under pain of death to have nothing to do with me. If I were to die tomorrow, which she says she hopes I will for I've shamed her so that she can never again show her face in the streets of Dublin, she's forbidden every one of them from attending my funeral.'

'Maybe you shouldn't open any more of her letters.'

'I think you're right. I'll see.'

'Don't do it as a penance, Frankie.'

He realized, once again, how well she knew him. 'I won't.'

Frankie's final day was a Tuesday. Bitterly cold morning winds carried the smell of snow, and Frankie worried about his successor, Father Boyle, slipping on the ice, which was thick as armour in places. He'd had breakfast with the elderly priest, then went to pick up the single suitcase he'd packed the night before. Returning to the warm kitchen, he said goodbye to Father Boyle but got no response. The old man was asleep.

Frankie went through the sacristy door for the last time and into the freezing church. His breath drifted like a cloud of incense. He walked to the altar and knelt. He bowed his head and tried to think of an appropriate prayer. It was too late to say sorry and he was certain that God didn't want an apology anyway. He whispered, 'Thy will be done,' then got up and walked down the centre aisle to leave by the main door, which he pulled shut behind him without turning round. The echo boomed in the cold, thin, empty air.

Frankie had sold his car when he first faced the prospect of unemployment, so Kathy had offered to pick him up, but he'd said he'd rather walk to her door from the station. In the last hundred yards along a secluded tree-lined drive, Frankie marvelled at how grand her house was. He arrived at the door rosy-cheeked and rang the bell.

It was almost a minute before he heard a sound and he was beginning to worry. Then the door opened and she stood there in tight black ski pants and a yellow T-shirt. This was the first time he had seen her casually dressed. He liked the fact that she'd chosen this day. He noticed that she had a tea towel in her right hand. She smiled. 'Sorry, I was doing the dishes. Come in.' She stepped back. He went in and stood in the big bright hall, looking up at the ceiling, which seemed very high. A triple-shaded light hung on a brass chain.

He realized she'd closed the door and he turned slowly, taking in the newness, the dried flowers in large pots on the black and white tiled floor, the polished table with Queen Anne legs, the almost see- through cream drapes. She watched him, his fine-featured face seeming childlike as he surveyed his surroundings. He wore a heavy overcoat bought from a charity shop. It made him look older; it was a middle-aged man's coat. She had seen the brown corduroy trousers before too, and the soft tan shoes. The suitcase, ancient as it was, was new to her. 'You can put your suitcase down here, if you want,' she said.

He nodded and bent at the knees, straight-backed to lower it to the floor so slowly it made no sound. 'Got nitro-glycerine in there?' Kathy asked.

Frankie shrugged. 'I didn't want to scratch your floor. The house is amazing.' He was looking through the door into a big room where a log fire burned in an inglenook fireplace.

'Come in and have a proper look. I'll take your coat. Do you want some tea or a drink? Beer or whiskey or something soft?'

He followed her into the room. 'A whiskey would be nice. Warm me up. It's cold out there. Nice but cold.' He smiled nervously at her.

'Sit by the fire. Get warm. I'll fix you a drink.' She went into the kitchen. He couldn't see her as she called, 'Want anything in your whiskey?'

'Some ice, if you have it.'

He heard the clink and she came back, a glass in each hand. They stood on the thick Indian rug in front of the fire. She raised her glass. 'Welcome.'

He raised his. 'It's nice to be here. I like your house. I never pictured you living alone in such a big place.'

'Probably psychological compensation for having nothing but a bed and a locker when I was a kid.'

'In the orphanage?'

She nodded. They sipped their drinks. 'You've done well for yourself,' he said.

'It doesn't really mean much to me, not anymore.'

He shifted awkwardly and drank again. She said, 'My priorities changed around fifteen months ago. Every minute that I've spent with you has meant more to me than any of this, anything money can buy.' He reddened and looked down at the rug. 'Don't look away from me now, Frankie Houlihan. We've spent almost a year and a quarter in small talk and I promised myself every night before I went to sleep that I wouldn't waste a single minute more…' She eased the drink from his fingers and put it alongside her own on the high dark stone mantelpiece. She took his hands in hers, held them softly and said, 'I love you.'

Letting her hands go, he opened his arms slowly, a gesture he had performed before only at the consecration of the Blessed Sacrament. She stepped forward and he gathered her in until her head rested on his left shoulder and her arms were around him. They stayed that way for a long time before Kathy spoke softly. 'If you knew how much I've longed for this.'

'Me too,' he said. 'I love you, Kathy.'

She held him tighter and her tears flowed silently in celebration. After a minute she wiped them and made space between her and Frankie so she could kiss him.

'God, this is the part I've been dreading!' he said, looking genuinely worried.

'Well, thanks a million!' she smiled, cheeks still wet.

'You know what I mean. I haven't done this since I was at school.'

'It's not rocket science, Frankie, just pucker up those lips.' She laughed.

Shutting his eyes, he tried to do what she said, making her laugh more. 'I was only kidding! You don't need to pucker up! Just relax.'

'Can I keep me eyes closed?'

'If you like.'

He did. She kissed him gently and primly for a few seconds, then pulled away. 'Here endeth lesson one. You can open your eyes, sonny.'

He opened them and they laughed together.

9

It was past noon when Brendan Gleeson woke in his bedroom in the Chequers Hotel in Newbury. He'd had to drive Corell to the airport before returning to the hotel last night, and he'd been determined to make up for lost drinking time. Checking his watch, he saw he was already ten minutes late for his meeting with the slaughter man. 'Shit!' he said and reached for his jacket, which lay on the floor. If he messed this up Corell would go crazy. From his jacket pocket, he pulled the fax with Hewitt's directions on it. He'd written the slaughter man's mobile number at the bottom. He dialled it, hands shaking from the effects of the alcohol. Monroe answered on the first ring and told Gleeson he was waiting for him downstairs. 'Gimme five minutes,' Gleeson said, and went to the bathroom to throw water on his face.

The slaughter man was sitting in the corner with two untouched half-pints of orange juice on the table. That was the sign they'd agreed on the phone so Gleeson would recognize him. It had been the slaughter man's idea; Gleeson was impressed but couldn't wait for a drink. Raising a thumb to the man and smiling, he motioned to the bar and went to get himself a drink. He carried a pint of Guinness and a large whiskey and lemonade to the table. 'Mister Monroe?' he said.

'Mister Gleeson.'

'That's right.' He put the drinks down and they shook hands. Gleeson sat across from him and drank half of the Guinness then nodded to the orange juice. 'Want a proper drink?'

'No thanks.'

Gleeson drank again, watching Monroe. 'You look worried, Mister Monroe.'

'Should I be?'

'Not so far as I'm concerned. I just wanted to put a little business proposal your way so you can make yersel a few quid.'

'Doing what?'

'Before we talk about that, you need to understand the importance of keeping this quiet. Whether you decide to do it or not, you can't talk about it. Not now, next week, next year, whenever. It's important for your own, eh, what do they say these days, quality of life?'

'You already said all this on the phone. I told you, I don't have a problem with keeping my mouth shut.'

Gleeson smiled and drank some more. He liked the fact that this guy was so easily wound up. He much preferred dealing with people he could boss around. Guys like Hewitt that had some sort of special brief from Corell and acted almost like his boss, he found hard to cope with. But the Monroes of this world let him act superior. He said, 'The people who gave me this project are very serious about confidentialism.'

Monroe frowned in puzzlement at the word. Gleeson continued, 'They are men that secrecy and loyalty mean a lot to.' Gleeson loved to hint about IRA connections; his accent was a bonus for this sort of stuff.

'Is that a threat?' Monroe asked.

'Not at all. I just want to make sure you know what the, eh, whole package is.'

'Well, I told you, I don't have a problem with it! ' His voiced was raised.

Gleeson looked around. They were alone in the bar. 'Keep the head, son, and I'll buy you a hat.'

Monroe's ice-blue eyes glinted with anger and he lifted a glass and drank some orange juice, put it back down and folded his arms.

Gleeson lit a cigarette and drank some whiskey. 'Now,' he said, 'this is the deal. You know the racehorses you get to take for the slaughter?'

'Yes.'

'Well I want you to take a little detour on the way to the slaughterhouse and let a friend of mine borrow them for a day.'

'Borrow?'

'Before you shoot them.'

'You're kidding!'

'Now why would I be flyin' from Dublin, payin' all that money in air fares to sit here kiddin' with you?'

Arms still folded, Monroe shook his head slowly. 'Where does your friend live?' he asked.

'Near Lambourn.'

'Whereabouts?'

'Are you interested?'

'What's the money like?'

'Two hundred and fifty pounds a horse, minimum.'

Monroe sat forward. 'How many horses?'

'As many as you can get - but they need to be racehorses and if you can get a good one the money goes up.'

'What does he want to do with them?'

Gleeson slugged from the whiskey glass then smiled. 'He's going to tie his washing between two of them and make them run round the garden until it's dry.'

Monroe didn't smile.

Gleeson said, 'It doesn't matter to you what he does with them, does it? You drop them off, then pick them up a few hours later, collect your money then go and do your job.'

Monroe stared at him for a while then said, 'OK. I'll do a couple and see how it goes. Who pays me?'

'My friend does.'

'Where do I take them to?'

'We'll drive up there and I'll show you. It's a hard place to find.'

'When do I start?'

'Yesterday.'

'We'd better move then.' He got up. Gleeson finished both drinks. Monroe jangled his car keys as he watched Gleeson drain the glasses. 'I think I'll drive, eh?'

Gleeson smiled at his sarcasm. 'Sure. So long as you can bring me back.'

They got outside and he said to Gleeson, 'If something happens and your scam goes tits up, I'll deny I had anything to do with it.'

'Listen, son, if anythin' happens you will keep your mouth completely shut. I don't exist. Neither does the guy we're going to meet. Understand?' Monroe scowled and turned away toward the car. Passing through Lambourn village Monroe said, 'Where did you get my name and number?'

'A friend of mine in Ireland. Said he thought you might be up for it.'

'What's his name?'

'It doesn't matter. You're here now so he was right, wasn't he?'

As they turned along the track leading to the house on the hill, Monroe said, 'I know this place. A guy called Kennedy used to train here. Went bust and did a moonlight about three years ago.'

'Is that so?' Gleeson asked in an uninterested voice as he looked out of the window at the thick woods bordering the narrow track on both sides.

Monroe said, 'How long's your man been here?'

'The less you know, the better for you, son. I just want you to meet Hewitt so you know where you're going and who's paying you.'

They trundled toward the big gates in silence, Monroe's jaw set hard and his eyes glinting with anger. He didn't like the way Gleeson spoke to him. As he braked to a halt, he noticed the closed- circuit camera mounted high on the black gatepost turn toward the car. 'Is that attached to a recorder?' he asked.

Gleeson didn't know but wouldn't admit to that. 'I told you, the less you know the better. If you want to ask questions, take your nice looks and go get a job on a quiz show.'

Monroe pulled the handbrake and turned to Gleeson. 'Listen, mate, two hundred and fifty pounds isn't a lot of money and you want me to risk my job for it. I'm not bringing a horsebox up here every couple of days for it to be caught on tape when I don't know what's happening at this place or where the tape's going.'

Gleeson smiled at him patronizingly. 'Stop worrying, son. If you don't want the job, just tell me now before I ring the bell. You can head back to the slaughterhouse and keep shooting cows for two hundred and fifty pounds a week if you want. Four horses a week for here makes a grand.'

Monroe looked away and revved the engine hard. Gleeson said, 'Is that a yes or a no?'

'I told you in the hotel, I'll try a couple. If I don't like it after that I won't do any more.'

'Stop whinging, then. Let's go in and see Mister Hewitt.'

As he drove Gleeson back to his hotel, Monroe wondered what Hewitt was doing up there, why he wanted the horses. He wasn't a horseman; Monroe noticed it when he shook hands. Hewitt had a pen and a little notebook in his top shirt pocket, and there had been a white garment on the arm of the chair in the room they'd been in. He'd thought it was a dressing gown at first but it had been more like a hospital gown or a lab coat. Still, Hewitt seemed much more civilized than Gleeson, had better manners. Monroe glanced at him as he pulled up outside the Chequers and decided that a chimp had better manners than the Irishman, so he probably wasn't paying Hewitt any compliments.

Gleeson got out then stooped and looked into the car at Monroe. 'Thanks. I'll say farewell. There'll not be any need for us to meet again unless you decide you're going to be a naughty boy.'

'Yeah, if I do you'll be the first to know, Mister Gleeson.'

'You're right. I will be,' he said, trying to look stern and dangerous. Monroe smiled dismissively, shook his head and drove away.

Gerry Monroe had a natural affinity with horses, especially thoroughbreds. Horses did things willingly for Monroe that they'd do for others only under duress. Horses would even run their hearts out for him and that quality alone would have made him a great jockey, which was what he'd wanted to be.

But his personal tragedy was that he was too heavy to ride on the flat, and he'd found out very quickly in his brief career as a jump jockey that he didn't have the nerve for it. As much as he trusted his own ability, however much his mount would give in effort, Monroe was terrified at the prospect of attacking those big black fences on half a ton of galloping muscle and bone surrounded by others, all travelling at thirty miles an hour, being squeezed up, jostled, forced into errors that might see him crashing to the ground.

During the twenty-seven races he rode in before retiring, Monroe could picture nothing but severed spinal cords, caved-in skulls, hospital beds, wheelchairs and coffins.

He quit at the age of twenty-three, staging a very soft-looking fall in muddy ground at Hereford on a gloomy November afternoon. He claimed the fall had damaged his back so badly that he'd never be able to ride again. For more than two years he'd taken his regular payment from the Injured Jockey's Fund, knowing it wasn't merited, knowing he was stealing it. Then they'd stopped paying him after a specialist could find nothing wrong. Embittered, Monroe had found a job.

He still worked with horses. Used his special affinity now in other ways to calm them, make them trust him, even as he placed the muzzle on their heads and squeezed the trigger.

He parked the red Volkswagen outside his council house on the western edge of the village and went inside. He was thinking about Hewitt and Gleeson. There was a lot of money involved in what these guys were doing. Had to be to take that big place on the hill, install cameras, bring dickheads like Gleeson from Ireland and pay him two hundred and fifty pounds a time to get their hands on a racehorse for a few hours.

In the small kitchen, Monroe filled the kettle then went to the bookcase by his chair and pulled out a thick softback with a picture of the Kray twins on the front. He liked to read about crime and criminals. He fancied he had the brain for it, and he'd dabbled in a few dodgy deals. He'd set fire to a stable once to help the trainer collect a big insurance pay-out, so he supposed he was a criminal really, but anything he'd done had been like what he was doing this time, working for somebody. As the kettle boiled, he stared through the steamed-up window; the thought that idiots like Gleeson could be high up in a criminal organization bolstered his confidence that he could, one day, make some very serious money.

10

While his father had been in England for a few days, Sean Gleeson had tried to clean the flat. He'd bribed his mates to help him, but had to throw them out after an hour because of their carry-on and messing around with the washing-up liquid and the mop and bucket. Now the floor was soaked. They'd been slagging him off too when they'd found his dad's dirty underpants and the bits of mouldy food and empty bottles and cans. And Barry McDonald had held his nose and said 'Dis place feckin' stinks!' and the others had laughed at what he'd said and the way he sounded and they'd all started saying it and holding their noses.

Sean looked around him. The place did stink. It had stunk even when his mother was there to clean it. The whole block stank, he thought. The living room light was the only bulb that still worked. His father wouldn't spend money on anything for the flat. Sean knew he hadn't exactly been brilliant himself at keeping the place clean. He'd made the best of the fact that his ma hadn't been here to nag him about tidying his room and clearing up after him.

But it was getting beyond a joke now, and his da was getting mad because the place was like this and she wasn't there to clean it. When he was drunk, he kept saying he'd go and find her and drag her back by the hair. Sean had seen her dragged by the hair before and he knew it was best to try and keep his da from going to look for her.

Close to midnight, Sean finally finished cleaning. He stood in the centre of the living room, then moved to make a final adjustment to the one easy chair they had, its cotton covering now so shiny with grime it looked like old canvas. Sean smiled and shook his head, he held his nose and said aloud, 'It might look better but it still feckin' stinks!' and he went into his bedroom and reached under the bed to pull out the last wads of hay from the bale he'd been given by the coalman for helping drive the horse and cart.

As he made his way downstairs, he heard his father coming, recognized the tuneless singing and the way he burped after each hiccup. Sean raced back up and climbed a flight beyond the door. He knew that if he was there when his da got in, he'd just force him to make spaghetti on toast for him then he'd slop half of it on the carpet. If he left him to his own devices, he'd fall asleep in the chair in five minutes. When his father was safely inside, he crept back downstairs with the hay.

In the square of tarmac in the centre of St Joseph's Mansions that had once been a playground, was Sean's iron-grey pony, Pegasus. He pricked his ears at the sound and smell of his owner and whinnied lightly as Sean approached saying, 'Hey, no noise after eleven! That's the rule. Ye'll get us thrown out of this fine accommodation so ye will.' Pegasus was tethered to the rusty railings. On his back was a rug made out of an old carpet and tied round his middle with four tatty elastic snake belts linked together.

The pony butted him, trying to get at the hay. He pulled a handful from the wad. 'Peg! Where's yer table manners?'

He stood close to Pegasus, comforted by his munching and warmed by his body on this cold February night. Scratching the grey neck lightly he said, 'Big race on Saturday, Peg, chance to make a proper name for ourselves.' He stared at the clear sky then put his hands under the pony's chewing jaw and tried to force its head up. 'Look, Peg, stars, that's where we're heading.' The pony butted him again. Stepping back and putting his hands on his hips and said sternly, 'Pegasus, you have no feckin sense of ambition whatsoever.'

Back upstairs, Sean eased the door open and heard the snores. He tiptoed into the living room and found his father in his usual position, half-sprawled in the chair, mouth open, dead to the world. As ever his jacket lay on the floor and his trousers were open at the waist. Sean scooped up the jacket and searched the pockets. It was the only way to get money out of him. He reached in, felt some paper and, as he pulled it out, he heard his father grunt. Shoving the paper in his pocket, he dropped the jacket and ran to his bedroom. He locked the door. When he felt for the paper he'd just stolen he realized it wasn't a bank note. He looked at it - some directions and a telephone number. He looked toward the room his father was in and said, 'You old bollix!' and threw the paper on top of the battered chest of drawers.

FOR YOU5 SAKE

11

After three months living together at her house, Frankie and Kathy were married at Cheltenham racecourse. The reception for a hundred guests was held on the top floor of the grandstand, in the glass-fronted restaurant where they could see in the distance the spot where they'd first met. Frankie's wedding gift to his wife was a miniature replica of the third-last fence made with black birch cut from the fence itself and mounted in a deep frame of oak.

She gave him a framed gift, too; the shoes they'd worn on their walks in the months after they'd met. His old, crepe-soled brown ones and her tan shoes with the leather laces which had now been tied to Frankie's laces and mounted in a wood and glass case with the gold-plated inscription, 'Frankie and Kathy, 100 miles of walks 'n' talks'. She gave him a new pair of shoes too, in the softest leather. She'd had them made for him in Italy.

Her secret present to them both was a thatched cottage in Winterfold Woods in Surrey. They'd happened on the cottage when out driving one day and Frankie had taken a wrong turn. They'd thought it beautiful and Kathy had noted the number on the For Sale board. She'd arranged with friends to move all their stuff while she and Frankie were away. Although he wouldn't know it until she took the 'wrong' route on their way back from the airport after the honeymoon, this was where they were going to start their marriage.

The wedding guests were all Kathy's friends. Frankie's sister Theresa had written saying that their mother had warned the whole family that anyone attending the wedding would be disowned by her, left out of her will and damned to hell for eternity. Then Theresa said she didn't care and would do everything she could to be there. But on the day, she didn't make it, and Frankie sat at the raised table staring at a gathering of strangers. He'd met maybe a dozen or so in the preceding months, and of those, he could recall only three or four names. His ordination, the only other major ceremony he'd been involved in, came to his mind; he couldn't think of a face in the front rows of the cathedral that he hadn't known.

But it was a brief sadness on a day that made his heart glad.

They'd head into the future relishing the promise it held. Apart from the joy of being together every day, Frankie felt he had a real contribution to make to the partnership.

He was now officially employed as Kathy's agent and had established a good relationship with a number of the editors she worked for. He'd also negotiated sponsors for her travels in the shape of a major airline and an international hotel chain. At the start, Frankie had lacked confidence and was almost afraid of calling up these experienced business people. But he'd found most of them behaved like perfectly ordinary, friendly folk and not at all like the hard-edged tyrants he'd imagined they might be. Kathy's name, of course, opened many doors.

Their honeymoon was to last three months. During the first year they'd known each other, when Frankie had been battling his demons and Kathy had been simply waiting in hope and getting on with her life, she had promised herself that if they ever were to marry, she'd take Frankie to all the wonderful places she'd been to.

So they wandered the globe for twelve weeks, climbing in the foothills of the Himalayas, parascending in Jamaica, rounding up cattle in Montana, diving in the Seychelles, sailing a yacht round the Western Isles of Scotland, travelling in a camel train in the Kalahari desert, white-water rafting on the Amazon, driving a husky team in Alaska, abseiling in the Grand Canyon...

On the flight home, they discussed future projects. Frankie made a list of all the things Kathy had already done and written about, pencilling tiny doodles against each as they both suggested new ideas. Frankie seemed enthusiastic and Kathy played along. She thought it best not to mention that she didn't want to go on with her career much longer. She wanted to have a baby. The growing urge over the past few weeks to get pregnant had surprised her with its force. The unspoken plan had been to wait a couple of years, although Kathy was now thinking that one year would be long enough. But she knew how much Frankie was enjoying his role in the partnership; she needed to wait for the best opportunity to start discussing her retirement with him. Here, halfway across the Atlantic, his mind spinning with ideas and hopes, wasn't the best time.

She looked at his list. He said 'What do you think?'

'Know what I'd really like to do? I'd like to ride in a race again.'

'Would you?'

'Win a race. I'd like to win one. Although I'd settle for completing the course this time.'

Frankie thought for a while then said, 'D'ye think we'd sell the idea again? You've already done it once.'

Playfully, she nudged his elbow. 'We could do it for fun this time.'

He smiled. 'You really want to?'

'I do.'

He closed his notepad with an air of decisiveness. 'Let's do it!'

12

Sean Gleeson loved that Saturday morning feeling of not knowing what the day promised, what adventure was laid out on that highway from dawn until dusk. Today he knew exactly what the afternoon held; something he loved even more than Saturdays...pony racing.

Sean had raced Pegasus against other kids and their ponies whenever he got the chance. Sometimes they'd race along dual carriageways just after dawn on Saturdays or Sundays. Occasionally they'd stage races in the streets of the city's deprived areas. Wild-eyed kids, some as young as nine, riding and roaring like Cossacks on the backs of piebalds and skewbalds, bays and greys, galloping along past cars and bus-stops, shops and houses, the click-clacking of the hooves sending echoes through the blocks of flats, drawing the dwellers to their windows to scream abuse or encouragement, to see some ponies slip and slide and fall, rolling their tiny jockeys along the road to collect high-speed cuts and grazes and the occasional broken bone.

People began betting on the outcome of these unofficial races. With money at stake, it was inevitable that one man would try to get an advantage over his fellows and some began helping with the training of the ponies. Boys were watched closely to see who had the gifts of balance and good hands, rhythm, calmness and a spark of fearlessness - boys who'd have the making of a proper jockey. And of the hundreds riding their street ponies, Sean Gleeson was recognized by the shrewd punters as being among the top handful.

Today Sean was to ride in his biggest race so far; down on the beach at Laytown. Mr Patrick Cosgrave, no less, a fine trainer of ponies, had booked him to come and have his first ride in this class of event, way above anything he'd ridden in before.

In loose silks of lemon and cerise, Sean sat on the back of a little bay pony called Shelley's Shebeen and circled quietly with the other runners for the third race at Laytown, where the only grass in sight grew in a few tufts on the dunes. Laytown races took place on the beach, and the most crucial aspect of organizing the meeting was ensuring the times coincided with the ebb tide.

Official horseracing at Laytown was a summer sport. Cosgrave, the trainer who'd booked Sean, had arranged this special racemeeting for ponies only. He'd paid for vets and a doctor to attend and had marketed the day much better than horseracing officials sold their days.

Sean felt the wind on his face and tasted the salt spray. The ponies tasted it too, chomping away, bridles clinking over searching tongues.

He wished his father was there to see him and be proud of him. His da loved the horses, but Sean had been too nervous to tell him about today. Besides, he hadn't been properly sober for weeks so Sean doubted he'd have remembered to come anyway.

The race was over six furlongs and Sean drove the filly along at a steady gallop at a speed he judged she could just stay in front, then perhaps she could quicken by ten per cent or so in the last furlong to hold them off. Sean concentrated on pumping rhythmically with hands and heels and he couldn't stop himself smiling. On the outside edges of his conscious mind, he was vaguely aware of the commentary over the PA and the blur of changing colours as he raced past the crowds on the dunes, but he felt completely at one with this speeding pony and it was the best feeling he'd ever known.

Sean and Shelley's Shebeen won their first-ever race together. Cosgrave threw his hat in the air, almost hitting a big herring gull. The crowds were glad, for the filly had been well-enough backed. And Sean, laughing with nerves and delight and wonderment at this feeling of triumph that he'd never known, rode the filly at a walk into the little makeshift winners' enclosure and everyone clapped and cheered. Clapped and cheered Sean Gleeson, making the first step on the ladder of his dreams feel like the top step.

On that Saturday afternoon, at around the same time as Sean was steering Shelley's Shebeen across the winning line, Kathy Houlihan, aboard the big bay gelding, Sauceboat, was being led by her lad around the paddock at Stratford in the English Midlands. Frankie walked quickly alongside. The horse was jogging, zigzagging on the strip of tarmac, ducking his head then raising it quickly, almost jerking the reins from the lad's hand.

'God, he's on his toes!' Kathy said, adjusting her stirrup leathers. 'I think my nerves are getting to him.'

'Mine too,' Frankie said, having to break into a jog himself at times to stay by the horse's side. 'He's like a boxer before a fight, isn't he? He's bobbing and weaving like Tyson!'

Kathy smiled at that and said, 'Hey, who's the famous writer here, me or you?' Sauceboat bucked, throwing her forward, making her shout, 'Whoa!' After falling off Zuiderzie at Cheltenham, she didn't want to suffer the indignity of landing on the ground before they'd even left the paddock. Sauceboat's trainer, Miles Henry, hurried across to take the rein on the opposite side from the lad who smiled at him in relief.

The trainer said, 'Not on his best behaviour, I'm afraid. It's not like the old bugger. He usually wanders round half-asleep.'

'He does, doesn't he?' Kathy said as she settled back in the saddle, conscious that the racegoers surrounding the paddock were watching, waiting for the only woman rider to be dumped on her bottom. She took a tighter hold on the rubber-clad reins, resisting the urge to clutch at Sauceboat's mane, too. She had hoped to ride Zuiderzie again but the horse had been moved from Miles to another trainer. Miles had recommended Sauceboat as "the ideal horse for you to ride over hurdles". She knew he was just too kind to speak the truth; "he's a quiet old plodder who won't exhaust you and make you fall off as Zuiderzie did".

And he'd felt safe and comfortable these past couple of months when she'd ridden him out at least three times a week. This was by far the most active she'd seen him, and she began to think that he might just have a better chance than his trainer and the bookies thought. Sauceboat had been placed four times but had never won. He was an outsider at 16/1 but as Miles led her out onto the track and released the reins, she felt raw power as Sauceboat stretched his neck and launched into a gallop toward the start. Frankie's cry of 'Good luck!' sounded faint as she accelerated away. From behind, he and Miles watched her shoulders and arms swing from side to side as she wrestled the straining animal for control.

Frankie, worried, glanced across at Miles. They'd come to know each other well in the run-up to this race. The trainer smiled and reached to put an arm around his shoulder. 'She'll be fine, Frankie. The fizz will go out of him before he gets to the start. Let's go and watch.'

They went into the stand and raised their binoculars.

Sauceboat was still on his toes at the start as he circled with the other fifteen runners. Miles had told Kathy the horse would settle himself naturally toward the rear of the field once the race started. 'Try and make progress as you come out of the back straight for the last time. You'll have to give him a smack or two, and he sometimes responds if you can lean close to his ear and shout something.' Kathy had said the only thing she'd be likely to shout was 'Help!'

Sauceboat pricked his ears as he heard the starter climbing the rostrum and he pulled hard to reach the lowered tape.

'Line up jockeys!' called the starter. The horses were seasoned handicappers and they came slowly but readily into line. 'Right!' shouted the starter and pressed the lever to raise the tape. Within twenty strides, Kathy found herself in the lead. Hauling at the reins, she tried to settle Sauceboat as they approached the first but he was ignoring her. Head down, neck outstretched, he skipped lightly over the hurdle and resumed his relentless gallop. Kathy glanced behind. They were already ten lengths clear of the others and she knew she was going far too fast. No way could Sauceboat keep up this pace. But there was no way, either, that she could hold him. She decided quickly to stop sawing at his mouth with the reins. It was best, she thought, to try to relax, try to look as stylish as possible for as long as she was in the lead - which, she was confident, wouldn't be for much longer.

But a circuit later, he was still well clear. With just two to jump, nobody was making any headway. In the stands, Frankie and Miles looked at each other in puzzled, happy wonderment. As they approached the last hurdle, Sauceboat was twenty lengths ahead and seemed, if anything, to be accelerating again. Frankie started shouting and jumping up and down, and when the pair cleared the last safely, he threw his arms around the trainer and they started bouncing on their toes.

Sauceboat galloped past the winning post carrying a bemused Kathy, whose dazed smile began to fade quickly as she realized the sweat and foam-streaked bay wasn't stopping. Standing in her stirrups and leaning back, she pulled as hard as she could, but it didn't slow him. She pictured herself, in what should have been a moment of glory, being carted around for another couple of circuits until this brute finally became tired of galloping. Approaching the top bend, she transferred her left hand to the right rein, hauling on it with both hands to try and turn him toward the white plastic rail in the hope it would act as a barrier.

Sauceboat turned toward the rail but didn't slow. He crashed through it, sending white shards like darts into the grass. There was another rail. He went through that too, still galloping headlong. Kathy found herself laughing nervously, hands still on the right rein, still hoping he would turn, slow down. Her thighs and forearms were burning, shoulders aching, fingers weakening quickly. There were trees ahead. That would stop him, surely. He seemed to be heading for them, a row of elms, a few leaves drifting from the branches in slow motion.

She thought of baling out, taking her chances in a certain tumble at thirty miles an hour before he reached the trees. But the experience she'd gained in all the dangerous things she'd done kept her cool, persuaded her to play the percentages. She knew that only a blind animal would run into a tree trunk. He'd change direction or stop - had to. Her view between his pricked ears showed the thick tree on the extreme right of the row rising like a long gun sight. He was going straight at it. In the final few strides before impact, she closed her eyes and Sauceboat wheeled violently right to pass the trunk. Kathy was thrown, her body whipping almost horizontally through the air the way it used to as a child when her father would swing her by her feet in the garden. The left side of her head was the only part of her to hit the trunk. The sound of her helmet cracking coincided with the clean snapping sound as her vertebrae parted, breaking her neck.

Sauceboat's trainer Miles Henry felt that his soul had died. At forty, he thought racing had taught him everything he'd ever need to know about life. But as he watched Frankie quietly stop the medics from lifting Kathy's corpse, he wept as Frankie bent and cradled her and held her as he carried her into the back of the ambulance. The medics closed the doors and as the white vehicle trundled away in the gathering dusk, Miles Henry wondered how he would be able to live with what had happened.

He was vaguely aware of the empty stands, the engines of horseboxes, loaded and ready for home. Miles knew he'd be unable to drive. He felt he might do well just to find the strength to uproot his feet from this spot and start to walk. He sensed someone approaching but couldn't take his eyes from the fading red lights of the ambulance in the distance.

'Mister Henry?'

He turned. It was Sauceboat's groom, Harry. Miles looked at the boy. 'Mister Henry, Pete said I should ask you if you wanted to travel back with us in the van. He said he'll arrange for your car to get collected tomorrow.' Miles Henry found himself nodding. He tried to move and couldn't. He found himself reaching out to Harry, opening his hand. Harry seemed uncertain but slowly he raised his arm and took Miles Henry by the hand. The boy led the man away.

When the horsebox-driver pulled into the yard at Lambourn, he helped the trainer down and took him into the house before returning to unload the horses. When he lowered the ramp, the first thing he saw was the big brown face of Sauceboat. The horse was lathered in sweat and shaking, almost vibrating as though leaning against a pneumatic drill.

Hurrying up the ramp, he saw that the horse was sweating so heavily steady drips fell from the gelding's belly. He ran down the ramp and across the yard to the office. The vet's number was pinned on the wall above the phone.

By the time the vet, Peter Culling, reached the yard, Sauceboat was in his stable, still sweat-soaked but heavily rugged to try and calm the shivers.

Culling shook his head and hurried into the box. Sauceboat's lad, Harry, peeled the rugs off. Miles Henry, more alert now, stood anxiously inside the stable door. 'What is it, Peter?' The trainer asked.

'God knows.' Culling opened his bag. He was a powerfully built man, standing five-ten. His receding sandy hair looked even thinner under the single strip light.

When the trainer saw Culling's face, he said, 'Peter, you look terrible, are you feeling alright?'

The vet looked away from him. 'It's been a long week Miles, late nights, early calls; you know the way it gets sometimes.' He bent to get a thermometer from his bag.

Miles Henry said quietly, 'You know what happened with this horse at Stratford today?'

The vet nodded. 'I was there. Terrible. Worst thing I've ever seen on a racecourse.' His voice was shaky. He eased the thermometer into the horse's rectum.

The trainer sighed and said, 'Kathy had been training here for months. She'd only married back in May. I thought she was ready, I honestly did. Especially with this horse, who's so bloody quiet you wouldn't know he was in the yard.'

Miles Henry was waiting for Culling to make some consoling noises, but as the vet raised his stethoscope he said, 'Can we drop the subject? I need to concentrate on trying to save the horse.' He spent almost ten minutes examining Sauceboat before turning to the anxious trainer. 'It's got to be something in his gut. He's in a lot of pain. I want to get him back to my place and put him under, have a proper look.'

'OK. OK, do that. I'll ring the owner. Don't do anything too expensive until I've rung the owner.'

'Well, make it quick, Miles.' He turned to the lad. 'Can you help me get him back in the van?' Harry nodded, seriously worried about 'his' horse now.

Peter Culling had converted part of his barn into an equine operating theatre. Harry and the box-driver led the shivering horse into the white-walled semi-padded room as Culling came through an internal door leading from his office. 'I've called my assistants, they'll be here soon. Thanks for your help. I'll ring and let you know as soon as there's some news.'

Harry stroked the horse's matted neck. 'I'd like to stay, sir, if you don't mind. I'll help.'

'I'm sorry, that won't be possible. It's outside the guidelines, I'm afraid. You'd be best back at the yard. I promise I'll call you very soon.' Culling looked exhausted. The boy handed him the headcollar lead and turned slowly away. The box-driver put an arm around the lad's shoulders as they went out.

45

When Culling heard the horsebox pull away, he opened his bag again. Taking out a syringe and a small bottle of liquid, he turned and injected Sauceboat just under his windpipe. Within a minute, the violent shivering eased. Soon it stopped completely. Culling led the horse out of the theatre and into a box adjoining part of the barn.

Stooped and almost dragging his feet, he went back to his office and called Miles Henry. The line was engaged. Minutes later the trainer rang him. 'The owner says do whatever you have to and bugger the cost.'

'I'll try, Miles, but we might not save him.'

'Mister Graham knows that. He'll stand the bill, don't worry.'

'OK, I'll get to it now. I'll ring as soon as I come out of theatre.'

Culling went to his drinks cabinet and poured a small measure of cognac. He sipped as he stared at the wall. Returning to his desk, he leafed through a notebook, and picked up the phone. It rang for some time before it was answered. Culling said, 'Gerry, I've got another one for you.'

Back in the silent house, Culling went to the conservatory and sat staring at the darkness. For almost two hours, he barely moved; then he checked his watch and wearily got to his feet. He made his way to the horse's box. Sauceboat was calm and still and his coat was drying. His eyes looked bright and when Culling swung a full hay net inside the horse began eating immediately. Culling filled his water bucket before returning to his office.

He dialled Miles Henry's number. Mrs Henry answered and Culling had to wait almost a minute before the trainer came to the phone.

Culling said gravely, 'Miles, I'm so sorry, we lost him on the operating table.'

At noon the next day, Gerry Monroe stopped the horsebox outside the vet's place, jumped from the high cab and strode purposefully toward the barn. Peter Culling had warned him that he wouldn't be at home, but there was a combination lock on the barn door and Culling had given Monroe the numbers. He dialled them in. A few minutes later, he was leading Sauceboat out to the horsebox. The horse was perky, and looked well considering what he'd been through.

Monroe loaded him without trouble, then went back and locked the barn door. The box he drove was an old wooden-sided one that rolled along the lanes of Lambourn, swaying gently and labouring as it climbed out of the valley up the B4001. Just before reaching the crest of the hill, Monroe wrestled the steering wheel round to turn the box along a track which ran parallel with the ridge a hundred yards or so above it.

Caution was needed here as potholes were scattered like craters on a shelled road, and the springs and wooden slats of the box groaned and squeaked each time a wheel dipped.

Approaching the end of the track Monroe saw that the big black gates to Hewitt's place had been opened as promised. He came off the last easy curve through the gates to find Hewitt waiting. Monroe led Sauceboat round the back of the big three-storey house, aware that Hewitt was watching the horse walk, studying his action, looking at his conformation. This was the tenth horse Monroe had brought since Gleeson, the Irishman, had approached him. The first time he'd met Hewitt, Monroe had been convinced he wasn't a horseman but he seemed to have been coping well, whatever it was he was doing with these horses.

Monroe put Sauceboat in the end box and turned to see Hewitt walking slowly toward him, smiling, counting out banknotes. Monroe folded the wad and shoved it into the pocket of his jerkin knowing he didn't need to check it.

'Thanks. Six o'clock OK to call back?'

'That will be fine. And you haven't forgotten my requirement, Mister Monroe?'

Monroe was sick of hearing this line but tried not to show it. 'No, Mister Hewitt, I haven't.'

'Do what you can.'

'Count on it.'

'Good. Come back around six. Just do your usual. You know where he'll be.'

'Fine, Mister Hewitt, no problem.'

He returned just after six cursing the driving, swirling rain that swept down the valley from the ridge, drenching him as he hurried to the back of the big house. Sauceboat was in the end box and followed him meekly when he tugged at the head collar, dragging his hooves slightly as they all did when he came back for them.

The bay gelding was more lethargic than most of the others had been and Monroe took some time getting him up the ramp. When he unloaded at the other end, at his place of full-time work, the horse seemed to have picked up slightly.

Monroe led him quietly through the doors into the dimly lit space with the white walls. Only one light burned in the building and that was inside this room. Monroe had to be extra careful; if his employers ever found out he was moonlighting he'd be in trouble.

He was talking to Sauceboat now as he turned the horse to face the door he'd just come through. He let go the halter and slid the door closed, then took up the rope again and steadily wound it in loops around his left wrist. Talking in low tones, he reassured the big horse that everything was going to be fine. With his right hand, he reached slowly behind him without looking, and eased his bolt-action rifle off the hooks on the white wall.

Moving his face closer to Sauceboat's head he spoke softly, reaching in his pocket for a Polo mint and holding it at waist level. The trusting horse lowered his head to lick the mint from his palm. Monroe swung the rifle dexterously until the muzzle rested in the centre of Sauceboat's forehead.

The horse stood calmly, crunching the mint, looking straight ahead, listening to the soft tones of this man who'd won his trust. Monroe said, 'Bye-bye big fella.'

13

The numbness held Frankie together until after the funeral. If he had any feeling at all, it was that this was not happening to him. He was an automaton making arrangements for the burial of a young woman. A few small things were to stir him: seeing their wedding guests return in mourning clothes; picking up his sister Theresa's tearful message on his phone saying that their mother had locked her in her room to stop her coming to him; finding unused wedding gifts stored in the cupboard under the stairs; and the grief of Kathy's adoptive parents when they'd come to see him on a dark day in Winterfold Cottage.

But there were no tears from him. Anaesthetized by whatever self-protecting chemical his brain was producing, the only time he felt any strong emotion was when he opened the card from his mother, the message causing him to throw it across the room. He'd received over a hundred cards. The words of sadness and sympathy had begun rolling into one another until he came to his mother's. It said, 'I hope she's burning in hell.'

Just after eleven on Thursday morning, Frankie Houlihan got into the red Subaru estate car that had been a present from Kathy. He drove down the rutted track away from the cottage. Rain fell softly. Every few seconds the wipers swished. Frankie was going racing for the first time since Kathy's death. Bobby Cranfield had talked him into it during several long phone calls.

Bobby Cranfield was PR Director for the Jockey Club. He had met Kathy when she'd made the initial approach about her plans to ride at Cheltenham. Kathy had introduced Frankie to Bobby, who had sorted out all the arrangements for Kathy - setting things up with Miles Henry, getting her a licence to ride, organising the early training.

As Frankie pulled out onto the main road, he managed a smile as he recalled Kathy's story of Bobby's call to tell her they'd got to get her down to Lambourn and let her sit on an old schoolmaster to start with.

Bobby did the Jockey Club job for love. He was a multi-millionaire from selling his international PR agency. He had horses of his own with several trainers, and the weekend after first contacting him, Kathy was in Miles Henry's yard, one of the top Lambourn stables, being legged up onto a quiet gelding.

And that had been it. The beginning. Over two years ago. And six weeks back had been the end. A fall to start it and one to finish it. Frankie's skin prickled coldly at the thought as it always did. There was the sick sinking feeling in his gut too. A parishioner had once told him that if there was really a God he must have a bitch of a sense of humour. Frankie had considered it blasphemous but since Kathy's death, he'd recalled it again and again. Six weeks without her. Long days and nights of trying to make sense of everything. Grief hadn't yet hit him, not properly, for there was something in him that refused to accept he'd never see her again.

He was heading for Wincanton in Somerset. Passing Stonehenge, Frankie thought how small it looked although it was a good way from the road. He and Kathy had passed it a few times and always promised to stop off on the next trip, but they never had done. It looked ghostly now through the fine, misty rain.

Frankie climbed the grandstand stairs and knocked on the door of box number thirty-two, which had a plaque saying Mr Bobby Cranfield. He went in and was surprised to find only Bobby there and the lunch table set for two. The box could hold at least twenty people and Bobby loved to entertain. He sat in his wheelchair smiling warmly; 'Come in Frankie. You look wet.'

Frankie shook his hand. A waitress appeared, smiling as she took Frankie's coat and offered him a drink. Frankie asked for mineral water.

He sat down in the only empty chair. 'How are you, Bobby? It's good to see you.'

'I'm as well as I've ever been, and even better now that I've got some decent company.' Cranfield's eyes shone with pleasure.

Frankie thought that nobody just seeing Bobby's upper half would know he was disabled. He looked fit and tanned and healthy with his thick, lead-grey hair. He was around fifty and he had a well- equipped gym and a pool at his big house in Oxfordshire, and Frankie had seen him work out in both. His party trick was launching himself into the pool from his chair by arm strength alone; then he'd exercise by keeping himself afloat moving only his upper half as his dead legs dangled.

Kathy had always seen Bobby as a living example of how she feared ending up. Every time they met, Frankie had seen a glint of terror in Kathy's eyes and when she'd learned that Bobby had been crippled in a fall from a racehorse yet had still gone ahead with her plan to ride at Cheltenham, Frankie thought it one of the most courageous things he'd ever known.

Frankie settled in the chair and silently counted the cutlery to gauge how long a lunch Bobby had planned. He was also wondering what was on the agenda with just the two of them there. He said to Bobby, 'My Holmesian powers of deduction tell me that the chef, at this moment, is not outside slaughtering a four-hundred pound pig to make sure nobody goes hungry here.'

Cranfield smiled. 'If you didn't have that accent I'd still know you were Irish. Who else uses ten words when one will do?'

Now Frankie smiled. Cranfield said, 'You're dead right. Nobody else is coming. We have the box to ourselves. Even Caroline,' at which point the waitress put Frankie's mineral water on the table, 'has agreed to leave us alone once she's served the starter.'

'So the starter's joining us too. Who's gonna get the races off in time?'

'Very funny. I'm glad to see you're in good heart.'

'I'm doing fine,' Frankie said, wondering when Bobby was going to explain why he'd asked him here.

'Managing to fill your days?'

Frankie nodded. 'I read. And walk a bit.'

There was a longish silence as they looked at each other, Cranfield with his kind smile and Frankie with the pain in his eyes still clear despite his affected jauntiness.

'Are you sleeping OK?' Cranfield asked.

'Not really, but self-pity never was the best sedative.'

'It's grief, Frankie, not self-pity. Perfectly understandable grieving. Don't give yourself a tough time over it.'

Frankie averted his eyes, sipped his drink. Cranfield said, 'Would it help to talk?'

'If I start I'll never stop.'

'That's what friends are for.'

'I'll take you up on it sometime, Bobby, but not now, if you don't mind.'

Cranfield reached across to grip Frankie's forearm. 'Of course not. Of course not! You know where I am when you do want to talk. Just give me a call.'

Frankie nodded. 'Thanks.'

Cranfield sipped white wine. Caroline brought two smoked salmon terrines then left again. Frankie said, 'I guess this has kinda messed up your timings, me not wanting to talk.' He looked at his watch. 'I mean, there's a full afternoon's racing to get through and there's just me and you. And I'm not talking. And me the best talker too, by far, of the both of us. It has the makings of a peaceful afternoon, does it not?'

Cranfield smiled. 'Oh, you'll talk alright, Frankie boy, maybe not about Kathy, but when you hear what I've got to say, you'll talk!'

Frankie boy. It was the first time anyone but Kathy had called him that and he suddenly felt an unreasonable stab of antagonism toward Bobby for saying it. But it passed in a moment as his curiosity took over. 'I'm listening,' he said.

Cranfield drank more wine then said, 'I want to ask a favour of you.'

'Uh-huh?' Frankie wondered what this multi-millionaire racehorse owner could want from him.

'I want you to help us out at the Jockey Club.'

Frankie's dark eyebrows moved closer together as he frowned quizzically. 'Help you out of what?'

'In the security department.'

'Doing what and for how long?'

'Working as an intelligence officer, an investigator.'

Frankie smiled, a forkful of fish halfway to his mouth. 'You know, you should've waited a few seconds, Bobby. I always wanted to do what they do in the films when somebody's so surprised at something over dinner they splutter food everywhere.'

'See, my timing's good. I'd have been in the line of fire.'

Frankie smiled. 'Stop winding me up.' And he ate.

'I'm not, honestly. There's a long-standing vacancy. They've interviewed for it twice and can't get the right person. You'd be ideal.'

'And how do you figure that one out?'

'Well you used to be a police chaplain at one time, didn't you?'

Frankie almost did splutter his food as he laughed. 'You're a case, Bobby. Now stop the kidding.'

'I'm not kidding. I remember Kathy telling me you spent some time as a chaplain to the Royal Ulster Constabulary.'

Frankie, his eyes still creased from his smile, looked at Bobby Cranfield and could tell he was quite serious. 'You're really not kidding, are you?'

'Really not. I think you'd do a great job for us.'

'The RUC chaplaincy was a joke. It was a politically motivated request to the archbishop in Dublin by a friend of his in Belfast who wanted a favour. The RUC has a tiny minority of Catholic members. My appointment was supposed to show that it was a cross-religious group. I ended up with so little to do I trained for my HGV licence so I could drive the horses around for the mounted boys and keep busy. That was the best part of it, in fact.'

'But didn't you have training in police procedure as part of your chaplaincy, or whatever they call it?'

'I did, but only to help me understand the lives of these fellas. It was hardly MI6 school.'

'But you got the same training as a new police recruit would have?'

Frankie shrugged and put down his fork. 'Well, a sort of sawn-off version, I suppose.' Kathy was never far from his mind and she seemed suddenly to be with him now. He could hear her laugh and see her shake her head and say to him, 'What a brilliant idea! What a great job! Go on, Frankie, take it, it'll be fun!'

Cranfield saw the change in his features. 'You're sort of warming to this now, ain't you?'

Frankie nodded slowly, reluctant to let Kathy go, wishing Bobby would disappear for a few minutes. And Kathy said to him, 'And remember, you're used to getting confessions out of people!' Suddenly he felt happiness, a peace he'd thought he'd never know again. That gag was typical of Kathy and he knew somehow that it hadn't formed in his own mind. He knew she was back with him in everything but body. His eyes filled. He thought quickly of Bobby, not wanting to make him feel uncomfortable, but he found himself quelling the instinct to dab his eyes with his napkin.

Frankie drove away from Wincanton before the end of racing, with an appointment in his diary to meet the Jockey Club's head of security in London next day; "just a formality" Cranfield had assured him. He pulled into the first layby, switched the engine off and sat staring at the darkening sky, willing Kathy to come back close to him the way she had done in box thirty-two. Willing it and wanting it almost like a drug. He concentrated, closed his eyes, recreated the conversation with Bobby in his mind, reached the same trigger point that had brought her to him. But she'd slipped back to the perimeter; he could see her there, waving reassuringly and he heard her say, 'Don't worry Frankie, I'll come back whenever you need me most. I'll always be here with you, watching over you, loving you. But live your life. Live your life!'

'I don't want to,' he said quietly, his face contorted, his throat sore from the constriction of grief, from trying not to cry. And he tried to say 'not without you'. His lips formed the words but his throat choked them to silence. Kathy receded, faded, still waving. She didn't turn away, just faded. 'Come back, Kathy!' he managed to say, although he felt his throat closing completely and the pain was intense. Then all the dams burst at once, convulsing his body as though the car had been seized by some earthquake, and Frankie's throat opened and out came a sound, a cry, so primal, so vital that he would always remember it with wonder. It was a sound he could not have created and it finally uncorked the well. In the deepening rainy gloom, Frankie writhed and wept and moaned, his limbs moving, out of control, hands trying to still his rolling head. It felt as though it went on for a long time and toward the end he began to feel himself emptying, draining of all emotion, of all movement and sound until he lay slumped in the seat like a boneless bag of flesh.

The ordeal exhausted him, purged him. Unable to move, he became aware of the deepest peace he'd ever known. Peace beyond what he'd believed possible. Peace so complete that it crossed his mind that he might have died or was dying and that this was the out-of-body experience he'd heard tell of. His eyes closed, slowly, in the way of a toddler when exhaustion overcomes him while he's playing. Frankie was vaguely aware of his breathing, much slower and deeper than he'd ever known it. He slipped into a blessed sleep.

Frankie spent the first two weeks in his new job learning about procedure. They teamed him with Geoff Stonebanks, who'd been a racing intelligence officer for ten years. Among other things, Jockey Club Security was responsible for providing guards at every racecourse to help prevent unauthorized access to the stables. These guards were employed on a part-time basis. The team of intelligence officers, six of them including Frankie, were full-time employees.

Geoff Stonebanks was as competent and cynical as his colleagues. He was an ex-policeman who lived in Lambourn. He'd moved there when he got the Jockey Club job because he thought that living in the racing village, with his ear as close to the ground, would prove an advantage. But he'd soon learned that the place seethed with rumour and counter-rumour. He'd long ago given up the notion that every stable lad was a potential mole of any reliability.

The worthwhile informants ran to single figures only, although Stonebanks had good relationships with all of them. When Stonebanks heard he was going to be 'inducting' Frankie Houlihan, he didn't relish the prospect. He thought even less of it when he heard Frankie's background. The fact that he'd been a priest didn't trouble him. But when he was told of Kathy's death, he felt awkward about spending a couple of weeks with Frankie.

Stonebanks had a reputation as a good listener. But it was a skill he'd worked hard at and one he preferred to lock up in his briefcase at the end of his working day. He lived quietly with Caroline, his wife of twenty years; they seldom socialized, and before he met Frankie, Stonebanks was worried that the ex-priest might want to extend their relationship beyond working hours. The man was due some sympathy, no doubt. But Stonebanks wanted to keep everything purely professional. So he felt some relief when a smiling Frankie Houlihan, dressed in a black suit and crisp white shirt, was introduced to him by their boss, Robert Archibald, on the morning of the first Monday in November.

They shook hands, and Stonebanks liked Frankie immediately for the openness of his face and the way he held himself when Stonebanks knew he must still be grieving, and nervous about the new job to boot. And he envied Frankie his comparative youth and slim, fit look. Stonebanks had been fighting a battle against being overweight for years and found it hard to get clothes to hang properly on his sixteen-stone frame. He smiled and said, 'Welcome to the craziest goldfish bowl in the so-called leisure industry.'

Frankie returned the smile. 'And are we swimming or throwing in the food?'

Stonebanks admired his quick wit. 'Depends how clean the tank is. Mostly, we chase our own tails.'

Frankie's induction was to continue by way of his meeting each of the three investigators who were not London-based. He'd spent a day at Plumpton with Gordon Drewery, two days up north at Carlisle and Ayr with Jamie Robson, and his final trip was to Warwick to meet Jack Webster, who was responsible for the Midlands. On his way to the track on what was the coldest Saturday of the season so far, a coughing and spluttering Webster called him to say he was dying with a cold and was very sorry but he wouldn't be there. Frankie said, 'Don't worry; we can meet some other time. Is there anything I can do at Warwick to help you?'

'You can tell Julie on the bar in members' to bring me a hot toddy after racing.'

Frankie smiled. 'I'll pass on the message.'

Frankie had been racing mad for years, and one of his ambitions had been to visit all fifty-nine British racecourses. He chalked up a new one with Warwick. This was his first visit and he thought it an attractive little course with a good atmosphere. As the first race came nearer and the crowds built steadily, Frankie wandered around, introduced himself to the stable guards and chatted a while with them, had a cup of tea and a sandwich in the members' bar and wondered which of the four serving girls was Julie if, indeed, she wasn't simply a figment of Jack Webster's imagination.

This was the first time since he started the new job that he'd been to a racecourse unaccompanied. He found himself seeing everything with new eyes compared with when he used to come racing as a spectator. Every huddled group in the bar was now made up of potential conspirators; stable lads leading their charges out of horseboxes all seemed shiftier than he could ever remember.

Who was that prosperous-looking man speaking to Crosby Allen, the bookie? They looked up to no good.

Frankie thought about it as he sipped tea, and found himself smiling at his own ridiculous thoughts. Still, he supposed that every new employee in any business was mentally primed like this in the early weeks. He wondered how long it would take to become as cynical as Stonebanks and the others.

Kathy was never far from his mind. When Frankie looked carefully through the Warwick racecard as he finished chewing his sandwich, his eye stopped at Zuiderzie, the horse Kathy had fallen from at Cheltenham the day he had met her. The impact of seeing the name stunned him. He stared at it as though it were the only thing that existed. It had been more than two years since he'd seen the horse, and many of the things that had happened since suddenly cascaded through his mind.

Miles Henry had phoned Frankie a few times after Kathy's death and sent flowers and a card. But looking at the racecard Frankie remembered that Miles was no longer training Zuiderzie, nor was the horse owned any more by Bobby Cranfield. After falling with Kathy at Cheltenham, Zuiderzie had lost his confidence over fences and his next few runs had been over hurdles. Frankie noted that today's race was a handicap hurdle, and that Zuiderzie was very low in the weights. The racecard form commentary told him that the horse hadn't won for more than three years. He was 33/1 in the betting forecast.

Come race time, Frankie made his way to the paddock. There was Zuiderzie, belying his eleven years and prancing around like a two-year-old constantly working the bit in his mouth and shaking his head until the metal jangled. He looked smart in his apparently new, dazzling scarlet rug with embroidered trainer's initials. Frankie leant over the rail as Zuiderzie danced past, tugging at the reins held by a smiling young blonde girl whose scarlet fleece matched her charge's rug. 'Hello, you old rogue,' Frankie said. The horses ears pricked and he turned his head slightly. Frankie smiled sadly.

As the bell went for the jockeys to mount, Frankie made his way back to the grandstand, uncertain whether his heart felt heavy or light. He was glad of this tangible connection with Kathy. So much time since the funeral had been lived in his head; memories, emotions, regrets, fears. Nothing to grasp. Nothing solid to grapple with or embrace. Now here was the horse that had brought him together with this wonderful, beautiful woman. And he felt her near him, sensed her presence. Not as close as the first time but comforting nonetheless. He smiled.

The PA boomed out the message that they were off. Frankie Houlihan raised his binoculars and watched Zuiderzie lead all the way and win by fifteen lengths. When he lowered those binoculars, tears spilled from the small rubber eyecups and left stains on his white shirt.

Belinda Cassell had only been in racing two months, and the seventeen-year-old was so thrilled with the victory of 'her' horse Zuiderzie that she hadn't shut up about it since rushing out madly to welcome the horse back in.

Belinda was his groom, and she just knew that if she looked after another thousand horses in her career she'd never ever forget this beautiful chestnut gelding, her first winner. Willie Creaney, the box-driver, had been charmed by her reaction at first (he fancied her anyway) but her non-stop chirruping on the way home was wearing him down and he was sympathizing in advance with whoever ended up as her husband.

Some racing people believe that a horse knows when it's won. In the back of the swaying box, Zuiderzie didn't feel at all special. He was shivering and sweating heavily.

When they reached the yard and Willy Creaney pulled the ramp down, he saw the horse and ran into the house to ring the vet. Peter Culling took the call on his mobile and told him he'd be there as soon as possible. Culling checked his watch and said to himself, 'Bang on time. Remarkable stuff. Remarkable.'

He smiled and accelerated toward Lambourn longing for a blue flashing light to stick on his car roof.

14

For a horse who, like Sauceboat, had supposedly died on Peter Culling's operating table the previous night, Zuiderzie was looking remarkably well when Gerry Monroe picked him up on Sunday morning.

The trip to Hewitt's place up the hill was getting so familiar now that Monroe recognized individual potholes in the road approaching the house. And there was Hewitt at the end of the drive as ever. Monroe was growing increasingly curious as to what the man was doing with these horses. The temptation to drive the box away after dropping Zuiderzie then creep back to the house on foot was strong, but Hewitt paid well and Monroe needed the money. If he was caught prowling around, he might lose the 'contract' or get another visit from Gleeson.

Later, on the journey to the slaughterhouse with the now drowsy animal, Monroe's mind went back to Hewitt's oft-repeated plea for a quality horse; he was thinking it was about time he did something about it. He knew nothing of the quality of the horses he'd already brought, didn't even know their names. He'd just collected them through his normal contacts. Their names and racecourse abilities had been of no interest to him. He assumed that if any famous horse were to be put down it wouldn't be himself who'd be pulling the trigger. Anyway, he'd be sure to read about such casualties in the *Racing Post*.

Four of the horses he'd ferried up to the big house had come from Culling's place. The vet had made a point of not being there when Monroe called (it dawned on him now that it had always been a Sunday morning when he'd picked them up after being contacted by Culling on the previous evening) and the horses, unusually in his trade, had seemed perfectly sound, quite healthy. When he got home, Monroe logged on to the *Racing Post* site on his PC and started doing some research.

The bookie, Compton Breslin, was not cut out for rambling or any other country pursuit, and the sight of his twenty-stone frame in wax jacket and plus-fours, leather walking boots polished to a shine, made Peter Culling snigger. The vet had insisted he'd only deal with Breslin on his terms and this was one of them; Breslin would never meet him in a public place or telephone him. After a coup, they'd meet in these woods halfway between Lambourn and Newbury, walking casually toward each other and passing in silence if anyone else came into view.

The vet would always be there first and try to make his way up an incline to force the fat bookie to climb those final hundred yards. By the time Breslin reached him, he'd be panting and sweating heavily. This Sunday afternoon was no different, and Culling hated him for the way he neglected himself, eating and drinking as though heart disease didn't exist. As though you were here forever and guaranteed good health.

At forty-three, Culling was convinced he himself would die soon. His father had been dead at forty- five, his paternal grandfather at forty-four. His maternal grandfather had died on the eve of his fiftieth birthday. Hearts. All of them faulty, diseased hearts. The thought of his male ancestors being freely allowed to breed, to pass on these genetic time bombs, would often drive Culling into a terrible rage.

Why couldn't humans be under some control? Why couldn't it be like the world of the thoroughbred, where the constant quest in breeding was to eliminate imperfections? How could his father be so selfish as to sire children knowing his own father had died so young, knowing his own heart was nothing but a clutch of quickly decaying valves?

If Hitler had won the war, he would have weeded out these people and he, Peter Culling, forty-three-years-old and wifeless and childless because of his own commitment to stop this Culling line of useless men who could not keep their hearts beating past their mid-forties, would never have been born. How, wondered Culling, can God put a child on this earth to grow up relishing each day, loving the sunshine and the women and the good life? How could he give someone such a tremendous appetite and ecstatic enjoyment of the fine things and then make him face the fact that it was all going to be taken away at a ludicrously, ridiculously young age? What kind of God is that?

Well, Culling was going to try and defy God and beat his father and his grandfather and all the other weaklings in the family line. He was going to try to live again through cryogenic refrigeration. Culling's own medical background confronted him with the strong argument against the likely realization of such an ambition, but his logic in pursuing it was that if it didn't work he'd be no worse off. On the positive side, he knew of the giant strides medicine had made in his own lifetime. It might take them a hundred years to bring him back, but what was a century against eternity?

As soon as he had enough money he was going to America, to die in the hands of the Everlasting Life Company of Michigan whose technicians would take him, within a minute of his heart giving out, and place him in suspended animation; freeze him in a metal cylinder that would be temperature- controlled by computer for as long as it took for medical science to come up with a way to bring him back - and keep him back. Then he would live properly! Then he'd marry and start a new Culling strain, a strong line of sons who'd never have reason to curse their father.

And here, arriving at the top of the hill, was this despicable animal who obviously did not give a toss about his heart or any other part of him. Especially his pride, if these stupid clothes were anything to go by. He knew Breslin dressed like a vaudeville clown on the racecourse, but he'd assumed that was part of his brash act to fleece punters. Here he was in civilization proper, dressed worse than that other ninny who was always on TV waving his arms around and yelling like a lunatic.

'Jesus Peter, can't we meet at the bottom of a hill sometime? This is bloody killing me! '

Culling smiled. 'Better vantage point here, we can see if anyone's watching.'

'We're surrounded by bloody trees! How can anyone be watching?'

'Trees are easy to hide behind.'

Breslin hobbled toward a fallen log and almost collapsed onto it, red-faced and panting. Despite his constant fears, tests had shown Culling's heart to be perfectly healthy and he was fit and proud of it. He was older than the bookie too, and he had to try hard not to show his contempt as he watched sweat drip from the fat man's brow on to the knee of his ridiculous blue tweed plus fours. Breslin looked close to cardiac arrest and the vet chided himself; he knew he should be protecting this valuable source of income, not putting it at risk.

Culling scanned the trees while he waited for Breslin to recover. The woods seemed silent but for Breslin's breathing. No birds sang. The grey squirrels who sometimes hurtled around were nowhere to be seen, and the air was still and cool.

Breslin seemed better. He leant forward, elbows on his knees. 'That was a nice one yesterday. Extra special because some heavy hitters were in there backing the favourite.'

Culling stuffed his hands in the pockets of his thigh-length brown coat and turned to the bookie. 'So you'll be paying me a bit more?'

'I'll be paying you what we agreed, but I'm thinking hard about your other proposal.'

'Well, the price has gone up.'

Breslin, annoyed, sat straighter. 'Since when?'

Culling smiled slyly, his inward-slanted teeth and narrowed eyes making him look wolfish. 'Since I've given you four winners in a row.'

'Well, what do you expect? I had to check what you were giving me.'

Still smiling the vet crouched low to Breslin's eye level. 'Well now you know how good it is.'

'So what's the deal?'

'Three grand to tell you the favourite will lose. Ten grand to give you the winner as well.'

Breslin found it hard to control his anger. 'It was five until yesterday!'

'Well it's ten now. Take it or leave it.'

Breslin stared at him for a long time. Culling held his gaze. Breslin said, 'Tell me who's actually doing it?'

'Why?'

'Because if there's a third party involved it's more risky. If someone else is doing the doping then—'

'Who said they're being doped?'

'Oh come on, Peter! For the first time in its life, that horse ran yesterday like the devil was up its arse!'

'And how many positive dope tests have you read about? How many out of the four I've given you?'

'None. Doesn't mean to say they're not being jabbed, it just means you've discovered something the lab boys can't detect yet.'

'You're wrong.'

'How are you doing it then?'

'None of your business, Mister Breslin! All you need to know is that the information is one hundred per cent. There's no third party involved. The next one will be in three weeks' time. Do you want in on it?'

'Will it be on a Saturday again?'

'Why?'

Breslin shrugged. 'The others have been, that's all.'

'And does it matter?'

'It doesn't bother me either way.'

'So do you or don't you want in on it?' Culling's impatience was showing.

'Maybe at the three grand price.'

'Not the ten?'

'Let me think about it.'

'Well before you start taxing your brain, maybe you'd like to count out yesterday's payment.'

All weekend, Frankie Houlihan had found it impossible to get Zuiderzie's victory out of his head. It was almost as though Kathy had steered the horse home from above. Frankie had wanted to go to the winners' enclosure and congratulate the owner and trainer and jockey, but he'd been unable to trust his emotions and didn't want to take the chance of embarrassing everyone, himself included and, potentially, his new employers.

So on Sunday evening he sat down and wrote to the winning trainer, Martin Broxton, a Lambourn resident he'd never met. And he ended up telling this stranger the whole story of the romance from meeting at Cheltenham right up to Zuiderzie winning at Warwick. It was the first time since Kathy had died that he'd written everything down, just let it flow, and it gave him much more comfort than he'd expected from it. Reading over his words again, he smiled as he doubted he could send this to a stranger. Then he thought, Why not? Why not let someone know exactly what she meant to me? Someone who didn't know her, who wouldn't feel awkward about hearing all this.

So he sealed the envelope and reached for his new Directory of the Turf for the address of Martin Broxton.

15

Gerry Monroe lived alone in a two-bedroom council house on the edge of Lambourn village. The second bedroom housed his computer, which sat on a desk he'd made from white pine. Every screw in the wood was flush, its slot at the same horizontal angle as its neighbour. Each surface was smoothly varnished, even the feet.

Monroe used the computer to trawl the internet for crime stories and for playing simulated empire- building games. Since collecting the last horse from Culling's place, he'd spent each evening searching the results pages of the *Racing Post* Online, checking Saturday runners. Using Timeform books, which gave a written description of the appearance of each horse, he tried to discover the identities of the horses he'd picked up from the vet.

Four nights' work produced a shortlist of nine. Frustrated, Monroe got up and paced the room. There was something lurking in his mind, the solution to this; he just couldn't tempt it to the surface. He checked the time; he believed in being in bed before midnight except at weekends. It was ten to. He went into his bedroom. Twenty minutes later, on the edge of sleep, it came to him.

Hurrying back to his computer he logged on again to the *Racing Post* site and went to the cuttings library. Any racehorse that died or was seriously injured had to be formally scratched from all its race entries. Monroe keyed in 'scratchings' in the search field. Within three minutes, his shortlist was down to four. Monroe returned to bed, smiling. His self-esteem was rising. So was his confidence.

Next evening, Monroe went to Culling's house and rang the bell. He'd heard the vet lived alone, and he was aware Culling had a reputation as a good, reliable, value-for-money operator. Other than this, he knew nothing about the man.

The light came on in the hall.

Monroe was just about to find out a bit more about Culling's character. As the shadowy outline through the glass door grew nearer, the slaughter man took a breath, tensed his shoulders, then tried to relax; this was his own first big test.

Culling looked surprised to see him. His eyes widened slightly but he didn't speak. Monroe, hands in trouser pockets, smiled. 'Hi, Mister Culling, hope you didn't mind me dropping by. I wanted to talk to you about those horses I've been picking up… on Sundays.' It was almost imperceptible but Monroe saw him flinch and said, 'I was hoping we could, eh, renegotiate the deal?'

Culling tried a bluff. 'Have you been drinking or something?'

'I don't drink much, Mister Culling, like to keep my wits about me if you know what I mean.' Monroe's smile had that glint of one-upmanship.

They looked at each other for a few moments then Culling stepped back and opened the door wider. 'Come in.'

Culling led him to the conservatory at the rear. The vet didn't like to give anyone access to any of the rooms he lived in. He'd had the conservatory built especially to accommodate visitors. It was a sort of sterile area; it held none of his belongings, gave no clue to his personality. There was a wicker couch and chair, each plumply cushioned, a smoky-glass-topped table and a single cactus plant in a big brown pot in the corner, no pictures, no reading material; one lamp with a weak bulb in the corner.

He indicated that Monroe should sit on the couch. The vet sat in the chair, put his elbows on his parted knees and clasped his hands together. Monroe's triumphant smile hadn't changed. He said, 'No, I won't bother with a cup of tea, thanks.'

Culling stared at him blankly, as though he hadn't heard the remark. Monroe's smile faded slightly. He said, 'I wondered what the names of those horses were, the last four I've collected.'

The vet shrugged. 'Why?'

'Professional curiosity.'

'To what end?'

'I think I can make some money if I know.'

'How?'

This wasn't going to plan for Monroe. He said, 'I came to ask questions Mister Culling, not to answer them.'

The vet sighed tiredly and ran his fingers through his thinning hair. 'I come to bury Caesar not to praise him,' he said, almost to himself.

'No burials here, Mister Culling. I've got some resurrections planned, but no burials.'

'You're talking in riddles, man.'

Monroe, smiling, opened his arms. 'You started it!'

Culling shook his head. Monroe said, 'Zuiderzie, Sauceboat, Kilkenny Lass and Broadford Bay.'

'Uh-huh?'

'Those were the horses.'

'So?'

'They all won the previous day. Unexpectedly. At a big price.'

'And?' Culling's face was losing a bit of colour.

Monroe cranked the smile up a few more watts. 'And you were the vet in attendance at each of the courses. And each horse was dead within forty-eight hours of winning. And I was the man who killed them. And you were the man who took the big profit. And now I want a favour... Enough "ands" for you in there, Mister Culling?'

Culling bowed his head. Monroe said, 'I don't want a cut of your take. I want you to get me access to the passport database for horses.'

Raising his head the vet said, 'Why?'

Monroe got up, feeling properly superior now, not having to wait for permission from his social 'betters'. He said, 'Never mind why, I want a complete copy of the database of passports of all horses in the UK.'

Frowning heavily, Culling watched him but didn't reply. Monroe said, 'Have it for me Monday and then you can get on with your business and I'll get on with mine.'

Culling nodded slowly. 'OK. OK, I'll get it.'

'Good. I'll call round. Same time.' It was an order. 'Aren't you going to see me out?'

The vet rose wearily and led him to the front door. Out on the step, breath white in the frosty air, Monroe said, 'I'll bet you I make more money than you do.'

Culling looked puzzled, then said, 'I'm sure you will, Mr Monroe. If you say so.'

Monroe's smile disappeared. He looked angry, hard. 'Don't patronize me, Culling. 'How much do you want to bet that I have more money than you one year from now?'

'Nothing! I don't want any bet with you! '

'Bet me! Bet me ten grand! Come on, you've got a head start. You're a smart man with a degree and letters after your name. I'm a nothing, an ex-jockey, a slaughter man with half a brain. You'll win, won't you? Bet me!' His voice was high and tense, ice blue eyes full of anger.

Culling lowered his voice almost to a whisper. 'Alright, I'll bet you. You have a bet.'

'Ten grand. One year from today. Money on the table. Whoever's got the least gives the other ten grand. Right?'

'Right. Right.' The vet sounded suddenly exhausted.

Monroe held out his hand. 'Shake on the bet!'

Culling reached slowly for his hand. They shook. Monroe pulled his hand away, sparks of rage still in his eyes. He raised a finger to face level and jabbed it toward the vet. 'I'll see you on Monday!'

He marched away across the block-paved yard, shoulders swinging, head high, ambition and self- congratulation almost consuming him.

16

On the first Sunday in December, Frankie rose, as he usually did, not long after dawn. His shaving mirror offered him as concise a summary as any doctor could have about his sleeping habits. Pale complexion, dark rings below his red-veined eyes; a generally haunted and hunted look. Frankie paused to stare at himself then looked down, thinking that Kathy would have hated to see him like this.

Bobby had been right, the new job had helped, and being with people was an advantage. Company had forced him to be as normal as possible, to be light-hearted when it was called for, to laugh from time to time, not to visit his troubles on others.

But the demons kept at bay in the daylight swamped him after dark, careered around in his head like malicious burglars returning to a property where they knew access was always available, where they could torment the demented, helpless caretaker all night long with pictures and film shows of his past.

Twenty minutes after daybreak he was dressed and sipping tea in the kitchen, standing by the window, watching the morning take shape. He ate some cereal and a piece of wholemeal bread and banana. He wasn't hungry but felt he should try and look after himself for the sake of appearance. Afterwards, he cleaned up, washed the dishes, pulled on a thick fleece and his old brown tweed cap that Kathy always laughed at and went out to welcome the sun as it rose over the frosty fields and woods.

Frankie returned just after nine and saw the message light flashing on his answerphone. It was Geoff Stonebanks, his colleague at the Jockey Club, asking Frankie to call him. They had their final day together on Friday. Frankie was now formally out on his own. He wondered, as he dialled the number, what the big man could want. It was the first time he'd ever called Frankie at home. Stonebanks answered on the second ring. 'Frankie, hope I didn't wake you?'

Frankie managed to find a smile for that. 'No, I was out. Sorry.'

'Don't apologize. Listen, we've got a bit of a problem.'

'Uh-uh?'

'You know Ulysses?'

'Uh-huh.' Frankie knew him alright; Ulysses was the ante-post favourite for the Cheltenham Gold Cup.

'He's been kidnapped.'

'When?'

'Last night, from his box at Jack Quigley's. The kidnapper left a note.'

'How much does he want?'

'Quarter of a million.'

Frankie wasn't sure what questions he should be asking or how he should be reacting. 'Who's the owner?'

'A man called Christopher Benjamin, a real fun guy. About as popular in racing as a sixteen-stone jockey.'

'Have you spoken to him?'

'I have. About ten minutes ago.'

'Is he paying the ransom?'

'Doesn't look like it, but he's of the definite opinion that as the police have no immediate solution to offer, we should be dumping all our other cases and getting his horse back for him.'

Frankie sighed. 'Sounds like a nice man to work with.'

'You bet. Can you meet me at Quigley's place at noon?'

'Surely. Near Wantage, isn't it?'

'About two miles north. Call me when you're close and I'll talk you in.'

The ransom note for Ulysses had been written with a black indelible marker in block capitals on a plain piece of A4 paper. Stonebanks had already been to see the police, and they'd given him a photocopy of the note. YOU REFUSED AN OFFER OF £500,000 FOR YOUR HORSE THREE MONTHS AGO. IT

SHOULD BE EASY FOR YOU TO PAY HALF THAT MUCH TO GET HIM BACK ALIVE. YOU HAVE FORTY EIGHT HOURS.

Stonebanks had met the owner, Christopher Benjamin, once before. It had been obvious when Benjamin introduced himself that he did not recall that meeting. Stonebanks chose not to remind him. They stood in Ulysses' empty box. Benjamin was impeccable in a light grey suit, white shirt, navy tie, polished shoes, the soles now ridged with a centimetre of reddish mud. In contrast, Ulysses' trainer, Jack Quigley, looked haggard and weary, unshaven. Frankie felt sorry for him.

They'd been over the story already with the police. The kidnapper had come in the night, poisoned the dogs, tied muffles (they reckoned, as no one had heard a sound) to Ulysses' hooves and simply led him out of his box. Frankie had noticed how uneasy Quigley was, constantly trying to avoid catching the obviously angry eye of Christopher Benjamin who'd been sniping indirectly at him almost since they'd arrived.

To no one in particular Benjamin would say things like, 'The Gold Cup favourite. How can he simply be spirited away in the night?' From a modern stable?' and 'How would people in normal business expect a valuable asset to be protected by those in charge of it? Is it right to rely on a few barks from a sleepy, vulnerable animal? Good God, surely not in this day and age.'

And Frankie would cringe a bit for poor Quigley, who was defenceless and knew it. Many top horses would have twenty-four hour stable guards prior to running in a major race, but there wasn't a trainer in the country who'd mount that guard four months before that event. OK, Frankie thought, maybe Quigley should have had some modern alarm equipment fitted but, as ever, hindsight was wonderful.

They went back inside the house. The trainer had builders in and the kitchen was a mess. He led them to a big basement room kitted out with a snooker table and a bar. A coffee machine stood in the corner and Quigley made them all a hot drink. They sat at the bar. Benjamin drew his fingers through his thick, silver-grey hair and looked at Stonebanks. 'Well, what next? Or should I say what first?'

Stonebanks said, 'We need to talk to all the staff, to the builders, to any suppliers who've been here in the past six months, to—'

Benjamin interrupted him. 'Wait a minute, wait a minute! We have forty-eight hours, Mister Stonebanks. Two days!'

'With respect, Mister Benjamin, we need to start somewhere. We can make a couple of assumptions but -'

Benjamin interrupted again. 'Look, the police have given me all this already. They seem to think this is about as serious as some ragamuffin kid stealing a kitten from a litter. I want Ulysses back safe and I want him back quickly.'

Stonebanks looked at him over the rim of his cup. 'Even if it means paying the ransom?'

Benjamin sneered in a half-smiling sort of way that said, is this man some kind of idiot? And Frankie disliked him even more. Benjamin said, 'I'm not paying any ransom, Mister Stonebanks. Don't we pay enough in fees all round to keep our horses in training, and people like you and your silent colleague in jobs?'

Stonebanks had been leaning back against the edge of the snooker table. He straightened. 'OK, Mister Benjamin. We'll do our best. We need to speak to everyone who's been on the premises recently. I'll start with Mister Quigley and my colleague Mister Houlihan will speak to the head lad.'

Talk fast then, Stonebanks. I want that horse back! Call me at my office within the hour!' Benjamin marched out, throwing the empty plastic cup on the floor to roll and dribble the dregs of its coffee on to the grey carpet.

Questioning of staff and builders and suppliers brought nothing. Frankie set about it with enthusiasm though Stonebanks told him it was all a waste of time and just went through the motions, despite a call from his boss who, in turn, was being harassed by owner Christopher Benjamin. Benjamin bullied the police into setting up a phone tap and by dusk, it was in place.

The dark grey cordless phone had been moved on to the old oak kitchen table. Frankie thought this smooth cold piece of plastic, which allowed contact with any other point in the modern world, appeared incongruous resting on the gnarled wood that looked a thousand years old.

For the first ten minutes, all four of them watched it. Jack nursed a large Scotch and the only sound in the room came when he raised it to his lips and the ice clinked. They stared as though the phone were a bomb; watched as though they were shackled there. Even their blink rates decreased with the concentration.

Then it rang.

As he put down the phone in the darkness of the remote call box deep in rural Oxfordshire, Gerry Monroe congratulated himself on his sharp criminal brain. He had upped the stakes with the Ulysses people, told them that he'd torture the horse and leave it in a hell of a mess if they didn't deliver the cash by midnight on Tuesday.

He wasn't expecting them to pay up. Not at this time. This first one was experimental. He needed to find out if he could get it all together, pull the whole thing off. The money didn't matter this time. He'd deliberately asked too much because he needed to see the reaction when they got the horse back dead. He needed to see how deeply they'd probe. Not very deeply, he suspected, but he had to see proof of that before taking his plan to the next stage.

Pulling on his helmet, he mounted the big black Kawasaki bike and fired up the engine. Under a moonless sky, the twin headlights carved a path through the blackness picking out squashed creatures and the faintest of white line markings.

Speeding through the night, he smiled behind the visor at his brilliant idea. How easy it had been to scare Culling into getting those files. Now he had access to information on all thoroughbreds registered in the UK. He had the markings for every horse in racing from its passport. He knew everything from each animal's overall colour to the pattern of hair growing on its flanks.

And he'd left not a trace behind.

Monroe whiled away the remainder of his journey planning how he'd spend his money once he was a millionaire. An expensive racehorse did not feature in his budget.

17

On Tuesday night in the dining area of trainer Jack Quigley's kitchen, Jack, Frankie, Stonebanks and Ulysses' owner, Christopher Benjamin, sat around the old table. The telephone was no longer the centre of attention. The kidnapper had said on Sunday that he would not call again until five to twelve on the Tuesday. If they had the money then he would arrange for collection. If they didn't, Ulysses would be dead by midnight.

Benjamin had no intention of paying. Nobody at the table doubted he had the funds to pay; he'd made millions trading in the international money markets. But he simply wasn't going to. He'd been there for most of the past twenty-four hours and had ruled like a prison camp commandant. The tension around the yard had grown almost tangibly as the hours ticked by. In the trainer's house, the atmosphere would have frayed the nerves of the calmest man.

Stonebanks and Frankie had spent much of the past two days liaising with the local police, interviewing Quigley's suppliers and ex-employees, talking to colleagues and paid contacts within the industry but they'd come up with nothing. And this laid them open to increasingly frequent thrusts of Benjamin's sarcasm and rudeness.

Stonebanks and Frankie thought that someone with a grudge against Benjamin was a much more likely suspect than anyone Jack Quigley had been involved with, but neither wanted to voice the thought.

At seven-thirty Eileen Quigley had offered to cook dinner. 'Nobody's hungry!' Benjamin snapped at her. 'Just make some tea!'

Frankie's eyes went to Jack when this happened and for the first time he saw a spark of real anger in the balding trainer's tense, tired face. But Quigley stayed silent. Frankie looked at Benjamin and just resisted shaking his head slowly. He was beginning to despise the man and he couldn't remember feeling that way about anyone before.

At nine-forty Benjamin looked at his big shining watch for the hundredth time that day then muttered something incomprehensible. Nobody had spoken for a while and Stonebanks said, 'Chances are the guy will give us an extension. He must know that forty-eight hours is a joke.'

All eyes turned to Benjamin. He said, 'And what sort of extension would you like, Mister Stonebanks? Would a year be long enough?' He shook his head slowly as if to say, 'Idiot'. He continued, 'Even if you had a year there would be as much chance of you people finding him as, as…'

'As you learning some manners,' Frankie said.

Benjamin froze for a few seconds then turned to Frankie. 'What did you say?'

'I think you heard what I said, Mister Benjamin.'

'What I heard was you being insolent and insubordinate. You've said so little in the past two days I was beginning to wonder if you were mentally handicapped in some way. I thought maybe you were on some special help scheme with the Jockey Club.'

'I'm not going to trade insults with you,' Frankie said.

'You're not going to trade anything with anybody, young man, especially with your local shopkeepers as you will have no salary to do any trading with when I speak to your boss.'

Frankie smiled.

Benjamin raised his voice. 'Do you hear me?'

'I hear you. I've said my piece. Let's all quieten down a bit. It's been a long day.'

'Don't tell me to quieten down, you little Irish bog man! '

'Talking of bogs,' Frankie said and got up and left the room.

'Come back here!' Benjamin shouted. Frankie kept walking. Quigley and Stonebanks fought hard not to smile. 'Are you his boss?' Benjamin asked Stonebanks.

'Unfortunately not.' Stonebanks said, thinking to himself that if he had been, he'd have recommended Frankie for a big salary increase.

'Then tell Robert Archibald I don't expect the insolent idiot to be in a job at the end of this week!'

'I'm afraid you'll have to tell him that yourself, Mister Benjamin.'

'Then you're a witness! I'll be citing you!'

'Fine.'

When Frankie came back five minutes later, he resisted a provocative smile or comment and settled back into his chair. It was just after ten o'clock.

Eileen Quigley walked in. Her slumped posture and general demeanour as well as her exhausted- looking, tear-stained face said everything about how the past two days had affected her. She was just the right side of forty but looked years older, even though she'd obviously put on makeup recently. She'd changed her clothes too in the past hour and looked smarter. In a hollow voice she said, 'Can I get anyone a tea or coffee?'

Benjamin turned in his seat. 'No you bloody can't! What you can get is a Yellow Pages! Do you have one of those or has somebody stolen that too?'

Frankie looked at Jack. The anger spark was even brighter. Eileen Quigley reached into the cupboard above the TV and took out a Yellow Pages directory. Wearily she brought it to the table, and laid it as carefully and apprehensively in front of Benjamin as she would have put food before a wild animal.

Benjamin threw it across the table at her husband. 'I suggest you turn to the section marked Transport and find someone who has a couple of horseboxes for hire tomorrow. If Ulysses is killed tonight, you'll be making calls in the morning to arrange for the removal of my other twelve horses.' Jack looked at him, his eyes showing the first real signs of defiance. But then he slowly picked up the book and started leafing through. His wife let go a sob, and sank back to lean on the short L-shape of the breakfast bar. Jack reached the page he wanted, took a pen from his shirt pocket and circled three telephone numbers. He ripped the page out. Then he walked around the table to where Benjamin sat. He put the page on the table in front of his biggest owner, the man who paid him almost £15,000 a month to train his horses, money that meant the difference between surviving in the life he'd always loved and going out of business. And he said, 'Put this in your pocket and get out of my house. Make the calls yourself. If Ulysses walked back through that door right now, I still wouldn't train another horse for you. I'd sooner starve to death.'

Benjamin was speechless. He looked at the torn-out page, then up at Quigley's angry but triumphant face. And what Benjamin saw was the source of his power evaporating, the loss of his control which was based on fear. He said, 'Sit down man, and don't be so bloody stupid!'

'No. You get up. I want you out of my house in the next sixty seconds and your horses out of my yard by noon tomorrow.'

'Listen -'

'No, you listen, you ignorant bastard! Get out before I punch you all the way to do the door and through it! Get out!'

Benjamin looked shaken as he got to his feet. Quigley suddenly seemed easily capable of what he threatened. The owner moved slowly toward the door. 'What about the call? What about Ulysses?' he asked in a much weaker voice than he'd been using earlier.

'We'll let you know in the morning when you come for your horses,' Quigley said.

'But I'm entitled to -'

Quigley interrupted. 'You're entitled to the same treatment, the same civility as you've shown us in the past two days, so you're entitled to be treated like shit. Keep walking.'

Benjamin stood and looked at his ex-trainer. Quigley moved toward him. Benjamin hurried out. There was a silence for a few seconds, and then Frankie started clapping. Stonebanks joined in as Eileen walked proudly toward her husband of sixteen years and put her arms around him. Jack Quigley smiled peacefully.

18

Things weren't panning out for David Hewitt the way he'd expected when he'd agreed to Corell's offer of the house and full lab facilities. Before moving in, he'd been worried about the supply of horses but they'd been plentiful - Hewitt had no complaints on quantity. It was quality he needed. He'd told that to Monroe often enough and now the slaughter man had come to see him with a proposal. Hewitt was nervous about calling Corell. Monroe wanted a lot of money, but Hewitt knew it would make a big difference to the project. Trouble was that in nine months he hadn't delivered a single thing although Corell hadn't put him under any pressure.

He sat on the arm of the chair in the library and watched the CCTV shot as Monroe's motorbike accelerated out of picture.

Through the tall window, the early-evening moon seemed huge, the richest yellow he could recall seeing it, like an enormous burnished coin. He was missing his girlfriend Marcia, and felt almost unfaithful when he spoke to her on the phone, as he had to lie about where he was. Corell had stressed the importance of nobody knowing what was going on in the big house.

The big house.

He'd walked around it all at the start, grateful for the space and the peace after the chaos of the university lab. Now the silence enveloped him, especially at night, a sinister silence. He played rock music and sometimes watched TV, but he'd found that keeping busy was the best way of warding off loneliness. He'd always had the capacity to lose himself in his work, and these past few weeks had shown him how valuable an asset this was. Hard work made the days seem shorter. It would also bring him more quickly to his goal. He'd have the professional satisfaction of leading his own field, not to mention a very big payoff from Corell and a share of future profits.

At the beginning, he'd tried to convince himself that this was a legitimate venture; that Corell was fully above board. But when he'd met him and his driver, Gleeson, and especially Gerry Monroe, he could no longer pretend, not even to himself, that these people were operating within the law. Monroe had just confirmed this with his proposal. Hewitt ran his fingers wearily through his thick fair hair and sighed. If he made this call to Corell, if he engineered the acceptance of Monroe's proposal, he was as good as colluding in whatever they were doing. Monroe had said, 'Don't worry about the names; you don't need to know anything in advance except that I can deliver. I'll tell you the names when I bring you the horses.'

He got up and went to the small table by the door. Kelly Corell's number was on a piece of paper by the telephone. Hewitt dialled.

Brendan Gleeson was in a Dublin betting shop when his mobile rang. Impatiently he pulled it from his pocket, about to switch it off so he could watch the end of the two-fifteen from Navan. Then he saw that it was Corell calling. He hurried outside and ran thirty yards down the street, making sure the blower commentary was out of earshot before he pressed to accept the call. His boss sounded a bit on edge and that made Gleeson nervy. 'Where are you?' Corell asked sharply.

'I've just come out of the supermarket, Mister Corell. Just getting something in for the tea for me and the boy.'

'Get yourself up here now.'

'Sure. Sure, Mister Corell.'

Gleeson ran to his car and drove fast to the club Corell owned. Twenty minutes later, he was on his way back to the docks. Beside him on the passenger seat was a grey canvas holdall with ten thousand pounds in Bank of England notes inside it. Gleeson had raced to the waterfront hoping to catch the 3.15 ferry, cursing everyone in his way. But when he reached the terminal, the ferry was still in port and the long queue of vehicles told him they hadn't even begun loading. The winter weather had done him a favour in delaying the sailing, but now that he was here, he wanted them to get on with it.

He watched the yellow-jacketed shore crew begin signalling them on board just after four o'clock. In the dimly lit hold, Gleeson parked and pulled his handbrake on tight, leaving his car in gear. Grabbing the bag, he hurried upstairs to quench his thirst. Ten minutes later, he was sitting at a table by the window through which the shore lights twinkled in the gathering dusk on the dark surface of Dublin Bay. In front of him on the pale blue table top were two pints of Guinness and two large Jameson's whiskies topped up with lemonade. He finished a glass of the whiskey in one drink then followed it by gulping a half-pint of Guinness. Only then did he relax, easing himself back in the seat, smiling as he waited for that familiar glow to take over and shift his troubles outside the worry zone.

Gleeson had no concerns about carrying the cash. He'd hide it on himself, among his clothes. When they searched at Holyhead, it was always the vehicle itself they checked. If he took the bag, they'd look inside it but he'd just leave it on board once he'd hidden the money. Easy. He drank half of the other whiskey. He'd need to be careful. He couldn't risk failing a breathalyzer on the other side, didn't want them to smell the drink off him especially as he'd persuaded Corell to let him bring the car. He'd argued it was just as quick by the time you'd taken into account the drives to the airports at each end and all the ballsing about with check-ins and stuff. There was also a much higher chance of being caught with the cash if he'd flown, with all that bag searching and frisking at the airport.

No, this was best.

An hour later, he knew he was drunk. The ship hadn't left port. They announced that the sailing might have to be postponed until the next day but they'd wait for just thirty minutes more to see if the weather in the Irish Sea improved. Gleeson judged that it was a hopeless case and decided to have a few more drinks. He'd drive confidently here in Dublin, even drunk.

But the ship sailed at five-thirty, and a cursing Gleeson eased himself out of the ridged seat and, swinging the grey holdall, walked unsteadily toward the illuminated toilet sign. On the way back from relieving himself, Gleeson noticed three men playing cards at a table by a big brown pillar. He walked over. A pile of notes lay on the table. Cigarettes burned in the glass ashtray, glasses with varying levels of Guinness rested on beer mats. Gleeson smiled. 'How'ye doin' lads? Mind if I sit in?'

As the ferry rode the swell past the North Stack to cover the last few miles into Holyhead, Gleeson was back in his seat at the window. The bag was empty. There was no money in his clothes except sixty-seven pence in change. Corell's money now belonged to three poker players who'd had almost equal shares in the past three hours. The anesthetizing effects of the booze were wearing off, and Gleeson stared into the night feeling as bad as he could ever remember. His face was desolate as the lights of the port glinted in his cold, resigned eyes. He'd be as well staying aboard and dropping himself quietly over the side halfway across the sea. It would save him time and worry and an awful lot of pain. He knew he was a dead man.

19

It had been a mild, wet autumn, and winter frosts had not yet been regular enough or sufficiently vicious to kill all the insect life. A swarm of flies fed on the bloodied wounds of the carcass. The horse lay in a shallow stream. Monroe had carried out his promise to mutilate the body and the big bay had been shot twice; once through the forehead, ploughing a hole like a dark sticky-edged pit in the clean white blaze, and again just below the left ear leaving brain matter smeared around the exit wound. The entry hole the bullet made lay submerged in the stream causing water to suck and blow, spouting at the flies, unsettling them for a moment before they crowded back. The horse's neck and flanks carried deep crescent-shaped slash marks. It was a week before they found him. The stream ran through an old abandoned construction site in Northamptonshire, on land that had been mapped out for a bypass until objectors got their way.

In Monroe's last call to Quigley, the killer had offered a clue; Think of being a bookie at Newbury. What's behind you and what's in front of you?' and he'd laughed and hung up. Nobody had been able to decipher the cryptic message. A man walking his dog found the body. When they went to recover it in a horse ambulance borrowed from Newbury racecourse, the meaning of the clue dawned on Frankie and he said to Stonebanks, 'If you're a bookie at Newbury, behind you is the water jump and in front of you is the new stand they're building. A construction site.'

Stonebanks nodded. 'He must have whiled away a nice evening thinking that up. Bloody lunatic.'

The police were there as Stonebanks backed the trailer as close to the bank of the stream as he dared. Stonebanks and Frankie, wellingtons on, waded into the water hauling the chain and Frankie winced as he lifted the eyeless bloodied head to let Stonebanks ease the heavy links around the horse's neck. A sergeant and a constable with a camera watched from above, a darkening sky behind them, as Stonebanks secured the chain and Frankie went back to start the winch motor. The mechanism ground noisily, gradually taking up the slack in the thick chain until it tightened around the horse's neck, squeezing brown blood from the eyeballs and exit wounds as the big body started moving slowly up the shallow banking.

Stonebanks could see that the underside was almost hairless, the flesh shrivelled from being submerged for so long, and he shook his head in disgust. He'd watched this horse racing more than once. It had been one of the most athletic, majestic jumpers of fences he'd ever seen. Those ripped and wasted muscles had propelled the half-ton thoroughbred around miles of track and over hundreds of jumps. And he ended up like this because of some madman.

They drove the carcass south to an abattoir to be kept in cold storage until the forensic people had seen it.

Back in his house in Lambourn, an excited Gerry Monroe had been waiting all week for the news to break.

It was late when Frankie got home. The cottage seemed even quieter than usual. It was a perfectly still night, barely a leaf rustled. A letter lay on the mat. Frankie went over by the window where, as ever, he'd left the lamp burning. He switched the kettle on and opened the envelope. It was from Martin Broxton, the trainer of Zuiderzie, and Frankie coloured a little as he recalled the emotional letter he'd sent pouring out his life story after Zuiderzie's Warwick victory.

It was a kind letter, handwritten and, Frankie thought, striking exactly the right note of sympathy and interest in Kathy's involvement with the horse. But Frankie's brows creased in the lamplight as he read the Zuiderzie had not survived more than a few hours after the race. The gelding had been struck by some mystery illness and had been put down. Broxton said he realized that this would come as a blow to Frankie on top of the troubles he already had, and that all at the yard missed the horse, who'd been a real character. But, said the trainer, 'That's racing,' a statement Frankie had heard and read hundreds of times over the years he'd followed the sport. That calm acceptance of the heartbreaks as well as the triumphs seemed to be typical of most people who were in the game in any professional capacity. Frankie identified with it easily, but the news of the horse's death hit him much harder than he'd expected. Zuiderzie had been the only living, breathing thing that he and Kathy still shared, as a memory, a touchstone. Frankie thought of his mother again, and of God, and wondered if he had indeed been cursed.

The other dead horse made front-page headlines in next day's *Racing Post*: ULYSSES SLAUGHTERED. KIDNAPPED GOLD CUP FAVOURITE FOUND DEAD IN STREAM.

There was a picture of Robert Archibald, Jockey Club Security Department Chief on page three. He said he'd been doing everything he could to find the killer of Ulysses and that all trainers should take precautions to protect their charges as another kidnapping could not be ruled out.

'Damn right it can't,' said Gerry Monroe aloud as he read it. 'Damn right.' He folded the paper and pushed it aside then spun on the swivel chair to tap his keyboard and bring the thoroughbred passport database on to the big bright screen.

After days and nights of research, Gerry Monroe decided on his next kidnapping target. He was going to have to travel north for this one if it was to be taken from the stable. He'd need to check the place out first. He knew Lambourn inside out, and he'd known how easy it would be to take Ulysses from Jack Quigley's place. But Graham Cassidy, who trained the very promising stayer, Angel Gabriel, was a stranger to him.

Cassidy's was a small stable up on the Shropshire-Cheshire border. The yard had never hit the headlines; it hadn't had anything good enough, but Monroe had checked the press cuttings and he knew Angel Gabriel had the right mix. The articles told him the horse was a precious family pet who all but lived in the house with the Cassidy family. The fact that the big chaser was also a live Grand National prospect was a bonus; it helped Monroe put a commercial value on the horse as well as a sentimental one. He wouldn't go so high this time because he wanted to have a realistic chance of collecting the ransom.

The press cuttings also told Monroe that the Cassidy family, with their very generous income from Mrs Cassidy's children's books, had no money worries. In fact, they seemed the perfect happy family with their twenty-year marriage and two smart kids, their beautiful cottage home adjoining the yard in the lush countryside away from all the backbiting and jealousy of the big training centres like Lambourn. The perfect happy family. Monroe smiled to himself and said aloud, 'Not for much longer.'

The postmark and the typeface of the address showing through the window told Maggie Cassidy that another royalty cheque had arrived. She loved how they tended to come on Monday mornings to make that normally dreariest of days much easier to face.

She kissed the envelope and carried it back to the sunny sitting room, where a half-finished cup of coffee and a just-lit cigarette in an ashtray sat on the polished circular table next to the big floral easy chair. Graham, as ever, was out with the horses. Billy and Jane were at school. A fine frost blanketed the countryside, working with the sun to cast that wonderful shade of winter light that Maggie loved. She'd had a huge picture window put in, almost half the size of the south-facing wall, so she could watch the weather and the light as the seasons came and went.

Maggie smiled as she luxuriated in opening the envelope, sliding her index finger into the gap at the top and slowly pulling the gummed ridge away. She didn't know how much the cheque would be for and she loved not knowing. Since the books had begun to sell really well and had been translated into more than fifteen languages, there was no way of keeping track of royalties. She just had to wait until the statement and the cheque came from her London agent.

This little ritual Maggie was going through showed her how much this money meant to her. All the years of struggling to survive made these moments so sweet.

The flap was fully open now. She could see the computer-generated codes on the edge of the cheque. She stopped and smiled, sipped coffee, drew deeply on her cigarette then eased the paperwork out and slowly plucked the cheque from the folds of the statement: £57,648.92

Her smile widened slowly and she read the figures again and checked the written amount to make sure she hadn't made a mistake. Almost sixty thousand. This was the biggest one she'd ever had. And her agent was working on an auction deal for her next three books, which he said, might bring in as much as half a million.

She laid her head back on the soft upholstery, closed her eyes and wondered, not for the first time, if this was really happening. They'd struggled for years as a family, working so hard, all of them, to try and fulfil the dream that had started as just Graham's - to win the Grand National. Not just to train the winner of the great race but to breed it, rear it, own it. At the outset, when they'd first met, Graham's dream had been to ride it too. But he'd been just twenty-five then. When he hit forty, he'd conceded that part of the fantasy to encroaching age and expanding waistline. But he still badly wanted the other two legs of what he called his 'dream treble'.

It was an obsession with him, one that had never dimmed. His determination, confidence and enthusiasm for realizing the dream had been a big factor in her falling for him. She loved the passion he showed. At the beginning, she'd have preferred that passion to be for her, but she accepted that even if it had been, it would have faded many years ago, tarnished by familiarity, and the ravages of time on her looks and figure. No, Graham's passion was sustainable because it never needed to be focused on just one creature. If a horse was never going to make the grade, it was quickly dismissed from her husband's thoughts, relegated to run in small races. A new focus was sought, a new horse, sleek, muscular, with a bold eye, a regal head; 'the Look of Eagles' Graham called it.

She'd decided it was probably best his dream wasn't of what she herself might achieve for him, or she would have been traded in and replaced several times over the years. She knew she'd never be Graham's number-one love, but he was rock-steady as a man and as a husband, and Maggie had come to value this above all. Some of her friends had much more 'interesting' spouses; life-and-soul types, romancers, off-the-wall men who could shock and surprise. But they could also be unfaithful, drink too much, abuse their wives and display most of the other flaws of unpredictable men. Graham would do fine for Maggie every time.

Staring at the cheque, she was trying to figure out what she'd buy him for Christmas. Her head went back again, her eyes closing slowly. This would be their third Christmas where debts would present no worries. Rather than resent money and what it did, or what lack of it did, as she'd done for most of her Christmases, she'd quickly learned to love it, almost to covet it. That scared her because this was the type of love stained by constant fear, a terrible worry that you'll lose your lover. That he'll up and go one day just when you were getting used to all the pleasure and security he'd brought. Disappear in the night, no forwarding address.

Maggie clutched the cheque tighter and tried to push the fear from her mind. She was almost fifty years old. If her agent could land this big deal, she could kill this terror, this dread of loss, once and for all. It wasn't as though she and Graham had another fifty years to survive. Twenty-five, maybe thirty. Half a million would be enough for that, wouldn't it?

She got up and went out to the yard. In the middle of the quadrangle made by the boxes, a chestnut mare called Mrs Molly stood sweating. Hazel, her blonde groom, held the horse's bridle while Graham Cassidy felt the mare's nearside foreleg for signs of heat, which would signify a return of the tendon injury Mrs Molly, had suffered more than a year ago.

Maggie tiptoed quietly toward them. The pitched roof of the stable boxes still showed a frosty collar just above the guttering where it was in the shade. Heat rising from the horses within had helped thaw the rooftops. But it was still cold, enough for the breaths of all four in the yard and the steam rising gently from Mrs Molly to be seen clear and white.

Hazel smiled as Maggie approached holding a finger to her lips, eyebrows raised. Graham was bent double. She stood behind him, waited until he straightened then softly put her hands over his eyes, still cradling the cheque in her palms. 'I smell money,' he said.

'How much do you smell?' asked Maggie, deepening her voice, mock-mysterious.

Her husband took a deep sniff. 'I smell enough to buy me that new suit I want for Christmas.' Maggie continued in the deep voice, 'Then you're only smelling the second line of the cheque.' She rose on tiptoes to push the cheque a foot away from his face, still holding it with two hands.

He opened his eyes. 'Good God!' he said. 'I should have said I smelt a new horse!'

Maggie laughed out loud. 'No chance!'

Hazel smiled but cursed them silently for not telling how much it was.

When Maggie told her children, at dinner, and showed them the cheque, their reactions reflected their characters and their own desires. Billy, thirteen, his thick light-brown hair, longish face and sharp jaw making him look already much like his father, spent most of his waking hours trying to come up with the 'big idea' that would make him millions. He scanned the internet for stories of young men like himself who'd made their fortunes in the world of e-commerce, even though he'd decided that all the seats were taken in that particular millionaires' stadium. Billy knew he'd have to invent something completely different to make his fortune. But he reckoned he'd a very good chance of doing that because all the entrepreneurs were falling over each other to come up with the next high- tech scheme. This convinced him that if he concentrated on the more practical, solid, day-to-day things people needed, then he'd be much more likely to succeed. He'd probably even overtake these guys. The internet bubble had to burst - had to. He was convinced of it.

'Aw Mum! Brilliant!' Billy said as he held the cheque. 'All that just for writing silly stuff for kids and drawing a few pictures! '

Smiling and reaching to take the cheque back, Maggie said, 'Yes, easy, isn't it? Why don't you try it, Billy boy?'

He shrugged. 'I would but it's too boring. I'd rather use my brain inventing things like what I've just come up with. And it's very lucky for you Mum that you've got that money 'cause now you'll have a chance to take a stake in my invention.'

'Which is what?' Maggie asked, pouring gravy over her beef and glancing at Graham and Jane, who were smiling knowingly and shaking their heads.

Billy chewed and smiled too and he was nodding gently as if to say, 'Go on, shake your heads and mock but one day I'll be rich and you won't be shaking your heads then.' He said, 'Mum, you need to promise to stake me for a patent application first.'

'Stake you? Stake you! Have you been watching those old gangster movies again?'

He coloured slightly. 'Nooo, Mum, that's what we say in the business. An investment for you.' Maggie nodded as though sizing up the proposal. She cut a piece of beef. 'And how much do these patent applications cost?'

'Oh, about five grand would do it, I would think.'

'Five grand! To send a letter to somewhere telling people what you've thought up?'

'It's not like that Mum, there's lots of paperwork and research and stuff to do. Five grand'd just be for the European rights to the Hot -' he stopped himself.

His sister said, 'To the hot what?'

Billy was annoyed with himself for almost giving it away. He looked across at Maggie. 'Mum, are you in?'

'I might be. Depends what comes after the hot.'

There was a big pause now and Billy felt the eyes of his whole family on him. They'd laughed at him before, plenty of times. He knew they didn't really mean to hurt him, but they did. He was the only one in the family who wasn't really great at something and he wanted to be, wanted to be the same as them. As good at something as his dad was at training horses; as good at something as his mum was at writing; as good at something as Jane was at being beautiful and having lots of friends and fund-raising and all the other stuff she did.

And coming up with ideas was all he could really do. He wasn't very good at school, didn't like it much. Hated being around girls because he felt so embarrassed and awkward at not having anything to say, to talk about, like being a good footballer or runner or PlayStation wizard like the others were. But the power of his mind was promising. He knew that, even if nobody else did.

'Come on Billy,' Jane said, 'The hot what? The hot water bottle? I'm afraid you're too late for that!'

They were waiting. Billy tried to look defiant as he said, 'The Hot Harrow.'

There was a silence for a few moments then Graham said, 'The what?'

'The Hot Harrow.' Billy was pleased that he'd stunned them with this one and his enthusiasm returned. 'It's especially important for you, Dad. I thought of it last weekend when we were harrowing the all-weather gallop. I know it's supposed to be all-weather but it isn't really, is it?'

'Not really, I suppose,' his father said.

'Because it gets quite hard packed if the frost gets into it and you need to harrow it for ages before a horse can even set foot on it.'

'Right, fine. But how does the Hot Harrow work?' asked Graham.

'Simple, the tractor's dragging the harrow. You harness the heat from the tractor engine and feed it to the metal on the harrow so it not only breaks up the frost with force, it melts it too, and that makes the whole thing much quicker.'

Graham nodded. 'How do you harness the heat?'

'Well, that's the bit I'm still working on,' said Billy, less confident now.

'The hardest bit,' Graham said.

'Not that hard, Dad. I just need to think about it a bit more.'

'Good. It's a good idea, Billy. Keep working on it.'

Billy smiled at the praise from his father then turned to his mother. 'What do you think, Mum? Are you in?'

'I think it's a good idea too. You solve the heat-harnessing problem and, er, get back to me. Isn't that what they say in the business world?'

Billy nodded, still smiling widely.

His sister Jane sat opposite him at the oval yew table. She could never remember a day when that table had not been there. Jane was certain she had memories of sitting at it in a high chair with a bowl of soggy mush on the plastic tray in front. She sat here now almost fifteen years later, a very pretty girl, small for her age, smaller than any of her friends, but with shining auburn hair, blue-green eyes and traces of summer freckles still spread across her delicate, slightly upturned nose onto her cheeks. Unlike most of her friends she wore no make-up or jewellery, had no piercings for studs and no intentions of letting anyone 'punch holes in her'. Her skin was smooth, blemish-free and her family were proud of her prettiness. Jane feigned indifference to her own looks but in her heart, she was proud of being different.

She swallowed some of her pasta and said to Maggie, 'Congratulations Mum. Were you expecting a cheque for that much?'

'No, God, no! Nothing like that much.'

Jane's eyes showed a tiny spark of triumph. 'Then why don't you give half of it to my Banish Blindness fund?'

Billy pretended he was choking on his food. 'Half of it! You're kidding! That's almost thirty grand!'

Maggie knew she wasn't kidding and she was stunned by both the request and the deviousness of her daughter's first question. And she was confused. She didn't know what to say in reply and Jane was looking at her, waiting coolly for that reply. Jane's fund-raising activities were something Maggie and Graham had always supported. The girl was tireless, had been since she was twelve and saw a TV programme about famine in Africa. And now she'd just proved she was also wily and a bit ruthless, and Maggie was suddenly seeing a new side to the first child she'd borne, and her mind and her emotions weren't quite coping. She looked at her husband. He raised his eyebrows in a way that said, "I can't help. Over to you."

She looked at Jane and said, 'Of course I'll make a contribution to your fund.'

'A half?'

Billy spluttered again. Maggie felt anger showing in her eyes and hoped that it would make Jane back off. But Jane stayed cool, waiting. Maggie didn't know if her daughter felt in any way uncomfortable at such an obvious confrontation, one she had cunningly engineered. What she did know was that Jane would be thinking that the end justified the means. Those people in Africa blinded by cataracts could be easily and cheaply treated, and twenty-eight thousand pounds would give an awful lot of people their sight back. If achieving this meant making her mother feel uncomfortable and embarrassed, then Maggie knew that Jane would be able to live with that. She made a decision. 'How much have you raised so far?'

'Just over six hundred and sixty pounds. Mum, this would make such a difference.' And her face softened and Maggie saw her daughter again, saw that pleading look which told how deeply she really felt about this.

Maggie nodded. 'And when does this particular campaign end?'

'I wanted to send the money off just before Christmas. Just think what a gift it would be for those poor people to know they were going into the New Year with the hope of being able to see again. To see their families.'

Maggie had been going to say that she would match the final total but now that seemed mean and paltry. She said, 'Whatever your final total is, I'll multiply it by ten and write you a cheque.' She suddenly had a quick flashback to Jane's devious setup question.

There was no telling of what manipulations her daughter might get into to jack up the final total, so she added, 'Up to a maximum of ten thousand pounds.'

Jane smiled and Maggie was relieved to know she wasn't going to argue with that. Not right away, at least. Billy said, 'Oh, Mum! That's twice the cost of a patent application, that's not fair.'

Jane turned to her brother. 'The Hot Harrow isn't going to make anyone see again, is it?'

Billy was lost for words and blurted out. 'OK, maybe it won't, but it could help people over there once they can see to grow crops and stuff! '

Jane said, 'And when was the last time there was frost in Africa?'

Billy went redder, mad at his sister, too clever for him yet again. 'Well, just a normal harrow then. I could help pay for those through sales of my Hot Harrow! Couldn't I Dad?'

Graham said, 'You could, I'm sure you could, but I think it's time we all calmed down and finished eating. There's evening stables to be done yet. You'll all need something hot inside you before we go back out into the cold.'

Billy groaned. Jane flashed a triumphant smile. Maggie found she couldn't finish her meal and got up from the table. 'I'll wash up.'

Jane scooped the last of her pasta into her mouth and through it said, 'I'll dry, Mum! '

Maggie turned to her. 'It's OK. I'll wash and dry.' She took Jane's plate. Their eyes met, and Maggie knew in that moment that her relationship with her daughter would never be quite the same again.

When the family came out into the half-lit yard to complete the ritual of checking the horses and giving them their last feed, Monroe could see their breaths pluming in the night air. He was crouching by the fence in the bare-treed orchard, the darkness offering all the cover he needed. The three square lights on the walls of the stables sent beams through the mist, making the Cassidy family look like ghosts as they separated and drifted away from each other to disappear into the shadowy boxes.

20

When Stonebanks asked Frankie if he'd mind covering Ascot for him on the Saturday before Christmas, Frankie was relieved and glad to accept. It rescued him from the seemingly inescapable assault of the coming festivities, and also gave him a solid excuse to decline Bobby Cranfield's invitation to have lunch and spend the day in his private box.

He'd thanked Bobby for the invite but had already said that he thought it was now inappropriate to be his guest at racemeetings. Bobby was PR director for the Jockey Club and Frankie was an employee. Nepotism was rife in racing. Without it, the game would probably grind to a halt. But now that he was getting into the job properly, Frankie was keen to prove himself through his own hard work; whatever he was to achieve, he didn't want people thinking it would be on the coat tails of one of the directors. Anyway, Bobby also owned quite a few horses now and Frankie had laughingly said to him, 'What if I end up investigating you or one of your trainers or jockeys sometime? I need to be seen to be acting absolutely independently.'

Bobby had laughed it off too and tried to persuade Frankie to come for lunch at the very least. But Frankie won the debate and Bobby, good-naturedly as ever, conceded. His parting shot was, 'Well Frankie, you're not allowed to have a bet so you wouldn't have been able to take advantage of my big tip for Saturday. My trainer reckons Arctic Actor is a certainty in the handicap hurdle.

When you see me in the winners' enclosure, you can at least shake my hand! '

Frankie promised he would.

Despite his failure to make any headway in the case of the kidnapping and death of Ulysses, Frankie was sharpening his skills and his confidence was growing. Few people on the racecourse knew who he was. He blended into the background wearing casual clothes, greens and greys and browns. He had a variety of sweaters and trousers that he wore in cycles, trying not to dress the same two days running. He had bought two new coats and now had five in all.

He felt it was important that none of the regulars began to notice the same man appearing frequently on the southern racecourses on weekdays as well as weekends, drifting around the betting ring, the paddock, the Tote windows, the stables area. Anyone who had noticed him wouldn't have seen much. He never approached a bookmaker or had a bet on the Tote. They wouldn't have known that he had a small but high-quality camera in his coat pocket. Nobody so far, Frankie was certain, had seen him taking pictures of 'interesting' people and who those people were talking to or drinking beside, or betting with. Sooner or later, they would twig him and find out exactly who he was, but until that time, he had an advantage, which he intended to keep for as long as possible.

At Ascot Frankie spent the first two races wandering around the betting ring; wherever he was in that noisy gathering he could always hear the braying voice of Compton Breslin, the well-known bookie.

Frankie couldn't pass him without smiling. Like himself, Breslin never wore the same clothes two days running but whereas Frankie dressed for anonymity, Breslin wore the most outrageously bright and stagey clothes imaginable. Frankie knew that this and his brashness, his sometimes personal and loud-mouthed challenges to circling individuals clutching cash, were all a carefully planned part of Breslin's strategy. Bookmakers were already the natural enemies of punters; if one gave cause for personal dislike as well, then all the more reason to try and take his money. And Frankie knew, as most did, that Breslin was the only winner in the long run. The fat bookie drove a gold Rolls Royce, of all things. From the moment he parked it and got out, he'd be shooting his mouth off at racegoers approaching the entrances, handing out gold-edged business cards to them, inviting them to come and take him on.

In the betting ring before the start of the handicap hurdle, Frankie had to concede that Breslin did at least put his money where his mouth was. Bobby Cranfield's horse Arctic Actor was a hot favourite with most bookies at six-to-four. Breslin called thirteen-to-eight and seven-to-four and was taking all the business on the favourite without reducing the price as most of them did to try and balance their books. Breslin just kept shouting the odds, coining in more and more cash while his colleagues looked on sour-faced. Frankie knew they'd all love to see the favourite win now so Breslin would be crucified.

Then he stopped and wondered at his use of that word, and felt almost as though he should apologize silently to Jesus.

He moved away to watch the race from the stands. If Bobby was right about Arctic Actor being a certainty, then Breslin would be taking a very cold bath indeed. Frankie made a mental note to go back into the ring after the race, just to see if Breslin could maintain the same confident demeanour when paying out.

But there was never any danger of the money bet on Arctic Actor going anywhere except into Breslin's bank account. An unconsidered outsider called Colonialize led from the tape, went well clear early and was never caught. Frankie watched him gallop past the post to an almost silent reception from the crowd. One of the things that had attracted him to racing many years ago had been the sheer passion of the spectators as they cheered their horse on; close finishes involving fancied horses were particularly atmospheric. But when twenty-to-one shots finished well clear of the others, things tended to be more funereal. Frankie smiled wryly; that's racing, he thought. He felt a twinge of sympathy for his friend Bobby Cranfield, but he knew there'd be no serious damage to the man's wallet. Still, Bobby would be embarrassed at tipping the horse to his friends. It had finished second, but not for a moment had it looked like catching Colonialize.

Three hours after winning the race, the tall narrow chestnut Colonialize was led shivering to Peter Culling's operating theatre, and the lad who looked after him was sent away. Culling injected the horse and stood watching as the shivers visibly slowed as though some internal battery was running down, then eventually stopped. He led the horse to a box and started rubbing him dry with some straw.

Back to the house then for a couple of hours in front of the TV before calling the trainer to report that the horse hadn't made it. Next, he rang Gerry Monroe and asked him to pick up the horse in the morning.

'I'm busy in the morning. I'll do it in the afternoon,' Monroe said.

Culling paused, trying to keep his temper. Since giving in to Monroe that night, the whole business had become fraught to the point where he couldn't manage the stress. He knew what it must be doing to his heart. He was nailed between the power Monroe now had and the dread of being caught by the authorities, a fate which grew more likely the longer the horses stayed on his premises. Culling had two assistants. Part of his strategy of doing his doping on Saturdays was that only he was on the premises on Saturday nights and Sunday mornings.

'It has to be in the morning, Gerry,' he said nervously.

Monroe's voice hardened. 'It doesn't have to be anything other than what I say, Mister Culling!'

'I didn't mean it to sound like that. It's just that, well, if things don't work out as planned, I won't be able to provide any more horses for you.'

'So? I'm sure there are some more bent vets around.'

Culling's face went red. His grip on the receiver tightened and he knew he had to get off the phone before his blood pressure rose any higher. 'Do it when you can make it then. The horse will be in the usual place. Goodbye.' He hung up and made himself walk away slowly to the conservatory to practise deep breathing.

Monroe had planned to spend one final evening up north to do a last recce on the Cassidy place.

Still, he already had a pretty good handle on procedure in the yard. On two days that week, they'd had runners. Graham Cassidy had driven the box so it was a fair assumption that when they had a runner, the boss would be away leaving just Mrs Cassidy and one groom. There were only eight horses in the yard and that didn't merit a head lad, which made Monroe's task easier.

He'd considered going on a raceday and simply leading Angel Gabriel across the fields to where he'd park a trailer. Mrs Cassidy seemed to go out very little and Monroe reckoned she locked herself away somewhere to work on her writing, but in the end, he'd decided not to take the risk. There appeared to be no form of burglar alarm. Three security lights came on if anyone approached after dark, but he'd noticed them do so when no one was around and suspected that small animals also triggered the beams.

The Cassidys had a couple of dogs who seemed to live inside most of the time. He'd yet to hear them bark. He was sure he could sneak in during the early hours of the morning and damp the big horse's hooves with rubber boots normally used for horses with foot problems. He had half-considered going in tonight, Saturday, but Culling's call had made his mind up for him. He'd head south again, pick this horse up from the vet's and take it to Hewitt's place.

He decided he'd steal Angel Gabriel in the early hours of Christmas Day, and as he made his way back across the fields toward his car, he congratulated himself on the irony of his timing. He smiled as he tried to recall the line from school lessons. He said it aloud: 'And the Angel Gabriel said to Mary, "You are with child." And Gerry Monroe said to the Cassidys, "You are without horse."' And he laughed at his cleverness and said, 'Shit, that's brilliant.'

21

Frankie couldn't face Christmas in Winterfold Cottage. He moved out on the Saturday night. His first impulse had been to find a hotel in London and book in for a week, but the intensity of Christmas, or at least the commercial side of it, would be even more acute in the capital. He recalled seeing an ad in the newspaper and he scanned through until he found the 'hideaway for those who hate Christmas!' It was a country house hotel in Builth Wells over the Welsh border, remote enough to lose himself for a few days but not that far from civilization. If needed he could be back in London quite quickly. He'd worked every week, already had a day off booked for Monday and racing stopped for three days on the run-up to Christmas. If he could have Tuesday off, that would give him a week away from everything; work, the cottage, Christmas.

As he drove west, he thought about where he'd really like to be going - to a monastery somewhere for a week-long retreat. He felt the need of God, of his comfort, much more at that moment than he ever had, but it was denied him because of what he had done. He'd convinced himself of this. There was no road back, especially for the hypocrite. He had a yearning too for his mother, for her forgiveness, her love. But he knew she despised him, was certain that if he knocked on her door she would turn him away.

At the hotel, he was relieved at the complete absence of Christmas paraphernalia and at the calm, professional welcome he received. The hotel was baronial, inside and the sound of his footsteps reminded him of the echo in the grand churches. His room was spacious and tastefully decorated, the big bed supremely comfortable. He'd arrived too late for dinner but had no appetite anyway, and he hung up his clothes and climbed in between the cool sheets.

He lay a while luxuriating in the softness as the bed seemed to envelop him, hold him tenderly, almost as though it were human and knew of his sorrow. And he slept.

Sixty miles north of Frankie, Maggie Cassidy lay awake beside her sleeping husband. Her mind had been in turmoil since she'd taken a call the previous afternoon from her agent. He told her with delight that the auction for her next three books had brought a winning bid of half a million pounds. The news stunned Maggie to the extent that, while she was saying to her agent how wonderful it was, she imagined that it was happening to someone else.

Maggie agonized for hours, then decided she would keep the news secret, deposit the cheque quietly in her bank and get on with life. That would be best for everyone, definitely.

After less than four hours' sleep, Maggie was awakened by the first phone call congratulating her on her good fortune. The story had made the Sunday papers. Maggie hurried to the bathroom and wept quietly.

After lunch on Sunday, Frankie went walking in the countryside around the hotel where lush, sheep- dotted pastureland covered the low swell of the hills. The weather was cold but fine and Frankie thought the sky looked a remarkably rich blue. He'd been out for an hour and his spirits had picked up considerably. Then he got a call from Bobby Cranfield.

'Frankie, I'm sorry to trouble you on a Sunday.'

'No problem, good to hear from you. Sorry about your horse getting stuffed yesterday.'

'That's why I'm ringing. You were on duty at Ascot yesterday, weren't you?'

'Yes.'

'Did you pick up anything unusual around that race?'

Frankie thought for a few moments. 'Not really… no. Nothing I can think of. Why?'

'Well something wasn't quite right about the way Colonialize won that race. He's run against mine half a dozen times in the past and never got anywhere near him, yet he won yesterday as though he could have gone round again. I've been through all the formbooks; it wasn't even his style of running to make all, he's always been held up.'

'Maybe that was the secret then,' Frankie said. 'Maybe the front-running tactics suited him much better.'

'I don't think so.'

Frankie noted the hesitation then deliberate pause before Bobby said, 'He ran as if he'd been doped.' Frankie's inexperience made him ponder as he tried to gather his thoughts. He said, 'Wouldn't he have been dope-tested after the race?'

'He was. We won't get the results until next week but I'll be awaiting them, as they say, with interest.'

'And no doubt hoping that you're wrong. The last thing we need's a doping scandal.'

'Dead right. Anyway, I also called to see how you were. I should have asked that first. Very rude of me.'

'Not at all. I'm OK. Felt I had to get away from the cottage for Christmas, so I've found myself a nice quiet country hotel. If I can persuade Geoff Stonebanks to cover for me on Tuesday I'm going to stay here for a week and just unwind.'

Bobby Cranfield sounded immediately concerned. 'Frankie, you mustn't spend Christmas on your own. Come and stay with us! We'd be absolutely delighted to have your company over Christmas.'

'No thanks, Bobby. It's very kind of you to offer but I really would rather be on my own.' He could sense the frustration, the exasperation in Bobby but the older man restrained himself. 'Well I understand, but Frankie, if you change your mind, promise you'll call me.'

Frankie smiled. 'I promise.'

'Good. Good. Well, I'll let you get on with your relaxation. Have a very happy Christmas.' It was out before he realized how hollow it must sound but Frankie quickly put him at ease.

'I will, Bobby, and I wish you and your family the same.'

'Take care, Frankie.'

As he pressed the 'End' button on his phone, the thing that had been niggling at his mind these past few minutes came through clearly; Compton Breslin. The bookie had been persistently offering longer odds against Bobby's horse than anyone else. That could mean that Breslin simply didn't fancy it or it could mean that someone had told him it was going to lose. And if Colonialize had been doped, not only had Breslin probably been told that the favourite would lose, there was every chance he'd have known that Colonialize would win.

Frankie considered ringing Bobby straight back. Then he thought about how he'd often heard Breslin shouting odds about a fancied horse, although he'd never paid particular attention to whether those odds were longer than those offered by his competitors. Yesterday was probably no more than normal practise for the big bookie. Frankie decided he'd wait until the dope test results were through before deciding what to do about Breslin.

The Welsh sky was still clear but a cold wind had got up. Frankie checked his watch, turned up his collar and headed back toward the hotel.

22

On Monday, the *Racing Post* carried the news of Maggie Cassidy's half-million-pound book contract on page three along with a picture of Maggie and Angel Gabriel. Reading it over breakfast, Gerry Monroe cackled with glee. 'Christmas has come early.'

Frankie too read the *Racing Post* over breakfast, checking through all the comments from Ascot on Saturday and looking at the betting analysis to see if he could glean anything from the race Colonialize had won. There were no unusually large bets reported on the winner.

Scanning through the rest of the paper Frankie noticed the piece on Maggie Cassidy and he found it heart-warming. She was a writer just like Kathy had been, albeit working in a different format. He held the page up better to catch the light from the big window behind his table; there was a resemblance to Kathy too in the woman's looks. She wasn't quite an older version, but she had the same shaped eyes and jaw line, and the same sort of mischievous look about her. The article went on to discuss Angel Gabriel's prospects in the Grand National and suddenly the image of the dead Ulysses in the stream sprang to Frankie's mind.

He left an almost full cup of tea and went to his room for his diary. In it, he found the number of Jamie Robson, his colleague in the north-west. When he rang, he heard a message telling him that Jamie was away for Christmas and that all business calls should be directed to the Jockey Club Security Department in London.

Frankie reached back into his briefcase and took out his Directory of The Turf telephone book. He found the Cassidy number and dialled; engaged. He tried for more than twenty minutes before getting through and was answered by an exasperated Maggie, who by now couldn't help but laugh slightly as she said, 'Hello, the Cassidy madhouse!'

Frankie guessed that every time she'd put the phone down it had rung again. He said, 'Is that Mrs Cassidy?'

'It is she.'

'We haven't met, my name is Frankie Houlihan. I'm a racing intelligence officer with the Jockey Club Security Department.'

'Oh, hello. What can I do for you?'

'I'm sorry to trouble you. Jamie Robson, who I think you probably know, would normally have rung but he's away on holiday.'

'Lucky him. I could do with one.'

'Would it be possible to speak to your husband? I'm sorry to be so formal but it's probably best if I speak to the licence-holder.'

'Is anything wrong?' Frankie could read the tone exactly and knew Maggie suffered from the same brand of fatalism as he did; if things were going outrageously well, then something bad was sure to come along.

'No,' he said. 'Nothing at all, just a sort of pre-emptive call on my part. Nothing really to worry about.'

She hesitated then said, 'Can you hold on? Graham's out in the yard. I'll just go and get him.'

'Sure, and by the way, congratulations on your good news.'

'Thanks. Thank you.'

He heard the receiver being put down on a hard surface, and he waited for what seemed quite a long time before he heard footsteps approach and voices growing louder. A rattle again as the receiver was picked up; 'Graham Cassidy. Can I help?'

Frankie introduced himself and went through the same spiel as he had with Mrs Cassidy. 'I hope you don't mind me calling, Mister Cassidy. I read the piece about your wife's good fortune in the *Racing Post*, and thought it was worth mentioning to you that the department believes that the person who kidnapped and killed Ulysses a couple of weeks back may well, eh, strike again, to use a tabloid phrase.'

'Oh, thanks. Thanks. We hadn't thought of that. Good point. I'm glad you rang.'

'That's OK.' Frankie was relieved. He'd been unsure of the reaction he might get, and had thought that grannies and egg sucking might have been mentioned.

The trainer said, 'Is there, eh, anything in particular you'd recommend we do? Security-wise, I mean?'

That caught Frankie out. 'Well, it's up to you really. I'm not familiar with the security you have in place at the moment.'

'Not much, really. We've got some lights that come on automatically in the yard at night if anyone approaches. But to be honest we don't pay much attention when they do. We're usually sound asleep by ten.'

'You've got no form of alarm system?'

'Well, there's one in the house but nothing in the yard. An alarm going off in the middle of the night would probably leave us with a stable full of nervous wrecks anyway.'

'Do you keep the place locked at night?'

'No, we're too afraid to. Had a fire here about ten years ago and three horses were trapped in a locked stable. To be honest, I'd rather they were kidnapped than burned to death if a fire broke out.' That left Frankie at a loss. 'Well, maybe you should contact your local police crime prevention people and see if they can suggest anything.'

'Good idea!' Cassidy sounded pleased. 'I'll do that. I'll give them a call.'

'Fine. Well, I'll let you get on with your celebrations.'

'Indeed, yes. Thanks.'

'Happy Christmas.'

'And to you and yours, Mister Houlihan. Oh, do I need to take your number?'

'You're welcome to.'

'Fine. I have a pen...'

In the twilight of Christmas Eve, Jane Cassidy finished laying a bed of fresh straw in the box of the animal she'd known and loved for most of her life. She had clear memories of her four-year-old self, clutching her mother's hand as she watched her father help the straining fat mare deliver the slippery sac of dark hair and legs that was to be christened Angel Gabriel and known to the family as Gabby. As mucus from the mouth of the foal dripped from her father's fingers as he cleaned it to open the airways, Jane has said, 'Has he been chewing gum, Dad?' She recalled how her mum and dad had laughed.

The racing public also loved Angel Gabriel for his spirit and his wonderful jumping. And Jane Cassidy loved him because he was all the things the public knew and more; gentle, intelligent and loving. When she'd been a child, it wasn't unusual for her mother to find her asleep in his box, curled up in the straw between his metal-shod feet. He was also a constant in her life. He'd always been there, had never scolded her or fallen out with her or teased her. Gabby had always been glad to see her, no matter how foul a mood she might be in. He seemed to hear her footsteps as she approached and he'd give a small whinny of anticipation, then nuzzle her warmly as soon as she reached him.

Jane forked the straw for the hundredth time, trying to make it level. A brand-new bed of this thickness was a rare treat. As with other yards, bedding was usually sifted each day and the droppings and wet straw removed. The remaining straw was simply topped up. But for Christmas, Angel Gabriel had a fresh, sweet-smelling cushion.

She put the fork outside the box and unbuckled Gabby's rug. Taking a stiff-bristled brush, she worked on his back and tail, cleaning away the wisps of straw and the dust; then to his mane, singing softly to him now, making his ears prick and swivel. 'Silent night, holy night...' Her voice was pleasant. The horse stood very still as though listening intently. 'You like that one, do you?' She asked and his ears flicked again. She spoke to him, 'Remember, I'm going away soon. Going to Ireland for a while to see Poppy. She's hurt herself. I'm going to help her get better. Be away for a while but Dad'll look after you... Doesn't Dad always look after you, eh? Don't worry. Will you miss me? I'll miss you. I'll miss your smell, well, not your poo, I won't miss that! And I'll miss the warmth of you when it's cold like this.' She was crouching beneath him now, doing his underside, knowing he'd be nodding furiously as he always did when she brushed his belly.

When she finished, she put his rug back on and filled his hay net and water bucket, then stood back and looked at him. 'You're all done up for the party season,' she said and moved forward again and hugged his neck. 'Happy Christmas, Gabby.'

As the Cassidy family finished eating Christmas Eve dinner, strong winds were whipping over the Shropshire fields. Maggie Cassidy washed up, taking pleasure in hearing the gale outside and listening to Graham and the children talking at the table, safe and warm.

The atmosphere was perfect. Everything was set for a proper, traditional Christmas. The tree glowed in the corner; logs burned in the big grate, warming the cushions in the inglenook. The dogs lay dozing on the rug and the family were in harmony. Even the horses were well. It was unusual not to have at least one animal down with something or other, but all were fit and healthy. December had brought three winners, a good bag for such a small stable. Graham was as happy as she'd ever known him. Above all, there was money in the bank and more on the way.

Maggie stopped for a few seconds, just stood completely still to make sure she took in this moment. She forced her mind to concentrate on the meaning of it, the beauty of it; for she knew she would never get it back.

Graham Cassidy had intended to keep the fire going until it was time for bed, but the wind blew with such a force outside that it funnelled gusts down the chimney, making the flames and smoke billow out dangerously over the hearth. Graham damped the fire down and decided to go and check on the horses.

Travelling north on the M6, Gerry Monroe was losing time. The sides of the horsebox caught the crosswinds like sails, and anything above forty-five miles an hour saw him using all his strength to keep the box on the inside lane. Although he cursed constantly, he wasn't too despondent. He knew the weather would be making so much noise around the yard, clattering every loose slate, screaming through each gap, setting every hanging thing swinging, that the trade-off was worth it. Unless Angel Gabriel spooked at it all, it should be an easy task to lead him out of the stable and away.

23

The storm battered Ballard Hall, Frankie Houlihan's hotel hideaway, with all it could muster, but the solid oak doors and two-foot-thick walls shrugged it off without so much as a rattle or squeak.

Yellow light shone from just one first-floor bedroom where Frankie lay listening to Faure's Requiem on the bedside radio. He was feeling emotional. Not just because it was Christmas Eve and Kathy wasn't with him. He'd just taken a call on his mobile from his sister, Theresa, who'd got the number from the message on his answerphone at home.

She'd told him that all the family was well, including Mother. It had warmed Frankie's heart to hear her voice, to hear her talk of their brothers and sisters. Theresa had tried to persuade him to call them all, wish them a merry Christmas. 'Maybe next year,' Frankie had said.

He was up early next morning out running in the wet, shining countryside of the Welsh borders. When he returned to his room, he found a message on his mobile phone. It was from a grievously serious Graham Cassidy. 'Mister Houlihan, I'm really sorry to be ringing you on Christmas Day but I'm afraid the worst has happened, as you warned. I'd very much appreciate a call whenever it's convenient.'

A seventy-five minute drive on almost-deserted roads took Frankie to the Cassidy place. On the way, he called Geoff Stonebanks and told him about the kidnapping. Stonebanks asked

Frankie if he could handle it until the next day. He could tell that the big man was distressed about this happening on Christmas Day, but not half as distressed, Frankie thought, as the Cassidys would be.

As he turned to go along the final rough road toward the Cassidy place, he felt guilty for feeling relieved that this had come up to break the melancholy, the monotony of these days. It was unfortunate that somebody had to suffer so his mind could be freed of self-pity for a day or two.

The door was dark green with a diamond-shaped window so thick that the glass distorted the light and movement inside. Below the window hung a huge Christmas wreath, its foliage damaged from the battering the wind had given it. As he waited for a response to his brief press on the bell, Frankie could see the scratch marks the holly had made in the door's paintwork.

When Maggie Cassidy opened the door and saw him, she knew somehow who he was. The man with the nice Irish voice who'd spoken to her the other night. He hadn't said anything yet, but she knew it was him. Just over six foot tall, she judged, slim, strong looking with thick dark hair, and eyes that were a vivid blue as the reflection of the pale sun on the glass caught them.

'Mrs Cassidy?'

She smiled and held out her hand. 'Mister Houlihan. Please come in.'

Frankie walked past her. The door opened into the kitchen. Frankie had seen so many of these kitchens now, with their big pine tables and Agas, their tiled walls hung haphazardly with pictures, framed and unframed; the deep windows, the brightness, the colour. Frankie had been at quite a few trainers' houses and all of their kitchens looked pretty much the same, like the Cassidys', although this one was the tidiest he'd seen. It was homely-looking but neat and very tidy. Frankie wondered if the Cassidys had a cleaner, although the 'memory' of Mrs Cassidy's handshake a minute ago suggested she'd done plenty of hard work in her own life. When shaking hands with women, Frankie was sometimes embarrassed by the softness of his hands, which had never done manual work.

Maggie closed the door and moved toward the table. 'Please sit down, Mister Houlihan. The kettle's just boiled if you'd like a cup of tea or coffee.'

'A cup of tea would be nice.'

She smiled. 'Fine. You look like a milk and no sugar man.'

'I am. I am indeed. I didn't know it was so obvious.'

'Ahh, it is. A slight turning down of the right eyelid at the corner. Always gives it away.' She was smiling warmly and Frankie was beginning to wonder if he'd come to the wrong place. He watched her pour the hot water into a pale blue teapot. He liked her, as he had done when he'd seen her picture in the paper and when he'd spoken to her briefly on the phone. She seemed naturally friendly and at ease, confident. He liked confident women. Admired was a better word, Frankie thought, under the circumstances. It wasn't right to like other women, that wasn't the expression he was looking for. You could admire a woman for her achievements, and being confident these days was, he supposed, an achievement in itself.

Maggie Cassidy turned toward him. Her shoulder-length hair was thick, and looked to Frankie as if the grey had been rinsed back to her natural rich brown colour. She said, 'Are you hungry?'

'No, thanks.'

'You had breakfast then before you left home?'

'I haven't been at home but I did have a fine breakfast this morning.'

'And what did you have then?' She asked.

'I had porridge and bacon and eggs, toast and marmalade and two cups of tea,' Frankie said, feeling rather like a child.

Maggie laughed lightly. 'If I'd eaten that at eight o'clock, I'd be a stone heavier by now!'

'Ah well, I went for a run beforehand,' he said lamely.

'Maybe I should take up running?'

Frankie shrugged and smiled then looked away, suddenly feeling awkward. Maggie brought two yellow mugs of tea to the table and sat down opposite Frankie. She pushed his across and he reached to take it. He smiled a thank-you and sipped. He could see the lines now around her eyes and mouth, and judged that she was mid-to-late forties. She wore a light covering of make-up; no lipstick but some sort of stuff on her skin and a trace of eye shadow and mascara. She returned his smile and he saw a deep intelligence in her hazel eyes, but there was vulnerability there too; she was obviously finding it tough to mask the stress of what had happened.

'How is your husband?' Frankie asked.

She was silent for a few moments, then said, 'Philosophical, I suppose. That would be the best way to put it. At least that's the face he's putting on to others. I know he'll be gutted at the thought of Gabby being away from him, never mind with some kidnapper. Graham's spent his life bouncing back from things; he'll find a way to handle this.'

'Is he around?'

'He's out with the horses. Getting on with things. Making the best of what's left.'

Frankie saw the facade drop away now; the lightness of the last few minutes collapsing as she looked tired and very strained. He was tempted to say something about there being a chance of getting the horse back, something to offer some comfort, but he knew it might just raise false hopes. He said, 'Have the police been?'

'Been and gone. Seemed interested from a novelty viewpoint but I'm afraid I wouldn't hold out much hope of them getting Gabby back.' She stared at the floor, looking almost blank for a few seconds then she looked up. 'Were you involved with the last kidnap?'

'Involved in trying to solve it.'

She smiled wearily. 'Of course. That was what I meant. Did you feel there was ever a chance of getting that horse back, what did you call him?'

'Ulysses.' Frankie felt suddenly put on the spot. 'It was a very tough situation. We had little contact from the kidnapper, just three calls in all. And the owner was...' Frankie knew he'd need to be particularly careful here. '... extremely upset and emotional about the whole business, perfectly understandably.'

'Did he ever consider paying the ransom?'

Frankie was reluctant to get much deeper in. The racing world was very insular. Nice as she seemed, he didn't know Maggie Cassidy or what her capacity for gossip might be, and the last thing he needed was Christopher Benjamin hearing on the grapevine that Frankie had been discussing his private business. He said, 'We would always advise that the ransom shouldn't be paid.' He thought he saw a definite look of relief in her eyes.

'How much did they ask for?'

'Quarter of a million pounds.'

'Did the owner actually want to pay?'

Frankie was growing increasingly uncomfortable but he understood what Maggie was doing. She was simply trying to prepare herself for the unknown. He said, 'Nobody wants to pay out that sort of money, Mrs Cassidy.'

'Please call me Maggie.'

He sipped his tea. 'My name is Frankie.'

She nodded slightly and looked thoughtful. Frankie said, 'Will your husband be out with the horses for a while yet?'

'Had enough of me, Frankie?' She smiled tiredly.

He felt himself blush slightly and raised his mug to try and cover his face he said, 'I just wondered if we shouldn't go through the questions together, all three of us. Just to save repetition.'

They found Graham in one of the boxes, grooming a dappled grey gelding, brushing methodically, quietly, unaware of their presence. Frankie saw a slight change in Maggie's face as she watched him and he couldn't interpret it. There was steeliness in it. He couldn't pin it down beyond that. Still, he had no way of knowing how this disaster would affect the Cassidys, what damage it might do to them. Crossing the yard he'd become acutely aware of what this loss must mean to such a small set-up. Losing any horse from here would be a major blow; to have the Grand National favourite snatched away, well, he just couldn't imagine how they must be feeling, for all Maggie's smiles and brave face.

He watched her. Her mouth was slightly open as though about to speak but seemed transfixed by the sight of her husband. He wore tan jodhpurs tucked into ankle-length rubber and canvas boots, and a dark green fleece top with a horse's head and the word Aintree large on the back. He looked very lean and fit to Frankie and still had a full head of hair although the grey showed through clearly even in the gloom of the box. There was no sound except for the brush sweeping a perfect rhythm down the horse's bright flank and Graham Cassidy's equally rhythmical breathing.

Maggie said quietly, 'You'll brush the spots right off him.'

'Bet I don't,' said Graham without looking up.

'How much?'

'Bet you fifty pence.'

'Better make it ten. We're saving up for a ransom.'

The joke seemed to end there for Graham and he stopped brushing and stood completely still as though he'd been knifed. She said, 'Cheer up, Mister Houlihan's here.'

The trainer turned slowly, a sheen of sweat on his brow. As he came toward the half-door, he forced a smile on to a face that looked ingrained with desperation and hopelessness and Frankie admired him hugely for the effort. The smile was fully formed as he reached for Frankie's hand. 'How do you do, Mister Houlihan? I'm so sorry to have called you on Christmas Day. Been bothering me ever since I put the phone down.'

Frankie took his hand, feeling the fine grit that layered his skin from the hard grooming. 'No need to apologize. I was having a very quiet time. It's nice to meet you. I'm just sorry that it's under these circumstances.'

'Yes. Well... don't worry.'

Frankie could see he was at a loss. He reached to touch the trainer's arm. 'I'll help in any way I can. Don't be thinking it's a lost cause, Mister Cassidy.'

'Graham, please,' the trainer said.

'Graham.'

'Frankie.'

'Typical men,' said Maggie, 'only met a minute ago and already into monosyllabic conversation.' All three smiled. Graham said, 'Shall we go inside and have a cup of tea? I'm sure you'll want to ask some questions then get back to your family and your Christmas celebrations.'

'Don't worry about me. My family are not around this Christmas, so I'm in no hurry at all.'

Maggie touched his arm and said, 'Oh, you'll have Christmas dinner with us then!'

Frankie blushed again. 'I hope you don't think I was angling for an invitation now, giving you some sad story! '

Maggie said, 'Of course we do!' as Graham was saying, 'Of course we don't,' and all three ended up chuckling. It lifted Frankie's spirits, cheered him to see the momentary relief of Graham's burden. Laughter had been the last thing he'd expected to find at the Cassidy house. Laughter and friendliness in a troubled place. On Christmas Day. Praise be to God.

On the way south with Angel Gabriel, Monroe had decided to stay off the motorways. He couldn't be certain when the alarm would be raised at the Cassidy place. That howling storm had helped him simply walk the horse out of its box. He couldn't believe how easy it had been - but that also planted a thought that he might be the victim of some set-up.

The eaves had moaned, the windows shook in their frames and the slates had rattled, but not a dog had barked. And there hadn't even been a lock on the stable door. He'd simply slid a couple of bolts back and led Angel Gabriel out. The horse had hesitated at the door and spooked slightly a couple of times on the way to the horsebox but otherwise had been a real gentleman. But it had all been just too easy, and Monroe wondered if he was being tailed or something.

There was also the factor of having to go even more slowly with the horse in the back and the strong crosswinds. It had been hairy enough at times, he thought, doing some pretty low speeds on the way up with maniac drivers suddenly finding themselves halfway up your arse. The last thing he needed was an accident. Anyway, as he was driving through the night, he could stick to the A and B roads. They'd probably be quieter than the motorways too.

He spent some of the journey refining his plan, plotting how best to handle things with Hewitt. If only he knew what the guy was doing at that big house on the hill and how the Irishman, Gleeson, was involved. Was Gleeson just the bagman for a bigger organization or was it some scheme of his own? Nah, couldn't be, thought Monroe, the guy surely didn't have the brains to come up with anything halfway decent. It had to be funded by someone else.

Whatever, there had to be scope in it for him to get a share. He'd proved in these past few weeks he was smarter than many. Much cleverer than some of the big shots who thought they were something in this game. He hated most of the people still involved in racing, despised them just for being at the hub while his fear and his past had condemned him to a life on the edges. Monroe the nobody - well, that's what they thought. The Cassidys wouldn't be thinking that when he rang them. He wasn't on the edges any more. He had the racing world by the balls. When news of Angel Gabriel broke, they'd be shitting themselves from Portman Square to Perth.

Much as Monroe wanted to terrorize the racing world by leaving butchered horses for them to find, Mrs Cassidy was a very rich woman and if he asked for half a million this time there had to be a chance she'd pay it.

If they did decide to pay, how could he make sure he'd get the money without the cops appearing from everywhere? He was smart enough to know that the establishment punished people like him a hell of a lot more severely for extortion than for killing horses. If he got caught trying to haul away a bag with half a million quid in it he knew he was probably looking at fifteen years in jail. There were other ways of making money from this. Long-term payback, maybe, but much, much safer. He'd need to think about it. In the meantime, he'd enjoy thinking about the rich Cassidys and how anxious they'd be, and there was only one person in the whole world who could ease that anxiety for them. And it sure wasn't Santa Claus.

24

In the Cassidy kitchen, they settled down to Christmas dinner just after three o'clock. Maggie and Graham sat on one long side of the big rectangular table. On the opposite side, Frankie sat between Jane and Billy. The tension was almost tangible; it had been building all day, and Frankie felt that his presence was a hindrance to the natural expression of anger and frustration that they must feel. Jane in particular looked very distressed. Her eyes were red and puffy and seemed constantly close to tears.

He'd left them alone for a couple of hours to go and visit the police. When he'd returned it was obvious that Jane and her mother had been crying. Since then it had been politeness in front of the guest and stiff upper lips all round, although Graham seemed to be the one trying hardest while suffering most. The trainer was obviously upset and anxious for the call they all knew had to come, but he strove to present an air of steadfastness, a sense that whatever happened they would plough on through life.

Maggie drank a glass of chilled Chablis. The others had soft drinks. Graham carved the turkey methodically while the kids and Maggie made comments about his carving style and Frankie smiled dutifully and even laughed lightly at some of the gentle ribbing. He knew it was mostly for his benefit, to try and make him feel more relaxed and he admired them for trying so hard, but when all the plates were filled with turkey and stuffing, roast potatoes and mixed vegetables, he felt it was time to say something.

Before he picked up his cutlery he said, 'I'd like to thank you all for making me feel so welcome. Especially on a day when you really should be alone with each other... If you know what I mean! Kind of Irish, I suppose! ' And he dropped his eyes as they smiled and laughed and he felt the blood come to his face again.

Maggie said, 'Don't be daft. If you weren't here we'd be fighting already, throwing sprouts at each other and knocking drinks all over the tablecloth.'

Graham nodded, smiling approvingly at his wife.

Frankie said, 'Thanks. What I wanted to say too was that you mustn't feel bad that you can't let rip because I'm here. I'm sure you're all very frustrated and very angry over Gabby and I know this dinner won't be sitting too well in your stomachs worrying about him. I want you to feel free to say anything you like if it makes you feel better.'

They went quiet. After a few minutes Jane said, 'Do you think he'll call today, Frankie, the kidnapper?'

'I hope he does. The longer he leaves it the more on edge we're all going to be.'

'What sort of ransom do you think he'll ask for?' Jane said.

Frankie shrugged and cut a piece of turkey. Mopping gravy with it he said, 'There's no way of knowing.'

There was silence again for a while then Billy, still chewing, spoke. 'I thought you weren't supposed to go to the police if somebody kidnapped you, I mean kidnapped your son or your horse or whatever.'

'I think that's what the kidnappers would certainly prefer,' said Frankie.

Billy said, 'Well, Dad called them right away.'

Frankie spotted the potential for conflict but was sure Graham wouldn't take what he'd said the wrong way. 'Your father was absolutely right in calling the police. For a start, the horse has been stolen. It might not even be the kidnapper; we're just kind of making that assumption.'

'But it looks favourite that it's the kidnapper, doesn't it?' Billy said.

'Coming so soon after the last one, I suppose it does. You're right,' said Frankie.

Billy warmed to Frankie then. Not many adults had ever told him he was right about something. Maggie had been watching,

FOR YOUR SINS

scanning each of the faces as they spoke. Frankie's sincerity, his mild blushing and lack of worldliness endeared him to her as though three children sat opposite. She said, 'How long have you worked for the Jockey Club?'

'I only started a few weeks ago.'

Billy said, 'Phew, this is a big job for you then isn't it?'

Frankie chuckled. 'I suppose it is if you look at it that way.'

Graham said, 'Were you in racing before this then?'

'Only as a spectator. Me da... my father loved the racing and used to take me to the Curragh and Leopardstown when I was Billy's age. Ever since then I tried to go as often as I could, which wasn't as often as I liked.'

'So what was your job before this?' Jane asked.

Frankie had been trying to prepare for answering this question. When Kathy had been alive, the question hadn't bothered him too much, because she was almost always around when it was asked and as far as she was concerned that was testament enough, that people could see her, see how easy she must be to love; so back then he'd answer easily, unfazed. But this was the first time he'd been asked since Kathy died. He had never been among people, socially, who hadn't known. Now they were waiting, these kind people who'd taken him in when they had plenty of troubles of their own. He knew as he opened his mouth to answer that his relationship with all of them was about to start changing, because he knew the questions that had to come next.

'I was a Catholic priest.'

Jane and Maggie stopped and looked at him. Graham and Billy carried on eating although Billy, chewing again said, 'I've seen priests at the races quite a few times. I used to plan to follow them to the bookies 'cause I thought they got tips from God.'

They all laughed.

Jane asked, 'How long were you a priest for?'

Maggie tutted. 'Jane! That's none of your business.'

'Oh, Mum! I was only asking!'

The first awkward silence. As the architect of it, Frankie thought it best that he filled it. 'I was a priest for eight years. I spent a year of that as chaplain to a police force. They gave me some training in police-type stuff and that, believe it or not, was a sound enough background to get me this job.'

'So, did you get made redundant from being a priest?' Billy asked.

'Billy!' Maggie said, although she was more curious than any to hear Frankie's answer, and she was relieved when Frankie raised a hand and smiled in a way that said, 'It's OK, don't worry.' He said to Billy, 'I sort of made myself redundant.'

Billy said, 'Oh, I've heard about that too. They do that in factories when they need to cut jobs down. They say there'll be voluntary redundancies. They do it when they've got too many workers. Is it the same? Did they have too many priests?'

Frankie was conscious that only Graham was eating now, showing no particular keenness to hear his answer. Maggie and Jane were riveted. Billy was just curious. Frankie said to him, 'Well, it wasn't quite like that. I sort of failed my own quality control test if you like, and decided it would be better for the Church if I found myself another job.'

Billy nodded, still chewing. 'So you found this one? Do you like it better?'

'In many ways I do. It's very interesting. And I get to have dinner with some very nice families.' Billy said, 'Is it a well-paid job working for the Jockey Club?'

'Billy!' Maggie said. 'It is very bad manners to ask questions like that! Especially of guests!'

Billy looked slightly hurt and embarrassed. He looked down at his plate and said, 'Sorry.'

Frankie said, 'No problem. And to answer your question, it's not that well paid and I'm sure you're bright enough to get a job that will pay an awful lot more. But then again, money's not everything.'

'Well said,' Graham put in.

Billy said, 'It is when you haven't got any.'

Smiles all round again. Frankie noticed that Graham had almost finished his meal and the others were well ahead of Frankie too, as he'd been doing most of the talking. Billy had done his fair share but hadn't let it interrupt his chewing and forking rhythm. Jane finished and wiped her mouth with her napkin. Frankie saw her glance slightly nervously at her mother then turn to him and he sensed, he knew, that a particularly awkward question was coming. As he steeled himself, the phone rang.

As Graham spoke to the kidnapper, none of the family, except Graham, could stay seated. They gathered around him, Maggie behind with her hand on his shoulder, Jane and Billy flanking him, their heads forward and tilting to hear what was being said by the kidnapper. Frankie stood further away, toward the opposite end of the table.

Graham said, 'That depends.'

'On what? It's a simple enough question,' said the voice on the other end. 'How much is he worth to you?'

'He's worth quite a bit.'

'Put a price on it.'

Graham kept calm. 'If we put him up for sale, we might get as much as two hundred thousand pounds.'

'But you wouldn't put him up for sale, would you?'

'No, we wouldn't.'

'So he's priceless.'

Graham disliked the smugness. He said, 'He is priceless. But we could have lost him in a fall. He could have broken a leg at exercise.'

'Are you saying that if you don't get him back, it'll be just one of those things?'

Graham hesitated, uncertain about the psychological game he was getting into. 'I'm saying that we care for that horse more than you could know, but things happen in racing. We've got over setbacks before.'

The pause was at the kidnapper's end now. The family knew there was a slight break in proceedings, as Graham looked at each of them in turn and smiled reassuringly. Maggie reached for her husband's free hand and squeezed it.

The kidnapper spoke. 'You seem quite a cold person, Mister Cassidy. How does the rest of the family feel? How does Mrs Cassidy feel?'

'They feel the same as I do.'

'Cold? They don't care?'

'I've told you how much we care. Please tell me what the ransom fee is.'

'Straight to the point, Mister Cassidy, I like that.'

Graham Cassidy didn't answer.

The kidnapper said, 'You'll be glad to hear that the ransom fee, as you put it, will not affect your standard of living in any way and that, unlike you, I am a very caring person. I care for how you people live and so I don't want a single penny of what you have now.' He paused. Graham waited, finding himself inadvertently holding his breath. The voice continued, 'I'll settle for the cheque your wife gets for her big book advance. Half a million pounds is the price.'

'No,' Graham said immediately, deliberately avoiding the eyes of the family. Jane was looking particularly anxious and frustrated.

'You're a very decisive man for a trainer, Mister Cassidy. Most of them are bullshitters who wouldn't know a straight answer if they fell over one. But I think that either you're in shock or maybe the police are there advising you to play the cool guy. You tell them that I'm the only really cool guy in this setup, because I'm holding all the cards. Ask them how cool I was last time with Ulysses. I don't mess around. I don't get panicked. I just get impatient. And I do what I say I'm going to do, so listen. I'm going to be very, very generous here and give you what is left of this year to think about this and make up your mind. I'm going to call you again on New Year's Eve to tell you where to collect your horse. If you decide to pay the money, I want it on New Year's Day, in cash, used fifty-pound notes. I am not going to be messed around with excuses about banks being closed over the holidays and so on, that's the reason I'm giving you almost a week. Half a million on New Year's Day and you get your horse back alive. Otherwise, bring the knacker's lorry for the carcass. And to help you make up your mind, ask the police what state Ulysses was in when they found him. I like to kill them nice and slowly.'

The anger rose in Graham's eyes. His face reddened. 'Don't harm the horse,' he said, swallowing the lump in his throat, surprised at his hoarseness. Jane guessed that her father had been listening to threats and she leaned into the mouthpiece and yelled, 'Don't you dare hurt Gabby! Don't you dare! I'll kill you if you hurt him! '

Graham's instinct was to cover the mouthpiece but he overcame it. He was proud of his daughter, although her yell caught Billy by surprise and he recoiled, grunting with fright as the tension was broken. The kidnapper said, 'That's what I like to hear, some proper emotion. This is an emotional time, Mister Cassidy; don't be embarrassed about joining in. It is Christmas after all.'

The line went dead.

Calmly, Graham held the receiver out toward Frankie who took it and unclipped the small microphone from the earpiece. Unplugging the cable from the grey Dictaphone, he rewound the tape. 'Is it OK to play back now?' he asked Graham. The trainer nodded as he hugged his daughter. They all sat down and watched the Dictaphone as it played out the conversation. When the half a million figure was mentioned, everyone except Graham looked at Maggie. Some colour left her cheeks; otherwise, she showed no reaction.

When the tape finished Jane, her pretty face still very agitated, looked at her mother. 'Mum?'

It was a challenge. The shortest and most clearly expressed question Frankie had ever heard. He was aware of the already tense atmosphere at the table beginning, almost, to crackle. Around the room, lights glowed; two lamps, the concealed bulbs below the rows of kitchen units, the Christmas tree, but as Jane posed the question, Frankie felt that everything else was fading, that the only place that that was really lit was this table, the only place that mattered in the world, never mind the house. And the faces; the anxiety, the troubles, the sense that all except Frankie had been involved in a long-running, high-stakes poker game and now just Jane, fourteen going on forty, and Maggie remained in the running for the pot.

Maggie said, 'We need to take advice from the police.' Frankie could hear the tiny breaks in her voice.

Jane said, 'Mum, what can the police do? What can they say? We need to pay the money! '

Maggie looked at her daughter. Frankie could see turmoil behind Maggie's eyes and he felt himself shift uncomfortably. He felt he shouldn't be there. Maggie said to Jane, 'Let's see what the police say. We have a week.'

'But I'm supposed to be going to Ireland tomorrow! I can't go knowing that Gabby might get killed by that man!'

'The police might catch him before the week's up,' Maggie said. 'We've got a recording of his voice.'

Jane stood up suddenly, and crossed her arms. 'They won't catch him! How can they catch him with just a recording of his voice? They don't keep voices like fingerprints or anything, do they, Frankie?' She turned to him and for the first time he saw the full power of her personality. It burned in her eyes, pulsed in the

121

clenched jaw muscles, glowed in the reddening cheeks and he saw her mother in her then, very clearly, and he saw something of Kathy. She'd said his name as a woman would, not a child. It had been a command to back her up.

He said, 'They might have some voice tapes, but not many, although that doesn't mean that this won't help them. They have experts who advise on things like accents and sometimes they can pin accents down to almost the street someone lives in, certainly to the village.'

'But how much time does that take?' Jane asked.

'Well, let me go down to the station now with this tape and get an opinion from them. There are other factors too. The way he talked about trainers makes it sound like he could be in the racing industry, or possibly worked in it and lost his job or something. This could be a kind of revenge thing, and if he was sacked, it might have been for some sort of offence. There's every possibility he already has a criminal record. If he has a record, it would greatly increase the chances of the police catching him.'

'In six days?' Jane asked, not at all comforted or convinced.

Frankie said, 'We need to report this anyway, so let's see what the police say when we do.'

Jane sucked in a breath and folded her arms firmly again. Her father said, 'Jane, do you really want to see this man getting half a million pounds for walking in here and stealing Gabby? Wouldn't you like to see him caught?'

Billy nodded. 'Yeah, you're the one who's always banging on about fairness and justice and all that other stuff for everybody in the world. It's not fair just to hand over loads of money to this bloke for stealing, is it?'

Jane said, 'Shut up, you! What do you know about fairness?'

Maggie said, 'Who's not being fair now? It's not fair to take out your frustrations on your brother. Especially when it's me that you're upset at.'

'Well, it just so obvious to me what the right thing to do is! You've got half a million pounds coming in soon, and it's money that you weren't really expecting to get so it will make absolutely no difference whatever if you hand it over to pay for Gabby! To get him back! ' She put her hands on the table and leaned across, her eyes filling now. 'Mum, I've been with Gabby since I was four years old! I grew up with him'

Billy said quietly, but in a point-scoring sort of way, 'I've been with him since I was two. I've grown up even more with him.' Jane ignored him and kept her eyes pleadingly on her mother.

Frankie watched as Maggie returned her gaze and he saw a change in Maggie's eyes; it was her turn to challenge. She said, 'So when my cheque comes in, Jane, do I give it all to the kidnapper? How many cataract operations would half a million pounds buy?'

Frankie glanced at Graham and saw him flinch slightly. The smile on Billy's face told Frankie that the boy considered it a masterstroke. Jane finally burst into tears. 'Oh Mum, that was a horrible thing to say! ' and she turned and ran out of the room.

Maggie looked defiant, defensive, prepared for criticism. Graham smiled at Frankie. 'Sorry, tension's a bit high.'

'Don't apologize. It's understandable.' Frankie got up. 'Probably a good time for me to go and try and get some time with the CID.' He picked up the Dictaphone. 'I'll call back if you like, or I can come in the morning and give you an update.'

Maggie, gathering herself, trying to regain her composure, looked at him. 'Won't you stay with us tonight?'

Frankie smiled. 'It's very kind of you to offer me a bed on Christmas night. More than the innkeeper did for a certain couple two thousand years ago. I think it's time to -'

'To get away from this mad family?' Maggie asked wearily, smiling.

'To let you have some time on your own, maybe.'

Maggie said, 'It's after five. It's Christmas Day. By the time you get away from the police station you're not going to find it easy to get into a hotel.'

'I'll make a few calls on my mobile on the way to the station and whatever happens, I'll call later and tell you what the police have said.'

Graham stood up and said, 'If you don't find anywhere, please come back. You're more than welcome to stay with us as long as you want. We're very, very grateful for your patience and for all your help.'

Frankie put the Dictaphone in his pocket and buttoned his jacket. 'For all my helplessness, more like. I wish I could do more.'

Graham said, 'Not at all. We realize it's an almost impossible task.'

'Don't resign yourself to losing him just yet. We've got a week.' Graham nodded, smiling gently. Maggie got up and so did Billy. Frankie said, 'I'll give you a call.'

As Frankie went out the door he heard Billy saying, 'Dad, wasn't it Christmas Eve when the innkeeper said no to Mary and Joseph?'

Frankie discovered that Maggie had been right, there were no rooms to be had within a fifty-mile radius, and he knew he was going to have to stay close by the Cassidys for the next few days. They welcomed him back warmly and he guessed that they had appreciated his effort to try and let them return to some form of private life. The children were in bed when he returned. Maggie showed Frankie to his room and offered supper. Frankie politely declined. She said, 'Will you have a drink, then and tell us what the police had to say?' Frankie asked for a whiskey.

All three sat around the dying embers of the log fire. The Cassidys didn't expect much from the police who had been straight with them from the outset, saying that wiretaps and call-tracing equipment and all the other stuff you saw on TV was expensive and time-consuming to set up, and very seldom produced results. Off the record, they'd said that the only realistic prospect of catching the kidnapper was to agree to pay the ransom then try to arrest him as he came to collect.

Frankie told them that the CID had pretty much confirmed this to him after hearing the tape. 'They said it would be a nice piece of evidence to help with the conviction if they did manage to arrest him at the pick-up point, but they stressed that it's against procedure for them to advise anyone to pay a ransom.'

Graham cradled a tiny amount of brandy in a large glass. 'Nothing more?' he asked.

Frankie shook his head. 'Sorry.'

'So the police would have us pay the ransom so they get a crack at this man?' asked Graham.

'Unofficially only. Pay it or arrange to pay it. They're not that concerned about the money. The pick-up is the key for them. If you decide to pay then whatever you agree with the kidnapper needs to be convincing enough for him to believe that when he turns up, every penny he asked for is going to be there.'

'Even if the suitcase, or whatever it is he wants it in, is empty or full of paper or something?' Graham asked.

'That's right. But if the cash isn't in it and the police fail to catch him - I mean if he escapes with an empty suitcase, then you're probably not going to get your horse back.'

Maggie sipped whiskey. She said, 'Or if he gets away with the full half-million but the police have chased him halfway across the country first, do you think we will still get Gabby back?'

'I kind of doubt it,' Frankie said.

'So do I,' Maggie said.

They were quiet for a while, then Maggie finally asked the question they all knew had been hanging in the air. 'Frankie, what do you advise? What's the Jockey Club line, should we pay the ransom?'

'The official line is that paying a ransom only means misery for someone else in the future. If it becomes known that people will pay up, then it won't be just this guy who'll be back for more. There'll be some proper criminals queuing round the block.'

'So you don't think this creep is a "proper" criminal?' Maggie asked.

Frankie swilled his drink and the ice tinkled. 'I think this guy is in the industry somewhere or has been. He's obviously used to handling thoroughbreds, familiar with the running of a racing stable. That reference he made to bullshitting trainers - I just think he's been in the business and somebody has done him down big-time. I get the feeling he's not just doing this for the money. He's got a major chip on his shoulder.'

Graham nodded in agreement. Frankie said, 'I'll start making a few calls tomorrow morning, digging around. Let's see what we come up with.' He sounded positive.

Maggie smiled and swallowed the rest of her drink. 'I suppose six days is quite a long time really.' Frankie nodded. 'God made the world in six days.'

Maggie's smile widened and she looked warmly at Frankie. 'A final plug for your last employer.'

'Final?' Frankie asked.

'Before bed, I meant,' she said, covering her mouth as she yawned. 'We can always try praying, I suppose.'

Frankie nodded slowly, almost regretfully and Maggie said, 'I'm sorry. That was thoughtless of me.'

Frankie smiled wearily. 'Ahh forget it. No offence taken.' He stood up. 'If you don't mind, I think I'll go to bed.'

Maggie got up. 'Not at all, it's been a long day.' She walked with him to the door leading into the hall. 'I put some clean towels on your bed.'

Lying in the darkness, Maggie and Graham spoke in low voices about the day's events and about Jane's planned trip to Ireland. It had been hurriedly arranged when they'd learned that Jane's cousin, Poppy, had broken her arm in a fall from her pony a week before Christmas. Jane was going to spend the remainder of the holidays with her to help her, cheer her up, although Maggie doubted she'd be cheering anyone up in her current state of mind. Maggie sensed that Graham had thought she'd been wrong to confront Jane with the theoretical option of what to do with the money. But he'd said nothing. It annoyed her that he would raise it when he thought it apt rather when she was ready to discuss it. In the final few minutes of silence before they drifted off to sleep she thought he might just bring it up and when he said, 'Maggie…' she became alert again.

'Uh-uh,' she said, feigning drowsiness to mask the tension rising once again.

'He's a very nice fellow, isn't he, Frankie Houlihan?'

'Yes. He is. Very helpful.'

'He has plenty of troubles of his own, I think.'

Maggie hesitated as Frankie's face rose sharply in her mind's eye. 'I think you're right.'

There was silence again for a while then Graham said quietly, 'He's very good-looking, isn't he?' Again, she hesitated. 'Mmmm. Yes, I suppose he is.' And she blushed in the dark.

25

The vet, Peter Culling, had monitored his food and alcohol intake closely over Christmas. Since his late thirties, death had never been far from his mind, and he'd formed the habit of counting down the days between Christmas and New Year. The annual achievement of waking up on 1 January brought mixed emotions. He was relieved to have survived into another year, to be able to build up his savings for the crucial 'suspension' of his life, but New Year's Day also brought the spectre of death closer, edged him toward his next birthday, dragged him nearer the cliff edge of mid-forties and certain heart failure.

He knew as well as any doctor what physical measures were needed to protect his heart as long as possible; he could have lectured on the subject with the confidence of knowing he practised what he preached. His diet was high in vegetables, omega-3 oils, and wholemeal bread. He took little fat and his weakness for alcohol was served by two glasses of red wine each evening - another heart booster and one of the few comforts in his life - and the occasional glass of cognac. He didn't smoke and he took regular exercise, always reaching, but never exceeding, the recommended pulse rate to maintain fitness safely.

What he wasn't so good at handling was the stress, which he knew, could be as bad for his heart as twenty cigarettes a day. And he found the stress unmanageable because it came from the fear of death that was with him almost constantly. The thought of not having enough money to pay the Everlasting Life Company of

Michigan to preserve his body tormented him. The deadline for getting that money shortened every day. Culling's interpretation of 'deadline' was literal; a hanging rope. In his mind, he saw nature herself hitching the noose that little bit tighter daily. Now there was added burden of Monroe knowing what he was doing. A ticking bomb, indeed. So with New Year's Day looming, he had decided to take a chance and do one at Kempton on Boxing Day

This was one of the biggest racemeetings of the year, and it took Culling far outside the guidelines he'd set himself. His scheme had been designed to work on smallish racecourses in bread-and-butter races, preferably not televised. He'd taken a slight chance at Ascot with Colonialize, but that race hadn't been on TV. This was Kempton's major meeting. They'd have their biggest crowd of the season and the TV cameras would be there. The press room was certain to be full and all eyes would be focused on the racing. When his chosen horse won, at the usual big price, the performance would be dissected much more carefully than if he'd chosen a little race at Huntingdon.

On the positive side, betting would be so heavy that day that he could charge Breslin, the fat bookie, a considerable premium for the information. Culling reckoned that this, plus maybe just two more in the next six months, would see him with enough money to feel secure. Every time this thought came, he wanted to put his head in his hands and cry with the relief of it. He longed for that day when he could finally stop all this, empty the stress from himself safe in the knowledge that the future was his.

Culling chose a horse called Gallopagos. As with the others, it led all the way. The winning margin was twelve lengths, the price 20/1. After the race, Culling was approaching the stables when he heard a Stewards' Enquiry called over the PA. He stopped, choosing not to enter the stables as mild panic hit him. What had the stewards found out? Had anyone seen him in the stables earlier? He knew he shouldn't have risked this one; it was too big a meeting. This was the one that would finish him. The panic was swamping him now, affecting his breathing, thumping his heart against his ribs.

Hurrying to his car, he locked himself inside. If anyone saw him like this, that would only add to suspicion. Five minutes later he heard the announcer say that the stewards had enquired into the poor performance of the favourite in the last race and had accepted the trainer's statement that he had no explanation.

Culling laid his head back and moaned in relief deciding he simply could not put himself through any more of these.

On Boxing Day, Graham Cassidy rose earlier than usual to feed the horses; Jane's ferry was due to leave Holyhead at ten-thirty and it was a long drive. Just the two of them were in the car and Graham was glad of that. The tension between Jane and Maggie had still been fizzing that morning. Jane hadn't spoken at breakfast despite urgings from her parents to talk about her trip. She had been so looking forward to seeing her cousin Poppy again, and had been confident she could help Poppy over her injury better than any doctor could. But she'd remained stubbornly silent other than to mutter the odd please and thank you, yes and no. And she'd taken leave of her mother coldly with a brief hug and a turned cheek.

Graham left her to her silence as he drove, knowing that she'd come out of it in her own good time. It was almost an hour before she did and when she spoke, she sounded sad. 'Dad, do you think we'll get Gabby back?'

'I don't know. I hope so.'

'What if we don't?'

He shrugged involuntarily. 'Then we'll get on with things.'

'With things?'

'With our lives. It won't bring the world to an end.'

She turned now and he didn't need to take his eyes off the road to know she was angry. 'How can you say that, Dad? You're the one who dreamed all your life of winning the National. You're the one that said Gabby was a miracle sent to us to help us get your dream, make it come true.'

'That's right. I was. I still have the dream but somebody's put it on hold for us for whatever reason, and there's nothing we can do about it.'

'So you just accept it?'

'What else should I do?' Graham had never found it difficult to stay calm, and it helped that he could easily anticipate most of his daughter's questions.

'You could tell mum to pay the ransom.'

'I wouldn't pay it myself if I had the money, so why should I tell her? If we pay the ransom, we're just sending the message that it's

OK to kidnap someone else's horse and make even more money. Do you think that's right?'

'I think anything that gets Gabby back is right.'

He paused for a few seconds then said quietly, 'You don't really think that. I know you don't.'

'I do! How can it be wrong to do whatever needs to be done to get him back?'

'Well, where do you draw the line? Would you kill this man who has him to get the horse back?'

'Yes, I would!'

'Oh, come on, Jane. Nobody loves the horse more than I do, but he's a horse, that's all. Even if he hadn't been taken, he could have walked out this morning and put his foot in a hole. Then we'd just need to get used to the thought of him not being there.'

'But Dad, that's not the way to look at things! You can't go through your life just accepting everything bad that happens to you! You'll just get dumped on all the time! What would you do if it had been me that had been kidnapped? Would you kill the kidnapper to get me back if you had to?'

'Oh, stop being so melodramatic!'

'I'm not! I want to know! I want to know if there is at least something in your life that will make you angry and make you stop being walked over! '

'The best I can offer you, Jane, is that I'd gladly give up my own life for you and for Billy or your mother. Gladly.'

She folded her arms, lowered her head and stared to the front again, and Graham felt the tension increase one more notch. He drove on in silence, angry with himself for having to play the dutiful father, having to try and give his daughter, his children, a perspective on life that would help them handle all their own disappointments. Inside he raged over the loss of this wonderful horse, cursed himself for not taking more precautions, hated the kidnapper with an intensity that made him feel that he too could easily kill the man. Above all, he wished he had the money to pay the ransom.

26

Sean Gleeson was worried. It had been almost three weeks since he'd seen his father. The word on the street was that he'd ripped Kelly Corell off for ten grand. Pat Pusey had already been at the flat three times looking for him. Sean had opened the door for the first time and Pusey had told him to tell his 'oul' fella' that if he didn't get the money back to Corell before Christmas then he wouldn't be seeing the New Year. The next twice, Sean had locked up and crouched below the window. Pusey roared through the letterbox so hard his spit ran down the inside of the door.

Sean was scared of him. He used the flat now only to sleep in, spending the day wandering the streets with Pegasus, riding him down by the canal and around Fairview Park. Sean had some money left, saved from his winnings over the summer on the ponies and from the hundred pounds Cosgrave had given him for riding at Laytown. Even if his father never came back, he'd survive. It wasn't as if he ever gave Sean any money anyway.

Life hadn't been too bad since his mother had left, but sometimes he missed her. He didn't want to lose his father too. Sean knew he could still be taken into care, and he couldn't face disappearing into the system to end up in some Jesuit-run place where he'd need to rise at five every morning and wear his knees out with the praying.

There was just Sean and Kevin's family left now in the Mansions, and the Corporation had boarded Sean's place up once already. But his mates had helped him rip the boards off and they'd burned them and roasted potatoes on the embers. Anyway, plenty of people just squatted in empty flats and houses and if he had to join them for a while, he'd cope, so long as he had somewhere to keep Pegasus. He'd handle it because it was what he was used to, and it would make his dream all the sweeter when he became a top jockey and bought a big house where you could stay in all day if you wanted without having to worry about the Corporation or the likes of Pat Pusey.

Sean untied Pegasus from the railings and scrambled onto his bare back. A tiny spur of rubber protruded from the heel of each of his black wellies and Sean prodded Pegasus in the ribs with them. The grey pony moved forward in a steady walk through the archway onto Killarney Street. Sean looked to his right, to the twinkling Christmas tree that bore the names of all those from St Joseph's Mansions who'd died from drugs. Dozens of names. He'd known them all; there was no need to read the list, which grew longer every Christmas. But he knew that no more names would be added after this year. He might not be here much longer, especially if his father never came back. And that only left Kevin and his parents. Rochelle, Kevin's ma, was the best fighter against the dealers the Mansions ever had. There'd be none of her family's names on any Christmas tree.

Sean turned left onto Portland Row, wondering where best to look for his father today. There was a rumour he was back in Dublin and Sean supposed it could be true. The last place he'd have tried was the flat, because he'd have known Corell's men would come there looking for him. But it would have been a brave or very stupid thing to return at all, unless he had Corell's cash. Sean knew what the gangster was capable of.

There were lots of stories about Corell. He was supposed to have killed his own girlfriend, cut her throat and left her on the stairs in St Mary's Mansions. The word was that two of his men had held Lampy McGurk off the top of one of the blocks by his shoes while Corell made poor Lampy watch him untie the laces. And what about the fella he'd nailed to the snooker table? Sean hoped his father wouldn't come home until Corell was dead, although Corell had a fear of nothing, they said, and he had a few of the Garda in his pocket so he could live a long time.

The pony's spine felt sharper than usual beneath him and Sean shifted to try and ease the discomfort. He'd noticed lately that his ankles touched Pegasus' sides a bit lower than they used to and he hoped he wasn't about to start sprouting.

It was teatime and the streets were quiet. The pony's hooves echoed off the tarmac. Sean thought of his father again. All he knew was that he'd left on the boat to Holyhead three weeks ago on a job for Corell, and hadn't been seen since. Something in Sean hoped that he'd stolen the money to use it trying to find his mother, who was in London somewhere according to his Auntie Phoebe, but he guessed the bookies would have given big odds on that one. He had probably drunk half of it and lost the other half on the horses.

He'd gone away on a boat. If he ever came back, it would probably be by boat too. For want of anything better to do, Sean turned the pony south and headed for the ferry terminal at Dun Laoghaire.

It was dark when he arrived there, and raining steadily. He sat on Pegasus close to the bus stop, and when everyone got on the first bus that came, he urged the pony beneath the green plastic canopy, taking up all the shelter and ignoring the mumbled complaints of the first three people who came to wait for the next bus. They moaned among themselves about it and Sean sat smiling, watching the comings and goings through the terminal doors, trying to recall what his father was wearing when he'd last seen him.

Four more people came toward the bus shelter. Steam was rising from the wet pony, filling the shelter. The queue frowned and held their noses and all joined in the grumbling. 'What the feck's goin' on here?'

'Bloody stinkin' horse!'

'Is that fella mad or somethin'? Waitin' to ride a pony onto a bus?'

'Hey, get that stinkin' gypsy horse outta here! This is for folk that can pay their fares!'

Sean turned to them, a glint in his eye. 'Ahh, sure we'd love to move, but hasn't the pony got well and truly stuck to the pavement here? The blacksmith was testin' out a new kinda glue, so he was, when he put shoes on him yesterday, and the stuff's gone and mixed very badly with the rainwater and stuck us to the tarmac as tight as yer own hair is stuck to yer head! '

The people looked at each other in puzzled silence. A woman said, 'Ahh, away wi ye! Yer havin' us on, so ye are!'

Sean raised a finger to his breast. 'Cross me heart and hope to die! It's the truth. The guards have gone to find the blacksmith and bring him up to set us free.'

'And how's he gonna do that if the horse can't pick his feet up?'

Sean said, 'D'ye see that manhole back there?'

They all turned.

'He's goin' down there with the fire brigade, so he is, and they're gonna bore up with a special tool and operate on his hooves from underneath.'

Some of them now looked as though they thought there might be something in this. Some said 'Now yer takin' the piss' and other such comments. At this Pegasus raised a hind leg in the way ponies do when they want to rest their weight for a while, so that the toe of his hoof was barely touching the ground. The queue moved forward as one, with a mixture of shouts and laughter and pushes and urgings to 'get out and give us peace'.

Laughing lightly, Sean nudged Pegasus in the ribs. As the pony ambled out in the rain, some people across the street stopped to see what the commotion was. One of them walked briskly across the road and was almost next to Sean before the boy noticed that it was Pat Pusey, Corell's hired thug. The plunging weight of fear in Sean's stomach dragged the laughter back into his throat.

Pusey gripped Sean's left calf as he walked beside him. Looking up he said, 'Here to meet yer da, Sean?' There was a triumphant note in Pusey's voice; otherwise, it was cold and hard.

'No, I'm not. I don't know where he is! Honest!'

'Don't lie to me, son! What boat's he on?'

'Honest, Pat, I don't know. I mean I don't know where he is. He's not on any boat, I don't think! '

'So what are ye doin' here, entertainin' the feckin crowds?'

They'd walked half the length of the terminal building on the opposite side of the road. Plenty of people were still around. Pusey reached for the reins and tugged viciously on them. Sean pulled Pegasus to a halt. Pusey looked up. 'Where is he, now?'

'I don't know, Pat! If I knew I'd tell ye, sure I would! I haven't a bleedin' clue. I just came down here to give the pony a bit of a walk out! '

'Walk out my arse!' And he reached and grabbed Sean by the front of his denim shirt and yanked him off to land sprawling in a puddle. Pegasus trotted quickly away, ears pricked, tail up. Pusey hauled Sean to his knees and started dragging him across the road toward the terminal entrance. 'Come on, I'm gonna be with ye when ye meet yer da in here! '

Sean stumbled after him shouting, 'Get off me! Leave me alone!'

Pusey forced him through the doors into the main terminal. People turned to watch and to tut disapprovingly, but nobody tried to help. Pusey went along the wall where the luggage trolleys were then stopped and spun Sean, forcing him against the hard tiles. 'Where is he? He owes us ten grand!' Pusey was really hurting him. Sean's jacket wasn't that thick, and the way Pusey was gripping him made his shoulder blades protrude and rub against the wall. Tears came to his eyes, though he tried to stop them, and he answered as he had all the times before, 'Pat, I don't know where he is. Honest!'

'You're a liar!'

Suddenly there was a female voice, angry, shrill, young, and a hand on Pusey's arm. 'Hey, leave him alone! He's just a child! Stop hurting him!'

Pusey, surprised, stopped shaking Sean. He relaxed his grip although he still held the shirtfront. Sean eased forward off the wall and stood balanced again, relieved, curious yet worried still. He saw the very angry, very pretty face of Jane Cassidy. Her eyes looked a sort of blue-green and Sean saw fearlessness in them. He wished she'd look at him but she just stared at Pusey, her hand still on his arm.

Pusey glanced around him, and saw some people nearby look away and shuffle off to distance themselves from this embarrassing scene. He glared at Jane and in almost a whisper said, 'Piss off, you little nuisance.'

'No I will not piss off!' She said very loudly and Pusey reddened. 'Take your hands off his shirt. You've no right to be assaulting him! I'll call the police!'

Pusey tried again, voice still low but more menace in it now. 'If you don't bugger off and mind your own little Miss English business, you'll be next.'

'What was that, you're going to assault me next?' She was shouting. 'You're planning to assault a young girl when you've finished with this boy! '

Pusey began to look panicky now as two men moved toward him from the terminal entrance. Jane saw them too and began screaming, 'Help! Help!' still holding on to the arm of Pusey's jacket but trying to make it look like he was holding her. The two men started running toward Pusey, who immediately let go of Sean and wrestled himself free of Jane's grip. He turned and ran, leaving Sean looking after him, dazed and confused at the speed of things. The two men stopped beside them and the taller asked, 'Are yous alright, now?'

'We're OK,' Jane said confidently. 'Thanks for coming to help.'

'Who was the fella that was botherin' ye?'

'He was tryin' to rob me,' Sean said. 'I think he was drunk.'

The tall man said, 'Give us a shout if you need us. We'll be in the bar over there.'

'Thanks, mister,' said Sean.

Sean and Jane stood looking at each other, he in his crumpled charity shop clothes, and she in her sky- blue Gore Tex jacket that had cost almost one hundred and fifty pounds. 'Are you alright?' Jane asked, and Sean could see that there was a bit of an actress in her, as there was in most girls. The question was asked with wide eyes and a sort of 'Uh, I don't believe what I just saw' expression.

He nodded. 'I'll be fine. Thanks.'

Jane stared, still frowning. 'Was he really trying to rob you?'

Sean straightened, adjusted his jacket and adopted an offended look. 'What are ye tryin' to say? Don't I look as though I'm worth robbin' then?'

She looked apologetic. 'No, of course not. I'm not saying that at all, it's just -'

'Just what? My clothes are needin' a bit of a wash from bein' dragged through puddles by that madman...' Sean paused and quickly looked behind him to make sure Pusey really had gone. 'And there's a few horsehairs stuck to me here and there and,' he looked down, 'I've got wellies over me Nike trainers to keep them dry and...' His expression changed from one of mock hurt to one of wide- eyed realization. 'Shit! Pegasus!' He hurried toward the exit.

Jane followed him looking worried. 'Pegasus?'

'My pony. Champion pony. Fastest in Dublin. That bastard Pusey scared him off.'

They went through the open door together into the rain. Jane said, 'Scared him off? When? You know that man? Who is he? Why was he trying to beat you up?'

Sean was looking in both directions. 'Ahh, yer a one for the questions, right enough, miss.'

'My name's Jane. And I think you should be a bit more grateful for my help, to be honest.'

Sean turned to her. 'Is that a fact, now? And what would you like me to do, kiss your feet? Be your butler for a year?'

They looked at each other in silence for a few seconds. 'It would be a start. Being my butler, I mean. I wouldn't let you near my feet.'

'Yer just scared I'd convert ye to wearin' wellies like mine, aren't ye?' They smiled, at ease with each other now. 'There's Pegasus,' said Sean. 'See ya.' He started along the road. The pony was grazing on a grass strip near the railway line.

Jane walked after him. 'Where do you keep him?'

Sean picked up the rein and zipped his clenched fingers along it, scooting off the water it had picked up dangling in the grass. 'Where do I keep him? In the paddock, of course, by the orchard.'

'Where do you live?' she asked, stroking Pegasus.

'In a mansion.'

She looked at him, a mixture of wariness and laughter in her eyes. He said, 'You're judging the book by its cover again, Jane. Just because of the way I'm dressed, you think I can't live in a mansion?'

She smiled slowly. He said, 'Look, I'll prove it. Hold this.' He handed the rein over and dug in the inside of his pocket of his jacket until he pulled out a library card. He held it close to her face, obscuring his name on the top line, showing the address. 'See, Joseph's Mansions.'

'And you're Joseph?'

'I'm Sean.'

'Who's Joseph?'

'Me da.'

'Your father owns a mansion with a paddock and an orchard?'

'He does.'

'And you've got raggedy clothes, a pony with no saddle and you get your books from the library?'

'I like plain living. I'm easy pleased.'

'And you know something, something that that man in there wanted to get from you.'

That brought Sean back to reality, and the smile that had been dancing in his eyes faded at the thought that Pusey would return - could easily be watching him now. As soon as Jane had gone, he'd be after him.

She read his thoughts, his hunted glance over her shoulder toward the terminal entrance. She said, 'I'll wait with you, if you like. My uncle should be here any time. Should have been here by now.' She turned around to look at the pick-up point outside the terminal. There he is, look, just getting out of the Mercedes. Come on, we'll give you a lift.'

'Err, aren't ye forgettin' somethin'? Where's Pegasus gonna travel, on the roof rack?'

She smiled. 'Don't worry. Uncle Fergus will go back for the trailer.'

'The trailer?'

'Wait here!'

She ran toward the big white-haired man who was looking anxiously around. Sean watched as she threw her arms around him, her rucksack bobbing on her back as her uncle swung her gently. Then they were coming toward him. The big man looked familiar. Could that be...? Jeez, it was, Fergus Gollogly, the racehorse trainer!

27

At the Cassidy place that evening, Frankie sat at the table with Graham and Maggie, trying to use logic and what little evidence they had to fashion some sort of plan. They'd decided they simply couldn't sit back and tick off the hours and days until the kidnapper called back. After half an hour with pad and pen, working through possibilities, they decided they were probably looking for someone who was or had been involved in racing, who, from his accent, came from south west England and who might well hold an HGV licence as a well as a grudge. They agreed that Lambourn, the racing centre of the southwest was probably the best place to start. Frankie said he'd ask the police to provide a list of HGV licence-holders living in the Lambourn postcode.

'And supposing you get the list, what will you do then?' asked Maggie.

'I'll call Stonebanks - Geoff Stonebanks, a colleague of mine. He lives in Lambourn and knows who's doing what down there. We'll take whatever time it needs to run through the list and see what we come up with.'

Graham nodded, looking suddenly less haggard, more positive. Maggie said, 'So you'll be leaving us for Lambourn?'

Frankie shrugged and laid his pen on the pad. 'Depends on what comes out of this. Let me call my contact now at the police station and see if he's still around. Can I use your phone?'

'Of course you can!' said Maggie and Frankie got up and went to the windowsill where the phone lay. Graham sipped coffee.

Maggie watched Frankie's reflection in the big mirror on the opposite wall.'She blew a plume of smoke toward the light as she listened to him ask for his CID contact. She watched every small move of his hands and head and shoulders as he turned slightly, seldom still. She'd noticed that about him; he was never at rest.

It took the police until late afternoon on 28 December to produce a list of HGV licence-holders living in the RG17 postcode; there were one hundred and thirty-four. Frankie worked through them, highlighting the seventy-three Lambourn addresses, then he rang Stonebanks and asked him to call back to save the Cassidy phone bill. Maggie and Graham were out with the horses.

Frankie heard Stonebanks grunt a bit as he settled for a long session on the phone. 'Sorry about this, Geoff, but it was the only thing I could think of. Otherwise I'd be sitting here waiting with the Cassidys, and I feel bad enough already that I can't do something for them, that the department can't do something.'

'OK, Frankie, no worries. I know what you mean. I just think it's a dodgy premise to be going on but in your place, I'd be doing exactly the same. Trouble is that a big part of your assumption is that this guy is someone with a grudge in racing. If you lined him up along with all the others with grudges, the ID parade would take a year. Don't hold your breath as far as drawing up a shortlist is concerned.'

'I'm not - but if anyone can help on this, it's you.'

'As the bankrupt Chinese stamp collector said, philately will get you nowhere.'

'Very funny.'

'Learned it from an old friend of mine.'

'Can we start?'

'Shoot.'

Almost two hours later Frankie had crossed through fifty-three of the Lambourn names. Of the twenty left on the list, Stonebanks reckoned that each was at least capable of kidnapping a horse and just under half of them willing to slaughter it. That gave Frankie eight people to concentrate on. He asked Stonebanks then to listen to the copy of the tape of the kidnapper's voice that he'd sent by courier. Stonebanks listened and said, 'I don't recognize it, Frankie. But I can't say I've heard all your suspects speak, certainly not recently, and I don't know any well enough to remember their voices. It takes a while for a voice to register in your brain, doesn't it?'

'It does. Don't worry. It was worth a chance. How would you feel about rigging the equipment up to your phone and calling each of these guys? We could get some sort of voiceprint comparison then.'

'We could. You get also get yourself a dead horse if one of them is the kidnapper. What's he going to do if he suddenly gets a call out the blue from the Jockey Club Security Department?'

'I hadn't thought of that.'

'Never mind. Why don't you get yourself down to London tomorrow, and we'll work on this shortlist and see what we can come up with?'

'I will, Geoff. I appreciate your help.'

'No problem. You can buy me a drink and a fillet steak.'

'It's a deal.'

Frankie sat by the log fire sipping whiskey with the Cassidys.' I'm going to miss this little ritual before bed,' he said.

'We will too,' said Maggie. She was sitting on the thick rug. Graham sat in the long-backed chair. They'd given Frankie the soft easy chair and he loved the way it enveloped him, made him feel secure, especially with the logs burning in the big fireplace.

'And I'm mad because I'll miss morning stables,' said Frankie. 'I've loved helping out with the feeding and grooming and stuff.'

Graham smiled. 'It's been good to have you. You'd make an excellent stable lad!'

Frankie grinned and raised his glass toward Graham. 'There are worse occupations,' he said.

'Well,' Maggie said, 'the pay's not brilliant but we could probably afford a bit extra for you.'

'I'd do it for nothing. The company alone is worth it. I've really enjoyed my time here. It's been great being back in a family atmosphere again.' And he realized with that little statement that he'd opened up part of his past that he didn't mean to. He hoped neither Maggie nor Graham would follow it up.

Maggie said, 'We've enjoyed your company too and we can't say how grateful we are that you gave up Christmas to try and help us.'

'No sacrifice, honestly. I just hope I can do something in the next forty-eight hours.'

Graham said, 'Even if you hit brick walls with your investigations over the next couple of days, will you come back and be with us for the call on New Year's Eve?'

'Of course I will. Of course.'

Frankie and Geoff Stonebanks spent the whole of the next day in the office. They were still there at ten that night. Frankie had learned that it was one thing having a short list of suspects and something else completely trying to get anything useful from it. He guessed that Stonebanks could have told him that before they started, and his respect and liking for the big man had grown because he'd said nothing, just beavered away all day at this lost cause. Frankie knew Stonebanks just wouldn't have wanted to discourage him at the outset on this, his first real case.

It had been a long slog of ringing people, reading files, seeking further possible contacts, trying to discover the whereabouts of everyone on the list on the nights in question and having to do it without being able to speak to the people themselves. Tough and tiring as it had been, there had been some comic moments, especially the frequent times when Stonebanks was ready to swear with frustration and had glanced at Frankie, unsure how offensive it would be for an ex-priest to hear such language. Frankie had played on it by frowning seriously when Stonebanks glanced at him, and the big man had taken it at face value and stayed silent or substituted softer curses.

At ten-past-ten Frankie said, 'Let's call it quits, Geoff, and I'll buy you that steak.'

Stonebanks, tie hanging loosely below his stubbled double chin, wearily closed the folder in front of him. 'And a large gin?'

'Two large gins, if you like, and I'll drive you home.'

'Ooh, a chauffeur too!'

'Least I can do. This has been an awful tiring day. We've got nowhere and you probably knew from the start how it would turn out. It makes me much more grateful that you stuck with it anyway.'

'You're not giving up, Frankie boy?'

'I ain't. If you'll put me up for the night I'll prowl around Lambourn for the next two days in the hope of finding something.'

Stonebanks looked at him for a few moments, and Frankie knew that he was deciding whether it was best to say what was on his mind. He said it; 'You know you're a million to one against here, don't you?'

Frankie smiled wearily and stretched and ran his fingers through his hair. 'I know, but I'm as well trying to do something as sitting around up in Shropshire waiting for this… this fella to call.'

A smile spread slowly on Stonebanks's face and he raised a finger to point at Frankie. 'You almost said a bad word then, didn't you?'

Frankie laughed. 'I did. You're right. I almost did. And earlier I almost said "a bitch of a day". My soul will surely be lost after another year or two in the company of people like yourself! Come on, let's go and get a drink.'

'Tell me what you were going to say first! '

Frankie got up, still laughing. 'Don't be daft! Come on.'

Stonebanks folded his arms. 'Nope. I'm not moving until you tell me.'

Frankie put his hands on the table and leant forward. 'It started with "b" and ended with "d".' Stonebanks got up and came toward him, put his arm around Frankie's shoulder and said, 'That's my boy! I knew you had it in you.'

Frankie straightened, laughing again. 'Come on, Crazy Horse, let's eat.' They walked to the door still linked by Stonebanks's arm. Frankie felt that the day had been more than worthwhile, for they'd got to know each other better in these twelve hours than they'd done in all the odd days they'd spent together back when Frankie had just started. He was pleased too that for the second time in the past few days he felt some real warmth toward a human being. Maybe his emotions were thawing. Perhaps life wasn't going to be so terrible after all.

Maggie and Graham Cassidy sat in their kitchen opposite Frankie and the man from the local CID who was called John Burnham. A pad and two pens were beside the phone, although the pens had seldom been out of the anxious fingers of one or the other of the party. Frankie had got back about noon and had told them over lunch his frustrations during the past couple of days. He and Stonebanks had done what they could using the list of HGV licences but had turned up nothing.

They'd only managed to eliminate three people on their shortlist of eight, and had simply been unable to gather enough information about the others to make judgement. Maggie had told him not to worry, and both had thanked him for trying. And since then, all they had done was wait by this phone, sitting and staring. Twice Maggie had picked it up and checked that there actually was a dial tone; that had made Graham smile nervously. They'd discussed what they were going to do; the money wouldn't be paid and there would be no bargaining.

The police had decided against setting up call-tracing equipment as they were convinced the kidnapper would be long gone by the time they got a car there. The Cassidys accepted this, and they conceded too that they weren't going to see their horse again unless the kidnapper had a change of heart.

They'd been waiting for eight hours, the last of them in almost complete silence. CID man Burnham had fallen asleep in the chair. Maggie thought Graham had looked increasingly sad as time went on; the stress of it all seemed to be ageing him as she watched. She said quietly, 'I can't wait for this to be over.'

Graham slowly stood. 'I'm going to check the horses,' he said quietly.

'Are you alright, darling?' Maggie called after him. There was no answer. 'Excuse me,' she said to Frankie and followed her husband.

She stood at the open door and watched him cross the yard in the glare of the security lights, his feet dragging, shoulders slumped, head down. He slid the big barn door aside and went in, seeing her as he turned to close it and waiting, watching her. She went to him. He looked completely dejected and very close to tears. Maggie had never known him like this. All she had ever seen in him was determination, hard work, obsession with his horses, a dedication to raising his children properly. Now here he was, a man almost broken.

And here she was, so protective of this money, of their 'security', she'd blinded herself to what was really important. She thought of everything they'd been through together, all the tough times when he'd always picked himself up, picked all of them up too and soldiered on. She loved him. She needed to show it, needed to practise it. Needed, somehow, to survive all this.

She put her hand out for his, and he lifted his right arm toward her and placed his hand in hers, and she felt it as heavy as though he'd been dead. 'Come into the tack room,' she said softly, 'it's too cold in those boxes.'

The tack room was small and had an old-fashioned gas stove. Maggie lit it and switched on the single striplight. Graham sat on a long bench he had bought from a school that had closed; it was heavy and shiny with dark brown varnish and had been in the school's gym for generations. Graham liked things that had a bit of history about them. She sat beside him on the bench, in front of the stove and beneath the racks of saddles and bridles and pictures of their horses and a couple of sponsors' horse blankets for races they'd won. Maggie took one of those off the wall; it was red with big silver lettering. She sat down and laid it across their knees and put her arm around her husband.

He hung his head and they sat in silence for a minute. He said dejectedly, 'We'd best go in. He might call.'

'Let him call,' she said, moving her hand to stroke his neck. 'We've waited long enough for him. He can wait for us.'

He was silent again for a while then said quietly, not looking at her, 'I want you to know and I want the kids to know how sad I'll be to lose Gabby.'

He sounded close to tears and it caught Maggie out. She'd thought he'd keep all this inside. 'I know,' she said, still stroking him gently. 'And for all Jane's histrionics the other night, she'll know how much Gabby means to you. Billy does too. They've grown up feeding on your dreams, for goodness sake. They'll know.'

'I just don't want them to think that because I try and take what life deals out, try to just get on with it, that I don't care and that I wouldn't fight if I could.'

She sensed there was more to come and stayed silent.

'If there was some way of getting to this guy, some way of meeting him face to face…'

'There is,' she said. 'We could pay the ransom.'

He looked at her. 'No. We've been through all that.'

'You're right, we've been through it but it's always been from my point of view and that's been ultra-selfish of me.'

And she saw the look in his eyes change and she knew he agreed with at least some of what she'd said.

But he said, 'Nonsense. You did what you thought was best, was reasonable. And you were right. Or should I say we were right.'

'Should you say we?'

She saw that look in his eyes again. He said, 'All things considered, yes.'

'All things considered meaning that you thought you didn't really have any say, because the money was coming to me and not you or to us?'

'Maggie, I was the one who said no to him on the phone last week, wasn't I?'

'You said no because you thought you had no right to bargain with money, with a cheque that had my name on it rather than yours, or ours. Isn't that right?'

He wouldn't answer, looked away again at the stove. Maggie said, 'Answer me one question, honestly. Just one and I won't ask any more. OK?' Staring at the floor now, he nodded. 'If you had half a million in the bank, your own money with no call on it for anything else, would you pay the ransom?' He kept staring at the floor. 'Would you?' she repeated.

'Yes.'

She lifted her arm from his shoulder, pushed the blanket aside and moved to the floor in front of him on one knee, and she put her arms around his neck and kissed him. 'Come on. We've got a kidnapper to make pick-up arrangements with.'

'You can't, Maggie, not just because of me.'

'Who else matters?'

He shook his head slowly. She touched his chin, pushed his head up. 'Who else matters?' she asked again, very softly, tenderly. And he put his arms around her and kissed her and pulled her close, holding her there for what seemed a long time. She shifted on her knees on the wooden floorboards and said, 'Graham, we need to go and we need to go now! '

He pulled her closer. 'Why now?' he whispered.

'Because my bum is burning! '

As far as Monroe was concerned, the phone call was to be a formality. There was no way the Cassidys were going to pay, and when they said they would, he had laughed. When he found out they were serious, he told them he'd call back to arrange for the pick-up and the delivery of the horse. And now, as he straddled his bike by the call box in the Berkshire countryside, he knew he was facing the true test of his criminal brain. He prided himself on being a sharp thinker and now he had to prove it. If he did he'd be half a million pounds richer. If he failed, he'd be spending a long time inside.

He sped back to Lambourn, to the abattoir he worked in. His own little house in the village held no appeal for him now. It just reminded him he had never made it as a jockey, never got to the top in racing, and as he rode along the wet roads in his leathers he wondered exactly what sort of house half a million pounds would buy. He knew that property up north was much cheaper and was aware that if he suddenly bought a big place questions would be asked.

Yet he wanted to stay close to Lambourn, wanted the bastards to see that he had made it. Trouble was that half a million wasn't enough to prove anything these days, and that was why he had the backup, the main plan. Once he had some serious money, he'd make sure nobody could touch him. They could ask all the questions they liked but he'd have answers. Answers for everything; for the big house and the Merc and the maid and the swimming pool and the tennis court and the long, long holidays. Barbados was the place, he thought. That was where all these rich racing bastards went to be with their own kind. Sunny Barbados where pond life like him couldn't afford to go. Barbados, the Newmarket of the Caribbean. Well, he'd be there and he'd outbuy them all. He'd let them see what it was to be able to spend!

And why not take this half a million to get him off to a decent start? He'd figure something out to make the pick-up safe. It couldn't be that hard, could it? It wasn't as though he had to bring the bloody horse along! He'd call them the next day and tonight he'd decide exactly how he was going to do this. To hell with the abattoir, he spent enough time there as it was. Anyway, the pubs would be buzzing in the village with New Year's Eve parties. He'd go there, have a few beers, make his plans for collecting the dosh then find some bird to bring in the New Year with, a new bird, none of the old slappers he normally ended up with. A new one for the New Year.

28

When the police heard that the Cassidys intended to pay the ransom, they pulled Burnham off the case and sent two new officers to speak to them. They went through all the warnings - by paying up they'd simply be encouraging the kidnapper to choose another victim, and handing over the ransom did not guarantee the safe return of their horse. But Maggie and Graham stuck to their guns, and were pleased that Frankie stood by them. He knew he should have taken the professional stance and sided with the police, but he preferred to support his friends.

The CID brought with them a much more sophisticated monitoring kit to record the phone call. When it finally came, the recorder silently switched itself on automatically.

'Still want your horse back?' Monroe asked.

'Yes,' said Graham.

'And you're still willing to pay?'

'That's right.'

'Well the price has just gone up. A million.'

Graham clenched his jaw and looked suddenly very angry.

Monroe laughed. 'Only kidding! I'm a man of my word, Mister Cassidy. Got a pen?'

'Yes.'

'Got the money?'

'We'll have it for when you want.'

'You've got forty-eight hours.'

'Fine. We can do that.'

'Good. Listen. Half a million pounds in used notes. I want you to go to the Charnock Richard services on the M6 at six p.m. on Thursday. You should park in the last row of the bays before the final exit for the petrol station. In that row, you will see a black Volvo 740 with a French registration plate. It is a left-hand-drive car. The door will be unlocked. Then get in the driver's seat; the keys will be underneath it. The car has a satellite navigation system and your destination will be pre-programmed. You'll hear audio directions as well as see them on the screen on the dashboard. The car also has special electronic equipment which detects mobile phone, police radio and radar output. I will be monitoring every sound. If you make any calls to the police or anyone else, you'll be collecting a dead horse. Tell the police that if they track you in any way, by road or helicopter or by fixing a bug to anywhere, tell them you'll be suing them for half a million. If you do everything right and reach the satnav destination without anything going wrong, you'll get your next set of instructions. Got all that?' Graham was scribbling. 'Yes.'

'Call it back to me. I don't want you blaming me if anything goes wrong.'

Graham read it back.

'Right… Good. One final thing; you need to remember this code word… Barbados. It's the one you will recognize me by. When you hear it, you'll hand over the money. What is it?'

'Barbados.'

'Good, now say hello to the nice policemen for me and to the Jockey Club guys.'

Graham said, 'When do we get the horse back?'

'As soon as I've counted that half a million. So make sure you don't get it all in fivers, won't you?' He hung up.

The younger of the CID men moved toward the tape recorder and started rewinding it. 'Right,' he said, 'let's start making plans.'

The abattoir wasn't due to reopen until the 6th of January, and Monroe knew he could safely take the rifle he always used as long as he returned it before then. He bound the weapon in thick black bin bags and strapped it to his bike using leather from an old bridle, although he had to reposition it a few times to make it fit comfortably under his right leg.

He'd been nervous making that phone call, but everything now looked fine and his confidence was high; the plan was a brilliant one and it bolstered his belief that he was set for the big time. He was sure it would work; certain he'd now get the money with the absolute minimum of danger to himself. What he did realize, as he put the final touches to the rifle strapping, was that with this 303 weapon that could kill a man at a mile, he was raising the stakes beyond the point of return. It was a calculated gamble; he reckoned that if they caught him he'd get ten years for the kidnapping alone, and ten years was as good as a lifetime for him. He'd be over forty when he got out, well past the age when he could hope to make his mark.

Carrying a gun would get him another five years at least, but for what he planned to do, he decided it was easily worth the risk. Research on the internet into past kidnap cases told him that a high percentage of people were caught at the pick-up point. He'd studied the various ways kidnappers had used to try and get clean away and some of them had seemed quite ingenious. Everything he'd learnt in those hours trawling through news archives had, he thought, served him well. He'd soon find out if he was right. Then they'd add his story to the archives - only he'd be one of the rare few who got away.

When Maggie Cassidy had made the bold decision to pay the money, she hadn't reckoned with the practicalities of getting the cash in forty-eight hours. The police had been unable and unwilling to help, and after much racking of brains, Frankie had volunteered to call his millionaire friend, Bobby Cranfield. Maggie had thanked him but said she may as well try her agent first. He was going to have to give a letter of guarantee anyway that the half a million was coming her way. Maggie knew he had some influential friends in the City and thought she should ask him if he could actually help get the cash.

The money was delivered next day by security courier. It was in a much smaller package than Maggie had imagined, but it was all in fifty-pound notes so she supposed it would be right. She spent an hour with Graham and Frankie counting it in the kitchen. After two attempts, they got it right and laughed nervously as the tension continued to build.

After dinner, Frankie called the CID. He returned to the table as Maggie lit a cigarette. 'Any news?' she asked.

Frankie said, 'They're still trying to get a result from the French police on Volvo 740s but they reckon they have things pretty much as they want them at the service station.'

'And there's no black Volvo in place at Charnock Richard right now?'

'Not as far as they can see.'

Graham shook his head. 'How the hell is this guy planning to do this?'

Frankie shrugged. Maggie drew on her cigarette and shook her head slowly. Graham said, 'He sounded so confident, didn't he? Surely he can be the only one who's dropping this car off? If this navigation programme is set from the service station, then who else could set it? Who else could take the car there?'

'He could get somebody to do it for him,' Maggie suggested, 'somebody who wouldn't necessarily be involved, He could simply pay an accomplice to do it, tell him what to put on the system when he leaves it and that's it. If the police picked the guy up we'd be no further forward and we'd have lost the horse.'

Frankie said, 'Don't worry. Whoever drops the car off won't even know the police are there.

They've got all sorts of thermal-imaging equipment and infrared cameras. They'll make sure they get some good video of him and if it's safe to track him, they'll try and do it.'

'What if it's not safe?' asked Graham. Frankie could see that now the commitment to pay had been made, Graham had grown much more animated, much edgier.

'They've promised not to do anything to jeopardize the horse's life,' Frankie said.

Graham said nothing for a few moments, then, 'Do you trust them, Frankie?' It was a plea for reassurance.

Frankie said, 'It's the first time I've worked with them. If we were stuck with Burnham, I'd be worried but these other two seem pretty slick. They have a final briefing meeting in an half an hour and they've asked me along so, if you don't mind, I'll leave you for a while.'

'Not at all,' Graham said. 'You'll be back for your usual nightcap, I hope?'

'Wouldn't miss it.' Frankie smiled.

Maggie and Graham sat together by the fire and talked of their plans if things went well next day, never entertaining the thought that they might not. Just before ten Graham got up. 'Frankie's getting dangerously close to missing his nightcap. I'll just go and have a last look at the horses.'

'Fine. I'll pour us a drink.'

In the barn, Graham was glad to see all was well. He spoke quietly to the horses as he stepped into each box to run his hand down a neck or a flank. He loved the warmth of them at night, the smell of them. 'Your old mate Gabby will be back tomorrow, God willing.'

Then he sensed someone behind him. At the same time, he felt cold metal digging into the back of his head. He froze; hand still on the half-shut door. Out of the side of his right eye, he could see the shadow of the gunman cast by the security lights. He held a rifle. He recognized the voice too when he heard him say, 'Barbados.'

29

They told Billy about the theft of the money. Maggie decided they had no choice, with the place swarming with police and the endless interviews with them, but they thought it best not to tell Jane. They'd just agreed a one-week extension to her holiday in Ireland as Poppy was doing so well with Jane's company, although Maggie was convinced that this lame duck she'd picked up, this Sean Gleeson, was more likely to be the reason Jane wanted to stay. Anyway, if she'd told Jane about the hold-up, about her father having a gun shoved in his face and the money gone, she'd have been rushing home to take over and comfort everybody. So they told her they were in negotiations with the kidnapper and that they were hopeful.

By mid-afternoon, Maggie was alone in the house, although two policemen were stationed outside; the condition Graham insisted on before agreeing to go to the station to look through some mug shots - a pointless bloody exercise, he'd told the CID man. The thief, the kidnapper had been wearing a black mask covering everything but his eyes which had been a vivid blue. That was all he could tell them, but the straw-clutchers had insisted that the mug shots might trigger something in his mind.

CID - Maggie shook her head slowly in disgust as she sipped coffee and lit her tenth cigarette of the day. At least they'd had the grace to be embarrassed at being so deeply taken in by all that French Volvo satellite navigation stuff. It proved to her that most policemen were no more well versed in handling kidnappings than she herself was. Apparently, Stonebanks, Frankie's colleague, had told him the Met would never have believed all that stuff. It was these 'country boys', as he called them.

And now Frankie was gone too, back to London to make his report.

She thought of last night when the man came in with the gun to Graham's head, her stomach lurching as she recalled it. Her first thought had been how glad she was that she had shown him some love these past couple of days, happy she'd agreed to pay the ransom even though it had ended in this trauma.

Poor Graham. He'd been devastated. She knew it was worse for men. In Graham's mind, he should have been able to offer protection, but he'd been as dumbstruck and afraid as she had been. And she knew what it had done to his dignity. Part of the reason, she thought, was that this whole thing had been panning out like some movie or novel and everybody knew what to do in movies.

The bad guy came in with the gun. The hero overpowered him or outsmarted him, maybe killed him but at least locked him up until the cops arrived. But when the scene came to be played, the cold reality was that the instinct to stay alive favoured inaction, compliance, surrender. And that's what they'd done, almost without a murmur. She realized it had affected Graham badly, that her presence had made his self-loathing more acute. She knew that worse was to come for Graham because of the guilt he felt about losing the money. If he hadn't agreed to let her pay, last night would never have happened. Now, not only had they been terrorized, all the money had gone and they held out little hope of ever seeing the horse alive again. Everything lost in a few minutes.

The tears rose once more.

Frankie and Stonebanks were in a basement bar off Oxford Street in London. Frankie had formally debriefed his own boss, Robert Archibald, and had his reassurance that there was nothing more he could have done. 'You went beyond the call of duty,' Archibald had said. 'There can be no criticism of you or of the department.'

Frankie was telling Stonebanks how guilty he felt at not being there when the gunman had come in.

Stonebanks said, 'Why? What do you think you could have done?'

'I don't know. What would you have done?'

'With a hunting rifle in my face? Probably started crying for my mummy.'

'You're just trying to make me feel better.'

'I'm trying to make you wake up and smell the coffee! This guy knew what risks he was running. He's just added armed robbery to kidnap and the killing of at least one horse. Do you seriously think he wouldn't have used that gun if you'd been there and tried to stop him? He'll get twenty years if they catch him and he knows that. Does he seem the type that would have just handed over the gun if you'd asked him? Or maybe you felt you could have rushed him or something daft like that? How quickly can you cross a room? Faster than a bullet? And if he shot you, do you think he'd have left the Cassidys alive? Come on, Frankie, there was nothing you could have done, even if you'd been there.' Frankie drank some beer and stared at the door. He knew Stonebanks was right; he'd just needed to hear it, needed to know that it was nothing to do with incompetence or lack of will, lack of courage. And he realized how petulant and self-pitying he must have sounded. What had Maggie thought? He felt he'd run off with his tail between his legs. Was that how she had seen it? And what about Kathy, watching from above, how had it looked to her?

'Look at the upside,' Stonebanks said, 'you'll have the whole department behind you now.'

Frankie frowned quizzically. 'That's an upside?'

Stonebanks laughed. 'That's my boy!' He raised his glass in mock salute and Frankie did the same. 'At least the Cassidys have had a look at this guy now, heard him speak, saw him move. What has it added to the picture?' asked Stonebanks.

Frankie sat back, legs stretched, hands in his lap, eyes to the ceiling. 'I don't know. Graham said he had the build of a jockey. He compared him to Derry Callaghan, remember him?'

'I remember him well.'

'Graham said that was who he reminded him off. Short and stocky, looked like he'd run to fat eventually but very fit looking, strong…'

'He was right, Derry did run to fat. He's about fifteen stone now.'

'Do you keep any sort of picture file of past jockeys?' Frankie asked.

Stonebanks shook his head. 'We issue them with licences, keep files on their medical histories and disciplinary records but no pictures as far as I know. Anyway, I thought he had a motorcycle mask on?'

'He did but Maggie said his eyes were very blue. Sky-blue. Very striking.'

'Lenses.'

'Pardon?'

'He was probably wearing coloured lenses. He's been pretty smart so far. If all he was showing were his eyes, you can bet he wouldn't be doing it knowing they were such a distinctive feature.'

'Maybe. But I wouldn't mind trying. What about the *Racing Post*? They'd have pictures of jockeys going back years. We could go and have a look there.'

'We could, if you've got a few years to spare. I think they file all their pictures by name rather than profession.'

'But surely their pictures will be on computer? They must have some sort of subheading for files?'

'Maybe. We'll check in the morning.' Stonebanks stretched wearily.

'That's twice you've said "in the morning" and now you're yawning. Are you dropping some class of a hint here?'

Stonebanks smiled. 'You're a fine detective, Frankie. With those powers of observation, you're sure to catch this guy.'

'Come on, Geoff, it's only half-ten!'

'Come on yourself! I've got to drive to Lambourn.'

Frankie smiled. 'I know you have. I'm only kidding. Thanks for your help and for your company.'

'Thanks for the beer. You staying much longer?'

Frankie sighed. 'Nah. Guess I'd better go home too.'

A slight tension filled the pause that followed, then Stonebanks said, 'You're welcome to come back with me.'

Thanks. I'll be fine. I need to face the hoovering and washing and cooking at some point. It might as well be tonight.'

'Sure?'

'Positive.'

Stonebanks smiled. 'See you tomorrow.'

'You will. Drive carefully.'

30

Apart from when they were asleep, Sean Gleeson and Jane Cassidy spent most of their time together. Uncle Fergus had let Sean ride some work and Sean found that sitting on a racehorse was everything he'd imagined it to be and more. It had made him rue his youthfulness and wish for the next five years to pass in a night.

They'd ride out in the mornings and again in the afternoon, no matter the weather. In between, they'd sit with Poppy, and Sean would tell tales of what the children in Dublin got up to and how the pony races were organized. They'd groom and feed the horses, and Sean would talk about the races he'd win when he became a jockey but as much as he tried to shut out the other world, Sean was growing increasingly anxious to find out what had happened to his father. But any time he said that, Jane would go mental, demanding to know how he could care what happened to such a horrible man, and Sean would regret then having told her some of the bad things his father had done.

The schools were due to re-open in a few days. Uncle Fergus had already been dropping hints to that effect. Nobody would care if Sean never turned up at school, but he'd been away from it too long. He wanted to have the education for after his riding career. He was aware most jump jockeys didn't last much past their mid-thirties and just wanted to be sure he could do something else.

But returning to school meant returning to St Joseph's Mansions. Jane had argued that it didn't. They'd been sitting in the hay barn, in a huge chair they'd made of bales. First, she said that he could go to Poppy's school. But Poppy attended a private school - that cost money. 'Well,' she'd said with her usual confidence, 'we can find another school near here.'

'That's a long way from Dublin city,' Sean said.

'You can move in here, with Uncle Fergus. Pay for your keep by working with the horses.'

'That would be just grand,' Sean said. 'But how would Uncle Fergus feel about it and what would we tell the school people? There's all that stuff about legal guardians and everything, and I don't want that.'

'Why?'

'Well, I want it, I want to be here. This has been the best week of my life and I'd love to stay here, but you'll have to go home soon yerself.'

'I can sort that. I can move here. You know I don't get on with my mum anymore.'

'Maybe. But I still have things to do, Jane.'

'What things?'

'Find out where me da is. And me ma, too.'

And Jane crossed her arms and furrowed her brow in the same way Sean had come to know so well. He wasn't looking forward to saying goodbye.

Frankie took the call on his mobile just after eight in the morning. It was Stonebanks. 'Sorry Frankie, but it looks like they found the Cassidys' horse. He's dead.'

'Where? When?'

'Outside the main entrance to Cheltenham racecourse, would you believe? The head groundsman found him when he arrived about half an hour ago.'

Shocked, Frankie sat in the car, shaking his head slowly.

'Shot and mutilated,' Stonebanks said. 'Very similar to Ulysses, so I hear.'

'Bastard,' Frankie said.

'Indeed,' said Stonebanks, surprised.

'Has anyone told the Cassidys?'

'Not as far as I know.'

'I'll call them.'

'Sure?'

'Positive. I'll call now. If I wasn't so far so south I'd go and tell them personally.'

'Drive up. Call them, then drive up. I know how close you are with them.'

'What good would it do? I'd be better off here now, trying to catch this, this…'

'Bastard?'

'Yes.'

'There are other things. You can check in with the police there. Maybe you'll pick something up from them. Get yourself on the move. Let me know if there's anything I can do.'

'OK. Thanks, Geoff.'

'No problem.'

Frankie pulled the car over, parked by the edge of the wood and sat looking down at the small screen on his mobile. The Cassidy number was programmed in. He scrolled to it and pressed 'send'. Maggie answered.

'Maggie? It's Frankie Houlihan.'

'Hello Frankie. How are you this morning?'

'I'm well. How are you?'

'I'm fine. Coping.'

He wished she hadn't said that.

'Is there something wrong?' she asked.

'More bad news, I'm afraid. They think they've found Gabby. He's dead.'

'Ohhh.'

'I'm so sorry, Maggie.'

'It's OK. It's alright.' He could hear the shock in her voice.

'I'm heading up to you now, if that's OK?'

'Yes. Of course.'

'I should be there by noon.'

'Good. Good. I'll tell Graham.'

'See you later then.'

'Yes. Bye.'

He cursed silently as he put the phone into its cradle - then it rang again. It was Maggie. 'Frankie, how did he die?'

He drew a breath. 'He was shot, I think.'

'So he wouldn't have suffered?'

'I don't think so, Maggie, no,' he lied. The horse had been mutilated. It was highly likely that happened after death, Frankie thought; there was no way this guy would have wanted to try and keep a pain-enraged horse still enough to shoot it through the head. But Frankie couldn't be certain that there had been no suffering at the hands of this lunatic.

'Good,' she said. 'That's not so bad then, is it?' She sounded completely stunned.

'No, it's not.'

'OK. Take care on your journey.'

'I will.'

As he drove north, he thought about the way people's lives worked out. There they'd been on the run-up to Christmas, the happiest of families. The Grand National favourite was safe in his box and in the post was a cheque that would make them secure for life, then bang. All gone. In tatters. He thought of his own misfortune and that of many of the parishioners he had served over the years. And he thought about justice and about God and could make no real sense of either.

Maggie and Graham decided to try and keep the news from the children until Jane returned the following week. It would mean asking Fergus to try and make sure Jane didn't see any newspapers or TV for a couple of days. They'd need to do the same with Billy, but that wouldn't be so hard as he spent most of his time trying to think up new inventions or playing computer strategy games. Luckily, he was still off school so none of his mates would alert him, although she'd need to screen his calls. Maggie rang Fergus who seemed devastated by the news, and agreed to try his best to keep it from Jane.

The *Racing Post* editor told Frankie Houlihan he'd be happy to help with the picture library, but that it was probably going to take a week to get it in the shape he needed it. Frankie thanked him and booked a day to go and scan through all the pictures with Maggie. He was still with the Cassidys. He'd travelled to Cheltenham with Graham who formally identified Angel Gabriel; Frankie found it a harrowing experience.

The horse had been so badly mutilated that Graham broke down in tears in front of Frankie and the clerk of the course. Frankie had seen many people cry and recognized the racking sobs of true shock and grief as he tried to comfort the trainer. The embarrassed clerk made comments about how terrible the whole thing was, and Frankie helped Graham back to the car before returning for an official interview with the man who had found the dead horse.

On the way back north, Graham, red-eyed, turned to Frankie. 'Frankie, let's not tell Maggie what he did to him.' Graham barely recognized the sound of his own voice, the croak through the tightness in his throat.

'Of course not. No, it's best to keep it between us.'

'Yes. Definitely.'

They travelled in silence for a while, Graham staring glassy-eyed at the road and seeing nothing. 'What about the press?' he asked. 'Will there be pictures in the papers?'

'Don't worry. I asked the clerk of the course to make sure nobody took any pictures. The police will want to take some for their files, that's all.'

'Good.' Graham bowed his head and said quietly, 'We can't even bring him home... They'd see what a mess he's in...'

'Don't be worrying about that. I'll make sure he's taken care of.'

'Thanks. You've been a tower of strength. I don't know what the family would have done without you, I really don't.'

'Ahh come on now, you're a great family. This has been a terrible, terrible thing but you all have the strength to get over it, to help each other.'

Graham shook his head and let out a long sigh. 'Jane will be inconsolable. My God...she's going to be completely devastated. She'll insist on having him home. She'll want him buried in the paddock. Oh Jesus!' Graham covered his face with his hands and started weeping again.

Frankie took a hand from the wheel and reached across to touch Graham's shoulder, to squeeze it softly. 'I'll sort something out, Graham, I promise. I know some good vets. I'm sure we can get one to work on Gabby, to get him cleaned up and his wounds fixed so you'll be able to bring him home.'

Graham nodded, face still covered, sobbing. 'If you, if you could...'

They drove on, and after five minutes Graham had recovered and composed himself. He apologized for breaking down.

'Don't be daft. It's perfectly natural, so it is. The grief's better out.'

'I just couldn't believe it,' Graham said. 'After he'd taken the money, I honestly thought we'd get him back. What on earth is the point of killing him? I thought he just came to the house to get the money to reduce the chances of the police catching him. What in the name of God did he stand to gain by killing Gabby afterwards?'

'I don't know, Graham. I really don't. It just makes me glad that you didn't try and tackle him the other night, because it's obvious now, if it wasn't before, that you'd have been tackling a madman.'

They talked about the police and their effectiveness, about the mug shots Graham had sat through for hours with nothing to show for it. Then they travelled in silence for a while until Frankie, driving, was aware of Graham turning purposefully toward him as he spoke; 'I want to do everything I can to help you catch this man. Apart from what he's done to Gabby, which I think I could kill him for, I want Maggie to get her money back. I want that more than anything else.'

Frankie considered saying that he was sure Maggie wasn't that worried about the money, but he knew that it wouldn't make Graham feel better so he just nodded. 'I'll put everything I can into catching him, Graham. My boss has already told me we have the backing of the full Jockey Club Security Department.'

'So what are the chances?'

'Depends on how solid our suspicion is that he might be an ex-jockey. If he is, and he doesn't wear contact lenses, our chances might be very good indeed.'

When Frankie brought Graham back home, Maggie asked no immediate questions. The shock and misery were etched in her husband's lined, grey face. Maggie realized that this man she'd known and seen almost every day for over twenty years was old now - old and tired and defeated. Alongside him, sympathetic and patient as ever, stood Frankie Houlihan, young still, and strong, with most of his tribulations to come, she thought. She went to her husband and hugged him. His head rested heavily on her shoulder and his hands barely linked at the small of her back. He started sobbing quietly. She looked at Frankie and knew he could see the pain in her eyes as he slowly raised a hand to chest height and backed away to slip quietly outside.

Frankie hated this feeling of helplessness. This was the second time he'd experienced it - the thug taking their money from under their noses had been bad but this was worse. He'd taken much more than money from Graham Cassidy. He'd taken his vitality and his dignity, his hopes and dreams, and there had to be something Frankie could do about it, there had to be.

He walked to the bottom of the drive. It was a gloomy day and away across the patchwork of fields, Frankie could see dark swathes of rain sweeping over the countryside. Turning up the collar of his coat, he went left at the end of the drive and walked along the hedge-lined road. He concentrated on emptying the emotion from his mind, tried to think logically and make some sense of what had happened.

The kidnapper was no fool; the way he'd conned the police over the pick-up proved that. It was almost certain that there was a reason behind everything he'd done. So why kill a horse if he'd been paid, a horse that was of no use to him? In killing it, he was killing his own chances of ever being paid a ransom again. And why the mutilation? It was senseless and this man didn't seem the type to do senseless things. Whether or not he was an ex-jockey whose picture was on file, there had to be something in his behaviour to work on. Rather than assuming, as they'd done in the last twenty-four hours, that the man was simply a violent lunatic, maybe the assumption should be that everything he did made sense to him.

Frankie walked on, vaguely aware of the sound of his feet on the fine gravel and the wind in the trees. He decided to start with the biggest puzzle of all: why kill Angel Gabriel? The killing of Ulysses was slightly more understandable as no ransom had been paid but, having said that, the deadline the killer had given for the money was ridiculously short, almost as though he hadn't wanted to be paid, as though he actually preferred to kill the horse.

Now, if he was depraved in some way, he could simply kidnap horses and kill them without running the risk of telephone calls and police involvement. Then there was the dumping of Ulysses in a stream - why? It must have been a hell of a lot of trouble to get that horsebox or trailer into position to place the body. The drag marks on the ground showed that he'd had to use some form of winch to get the horse properly into the water; why hadn't he just winched it out and dumped it in a field?

And why hadn't he left it in a public place, as he'd done with Gabby? It was as if he hadn't wanted Ulysses found for a long time, yet he'd taken the opposite tack with Gabby. Frankie couldn't figure it out. He walked for twenty minutes then turned back as the rain shadows moved nearer and the wind rose.

In the kitchen, Maggie Cassidy sat alone, smoking, sipping cooling coffee, trying to block everything out. A knock at the door made her jump. She put down her cigarette and opened the door. Frankie stood there, dark hair and pale face framed against the gathering storm clouds. She said, 'Come in. No need for you to knock.'

Frankie took the step up into the kitchen and she closed the door quietly. She saw him look around the empty room. 'Graham's gone to bed. I think it's all finally hit him.'

Frankie unbuttoned his coat. 'Poor fella. The strain's been terrible on all of you this past week.' Maggie clicked the kettle switch. 'Take your coat off, I'll make some tea.'

They sat in silence for a while, cradling the hot mugs. Then Maggie said, 'Will you stay for a few more days, Frankie?' She hoped it hadn't sounded like a plea. She couldn't gauge what he was thinking as he looked at her but she knew he was going to decline.

He said, 'I want to get back, Maggie, and get working on this. I want to find this man. And... and I think you should have time on your own with the family to come to terms with all this, if you don't mind me saying.'

She reached for another cigarette. 'I'm not sure I want to come to terms with it now. After he took the money, I was confident we'd get Gabby back.' She lit the cigarette, drew hard on it and rested her head on her right hand as she exhaled. She looked suddenly tired. 'I never thought what we'd do if we didn't get him back. Didn't prepare for it. And now it's happened so suddenly, I don't know what to do. It's sort of the end of everything. I just wondered if you could stay with us for a while.'

'To save you from facing up to things?'

She looked at him. It was the first time he had ever been blunt with her and she couldn't decide if he'd done it deliberately or had just put it awkwardly. 'Yes. I suppose that's part of it.'

'Maggie, I feel useless here. I feel I've been useless to you all throughout this and I want not to be useless.'

'You're not, don't be silly. You've been a great friend and a great help.'

'But I didn't stop him stealing your money or your horse. I didn't do my job properly, and I want a chance to try and make amends because I think we can catch this fella.'

'It wasn't your responsibility. You did all you could. You even phoned to warn us to be careful. It was our own stupidity that cost us Gabby.'

'And half a million pounds.'

She nodded.

'Well I'd like to try and help get it back,' Frankie said. 'I've arranged a meeting soon for you to look at some pictures and they might just throw up a good clue. And if I can get my brain working properly, I think there's some sense to be made out of all the mad stuff that's gone on.'

'So you're going back to London?'

He nodded. 'London, Lambourn, wherever I need to go to feel I'm actually doing something, to feel I'm working.'

She looked at him. 'I'd like to feel I was doing something too. I'd like to help.'

'Fine. I think it'll do you good. Maybe you could start by doing what I'm doing and concentrate on trying to think like this fella. Try to put yourself in his shoes and come up with a good reason for what he's done. Assume he's smart and emotionally stable. Have you a pen and paper?'

She went to a small plastic pot that stood on the windowsill and picked out a pen. Then she opened two drawers before pulling out a dog-eared writing pad. Bringing it to the table she scribbled lightly to get the ink running. Frankie said, 'Right, let's go back to the very start.'

31

On the 6th of January, the abattoir Monroe worked in was due to reopen after the Christmas break. He had twenty-four hours to carry out the next stage of his plan. He regretted his haste now in dumping the carcass so publicly at Cheltenham. His motive had been to have the horse found quickly, to confuse the police if possible, making them wonder whether it was a kidnapper or a psycho of some kind they were dealing with. And he had to admit to himself that he'd done it to illustrate his power too, to have owners and trainers all over the country wondering if they were going to be next.

But he'd forgotten to check Cheltenham for CCTV. Although he'd arrived there at three o'clock in the morning, there was a chance that the system, if they had one at the gates, had been switched on. It was a remote possibility and the fact that it had been so dark made it even more unlikely that he'd have anything to worry about. But if the horsebox had been filmed, Monroe reckoned he could turn it to his advantage.

He booked the horsebox on the last ferry to Dublin on the 4th of January. Once on board, he hid in the cab until the hold had been secured, then settled on the padded bench seat to wait out the journey. The silver-coloured suitcase containing the half-million pounds was beside him. He stroked the surface, liking its dimpled, steely feel, and he was glad he'd bought the best to hold the money, his money now, money that was just the beginning. He passed the time counting the bundles then secured them again as the ship slowed and turned to enter the harbour. He shut the case in the overhead locker.

It was dark when he drove off the ferry. His journey was to be one he'd last made as a child when his grandparents had a farm overlooking Laura Lake in County Leitrim.

Monroe had spent a long summer holiday there by the lake. Running down the hill from the farm and diving into the cold blue water. That steady, gradual slope, that deep water was what was drawing him back there now. That and the knowledge that Laura Lake was one of the few in Ireland with a road bordering most of the shore.

His grandparents long dead, Monroe knew the old farm lay deserted and partly ruined. Tree branches swept and scratched the horsebox. Slumbering water birds woke and flew off. Monroe wrestled the wheel to full lock and turned up the hill, then entered by the top driveway. Along past the front of the old house then a right turn to face the moonlit lake at the foot of the bottom driveway.

Another advantage of being about thirty feet above the lake was that he could easily see headlights. The lake road was in poor repair and little used, but Monroe waited until after midnight to maximize his chances of going unseen.

He took a heavy flashlight from the overhead locker and climbed out. Cloud obscured the moon and he could see little outside the flashlight beam, which he trained on the slopes leading to the water's edge. He knew from his childhood swimming days that the shore side water was fairly shallow but he remembered only too well his grandfather's warnings about how deep it got after you reached the end of 'the shelf'.

He only had to make that shelf. The box would keep going and drop beyond it. The final depth was more than sufficient to swallow the big vehicle forever. The rocky ground running down to it was steep enough to give the horsebox the necessary momentum, but the road was narrower than he'd remembered it. The real risk was going to be in getting the box nose on to the drop-off point, then inching it past its centre of gravity. Once it started toppling, a quick jump clear and he was away.

Monroe set two rocks at the road edge to guide him then he returned to the box, lowered the ramp and rolled his Kawasaki out. He took the suitcase from the overhead locker and left it beside the bike, which he'd fitted with false number plates. He got back in, started the engine and sat for a few seconds. Did he really want to risk someone happening by, catching the silver suitcase in his headlights and stopping to investigate? He jumped down again and brought the suitcase back into the cab, conscious of how loud the clattering engine sounded in the rural darkness. He'd have to hurry. He released the handbrake.

He reached the marker rocks.

Just the final few inches forward now into the water. The wheels on the uneven bank caused the box to lurch sideways. Monroe gripped the suitcase handle with his left hand and opened the door with his right. It swung closed again. Once more, he tried. It closed again. He let go the case and put the handbrake on, then he pushed the door open wide until it fixed on its struts and held. Now he released the handbrake, grabbed the suitcase, and as the box moved he turned quickly to jump clear. But as the left front wheel dropped over the edge, the door swung violently inwards as Monroe was halfway out; the metal frame hit the crown of his head, fracturing his skull and knocking his unconscious body back into the cab.

The front bumper broke the cold, dark waters at forty-three minutes past midnight. Two minutes later, the moon found a gap in the clouds and glinted on a patch of oil on the surface of Laura Lake. It was the only sign that anything had happened, and the small slick was already dispersed by the wind and the choppy waves.

32

After leaving the Cassidys, Frankie spent the next couple of days travelling between Lambourn and London, having brainstorming sessions with Stonebanks and other colleagues. The racing intelligence officers based around the country promised him they'd mine all possible contracts to try and find the smallest lead. He rang Joe Ansell, the vet who was trying to repair Angel Gabriel's mutilated body. His assistant asked if Joe could call back in a while. Frankie knew Joe had been working hard since the carcass had been delivered. The wounds would hasten decomposition, and Joe was restricted to doing his cutting and stitching in what amounted to a makeshift cold storage unit at the Horseracing Forensic Laboratory in Newmarket. Joe had promised the horse would be ready to go back to the Cassidys by the end of next week.

Frankie called Maggie to find out how they planned to handle the burial. He first asked about Graham and the children.

'Graham hasn't left his bed since he came back from Cheltenham,' Maggie told him. 'All he does is sleep. The doctor says it's a combination of shock and depression, and that the medication will steadily bring him out of it.'

'Poor fella. You should have Gabby home by the weekend. That might help him, eh? I'm just waiting for Joe Ansell to call me back with confirmation. Will Jane be back by the weekend?'

Maggie sighed. 'If I can get her away from Sean.'

'First boyfriend?'

'First proper one. Seems a real character. Fergus likes him too.'

'Sounds an interesting kid.'

'To say the least!'

'What about Billy, how's he been?'

'Oh, Billy won't change! Spends most of his time in his room on the computer. Still trying to dream up get-rich-quick schemes.'

'Like the Hot Harrow?'

'He told you about that?'

'He did. Among others. He's a good boy. Be a millionaire one day.'

'Huh!'

'Don't knock it. They say an ounce of perseverance is worth a pound of talent.'

'Who says? I've never heard anyone say that.'

'You just heard me.'

'And I think you made it up! '

'I probably did. It's good to hear you sounding a bit brighter.'

'Oh, nil desperandum and all that.'

'Give Graham and Billy my best. I'll see you at the weekend.'

'Look forward to it.'

The cottage in the woods felt as though it had been deserted for ages, much longer than the time Frankie had actually been away. He laid his bag on the bedroom floor and began to unpack, stopping to open the windows, then reaching round to the outside of the pane to scrape off the wet leaves stuck to the glass. The place smelt damp and stale, felt cold and unwelcoming. He hadn't the will to set about it the way he knew he should to try and put some warmth and life back into it, and as he stared through the open window to the trees beyond, he realized that the wish to keep this as a proper home had died with Kathy.

But he had nowhere else to go, and he needed a base. He knew that he also needed to discipline himself, push himself to do the chores that had to be done. So he changed into his old jeans and the red sweater Kathy had liked and he set about cleaning and tidying, airing and washing, and he found that the busier he became, the more his spirits lifted.

The worktop area in the kitchen closest to the door was where he tended to dump things; letters, bills, the contents of his pockets, his watch, and as he sorted through the collection he found the letter he had meant to answer, the one from Zuiderzie's trainer, Martin Broxton. As he picked the letter up, his mobile rang.

'Frankie? It's Joe Ansell.'

'Hello, Joe! Thanks for calling me back.'

'No problem. I wasn't far from the phone when you rang, but I was just trying to be absolutely certain about something I'd found before I spoke to you. Just left the horse a minute ago.'

'Angel Gabriel?'

'Well, yes, the one who's supposed to be Angel Gabriel.'

'Supposed to be?'

'I've just spent over two hours removing dye from his head. Underneath the dye this horse has a lovely white star.'

'White? White hair?'

'What do you think, white corduroy?'

'Angel Gabriel had no white on him.'

'That's why this horse isn't Angel Gabriel.'

When Frankie finished the call, he stood staring out of the window, trying to gather his thoughts. What the hell was this guy up to? Was Angel Gabriel still alive? If so, what did this madman plan to do with him? He already had the ransom money. Broxton's letter caught his eye and he picked it up again. The picture of Zuiderzie in the paddock at Stratford came back to him, followed immediately by the picture of the corpse of Ulysses. He recalled thinking how alike both horses were.

Running upstairs, Frankie grabbed his diary and skipped through, checking the date he'd gone to Warwick against the date of the first kidnap - close, very close. He ran back downstairs and took his *Directory of the Turf* from the shelf to find Martin Broxton's details. Halfway through dialling the Lambourn number Frankie stopped. Was his inexperience and over-excitement making him act stupidly? Maybe something was going on, but he shouldn't discount the fact that Broxton himself might be involved. A call to Stonebanks would be much more sensible.

On the way to Stonebanks's place, Frankie considered ringing Maggie Cassidy and decided against it. The last thing they needed, especially Graham, was to have their hopes dashed a second time. Best to wait until he had something more solid. Then he remembered he'd have to ring, have to tell them something. They were expecting the corpse for the burial within the next couple of days. He'd told Joe Ansell he'd come back to him. It was almost certain they'd need to preserve the corpse now, pending a criminal investigation. He'd sound out Stonebanks.

Stonebanks was working from home, something he tried to do a couple of days a week. He wore a pair of black chinos and a grey polo shirt; it was the first time Frankie had seen him without a collar and tie. Stonebanks nursed his coffee, clutching a mug with his initials on. He said, 'You think both horses are still alive?'

'I think they could be,' Frankie said, trying to contain his excitement, to appear calm and professional.

'And the horse we dragged out of the water was Zuiderzie?'

'That's right. I think he put him in the stream as part of the mutilation process. Remember how decayed the skin was where he'd been lying in the water?'

Stonebanks nodded. 'And the horse Joe Ansell's got isn't Angel Gabriel?'

Frankie nodded, finding it hard now to mask an almost childish triumphalism; it was shining in his face. 'If you're right here, Frankie boy, you've made a major name for yourself! Now talk me through it and I'll try to pick some friendly holes in it.'

Frankie put down his cup and settled forward, elbows on knees. 'If I'm right and yer man has just found lookalikes for these horses, what's to stop him finding a couple more that are alive and racing and putting these top horses in as ringers in their place? What a killing he'd make on the betting side!'

Stonebanks said, 'It'd be a damn sight harder to find lookalikes that good when the horse had to be left alive, if you see what I mean? I accept that a distraught owner, expecting to see his horse dead, wouldn't look that closely at a mutilated body but it would be different on the racecourse; much tougher.'

'Fine, but let's assume, for the moment, that the horse's connections are in on the scam too.' Stonebanks shrugged. 'Fair enough.'

'Ulysses and Angel Gabriel are young enough for him to be able to wait a year or so to get things right, and if he did, he'd make an awful lot more out of the bookies than from ransom payments.'

'And who'd be training these horses in the meantime, keeping them reasonably fit and happy?'

'Not a big problem, is it? If I'm right and he's got hold of the carcass of Zuiderzie then there's every chance that he's in the business just now. He might even be a trainer rather than an ex-jockey.'

'God forbid,' said Stonebanks, shaking his head. 'So finding out what happened to Zuiderzie after he was put down is a key factor, you're right.'

'So what about Martin Broxton? Do you think it would be safe to talk to him upfront?' Frankie asked.

'Straight as a die, Broxton. No problem there at all. You'd just need to be careful not to make too big a thing of it or word will get out that something is cooking. Just take it easy with him, tell him it's a routine check on horses that, eh, what can we say...? Did you mention that Zuiderzie won on the day he was put down?'

'That's right. I was there. He absolutely hacked up after leading all the way. Won at a big price.' Stonebanks stared at him for what seemed a long time then put down his coffee mug and started massaging his jaws. 'Won easily and very unexpectedly at a big price and the next day he's dead?' Frankie nodded slowly. Stonebanks said, 'Have you checked his dope test?'

Frankie shrugged, open-handed. 'No. Should I have?'

'I don't know. It just seems odd.'

'Now you mention it, I remember noticing how on his toes Zuiderzie was in the paddock that day, which was very unlike him. Kathy always used to say how docile he was, how laid-back. I just put it down to some class of rejuvenation or something since he'd left Miles Henry and joined Broxton's yard. If it had been a positive dope test, we'd have heard about it by now, surely?'

Stonebanks got up and went to the phone. 'Somebody might have heard about it, but it wouldn't necessarily have made its way back to us. Let me call the lab boys.'

Fifteen minutes later, he got a call back from Newmarket with the result of Zuiderzie's Stratford dope test. 'Thanks,' he said and hung up, then turned to Frankie. 'Negative. I suppose that makes it easier to go and talk to Broxton. We don't have to worry about him being involved in anything.'

'Are you coming along?' Frankie asked.

'No, it would seem over the top then. He might get suspicious. Why don't you just make it look like a social visit? You mentioned you'd exchanged letters, no reason for you not to drop by and introduce yourself, reminisce about old times, get him talking about the horse.'

'Good idea, Geoff. Good idea.'

When Frankie called Broxton, the trainer seemed happy to hear from him and invited him for breakfast and to watch some schooling next morning.

Frankie and Martin Broxton got on well, and chatted about racing in general and their respective careers. It was after breakfast as Broxton showed him round the yard that Frankie brought the subject back to Zuiderzie, saying, 'It must have been a real shock to lose him after he'd won his first race for you.'

'We couldn't believe it, Frankie. It happened so soon after it too. He'd just got home and we had to call the vet out. It must have started on the journey back. The poor bugger was standing there shaking like he was made of metal and somebody had hit him with a hammer. Shaking like a bloody tuning fork, he was. Culling operated on him that night, within an hour, in fact, but just couldn't save him.'

'Culling's your vet?'

'That's right. Good man. Good vet. If Peter Culling couldn't save him, nobody could.'

'And what was Mister Culling's verdict? What killed him?'

'Aggravated colic, I think he called it. The non-aggravated version is bad enough, I can tell you. I don't want to see this other type again.'

'Pity the owner.'

'Yes, and his lass. Zuiderzie was Belinda's first winner. She's still not over it. Still keeps a lock of his mane in her locket.'

'Poor girl. So did the owner take him home, have him buried?'

'Nothing so romantic, I'm afraid. There ain't too many can afford to do that these days. We let the vet dispose of him through the local knacker's man, helps pay a bit off the final bill.'

'Yeah, I suppose.'

Broxton smiled as they stopped by the box in the corner of the yard, and a big brown intelligent head appeared over the top of the door. The horse sniffed at his trainer's shoulder and began nuzzling him. 'Never mind,' Broxton said, 'here's the next serving of hope, the thing that keeps us all going. Frankie Houlihan, meet this year's Triumph Hurdle winner, Barabbas. Barabbas, meet a man with very good connections!' Frankie smiled and reached to stroke the big nose.

Frankie returned to discuss things with Stonebanks before ringing Culling to arrange an appointment. Stonebanks said he'd known the vet for years and although he seemed quite a reclusive individual personally, he had no reason to believe he was anything other than a hard-working vet. He was properly licensed, long serving and he covered a number of racecourses in an official capacity as well as running his own business in Lambourn.

When Frankie rang and introduced himself, he felt that Culling had been thrown and that the vet had been shocked too when he'd mentioned that he wanted to come and speak to him about Zuiderzie. Culling had tried to cover his reaction by claiming he was on his mobile giving emergency advice and could he call Frankie back in a few minutes? So Frankie gave him his mobile number and sat in Stonebanks's kitchen waiting for the call. He and Stonebanks probed and twisted what they had so far to see if they could squeeze anything more from it.

Then Frankie remembered what he had to do. 'Geoff, we've got to find some way off keeping that horse at Joe Ansell's above the ground and in decent shape.'

Stonebanks looked puzzled for a minute the said, 'Ahh, you're right.'

'Not exactly the easiest thing to store, is it?'

Stonebanks shook his head. 'You can say that again. He'll need to be frozen or he'll be stinking in a week. What's happening with him where he is?'

'Joe Ansell's put him in a cold room he uses but that was just to allow him to be able to work with the cuts and stuff. I don't think he's got anywhere he can actually freeze the body.'

Stonebanks looked thoughtful, then said, 'I know a guy who has a big meat processing plant. He might have some sizeable units there. I'll give him a call.'

33

Culling couldn't stop sweating. It was chilly in the conservatory where he paced the tiled floor, wide- eyed, unable to calm himself or control his thoughts. They were onto him. Everything was crumbling, about to collapse, all that he'd worked so hard for this past year. He was so, so close to finalizing everything, to getting to America, to his own Promised Land and now this. The Jockey Club Security Department. Jesus, what had tipped them off? Why Zuiderzie? Oh, but that was the way they worked, wasn't it? They'd have the evidence for all of them but they'd just pursue one case, the only one they were surest of, one was all they needed.

He loosened his tie. Suddenly the image of the fat, sweating bookie, Compton Breslin, came to his mind, and he hated to think of himself in the same state as that slug used to get into when he'd made him climb the hill. What about Breslin? Had the security people approached him? Had he given them some sort of tip-off? Or had Monroe finally opened his mouth? There was no reason why he should. Come to think of it, there was no reason in Breslin's case either. He'd had a call from the bookie just the other day to see when the next one was planned.

Well there'd be no next one now. God, he'd promised there'd never be a next one if only he could get away with this. A conviction would see him turned back at the barrier at any US airport, deported as a criminal. Culling made himself stop and sit down in the wicker chair. He held his head in his hands, gripped his cheeks in clawed fingers that pressed white islands into his sweaty, flushed face. He had to stop panicking and make himself think rationally.

OK, worst-case scenario. They know I've put all the horses down. They know all have won at a big price the same day. They know the dope tests came up negative. The horses can't be tested again. But let's say Breslin has opened his fat mouth and said he's paid me money.

But why? Why kill the golden goose and all that? No reason unless Jockey Club Security have nailed him for something else and he's offered me as a sacrificial lamb.

I could leave now, head for the States, sell the house to get the last bit of money I need. But they have an extradition treaty; I'd just be brought back humiliated... Unless I could manufacture an early death. Something that wouldn't poison my system, jeopardize my chances of being revived...

Culling got up and hurried to his library.

After half an hour waiting for the vet to return his call, Frankie said to Stonebanks, 'How far is Culling's place?'

'A couple of minutes' drive.'

'Will you take me there now?'

'Think that's wise?'

'He sounded awful flustered by my call, promised to call back in a few minutes.' Frankie looked at his watch. 'That was half an hour ago.'

Stonebanks hauled himself out of his chair. 'OK, let's go.'

They drove past the vet's place first. Through the gates, Frankie could see a green estate car on the gravel in front of the bungalow.

'Is that his car?' he asked.

'Yes.'

'So he's still at home. Park up somewhere, Geoff, would you? And wait for me.'

'No problem.' Stonebanks pulled over.

'Thanks.'

The big man switched off the engine, unclipped his seatbelt and turned to smile at Frankie and give a small salute. 'Good luck!'

'If I'm not back in quarter of an hour, come in with all guns blazing.'

'Yes sir!'

As Frankie got out and walked the short stretch of pavement to the gates, he smiled and shook his head. He realized Stonebanks's tone of voice and knowing smiles meant that he thought Frankie was going off the deep end, that he was willing to let him make his own mistakes.

He rang the bell beside the brass plaque that said Peter H. Culling MRCVS. He heard Culling's footsteps coming down the hall and saw the rippled outline through the bubbled glass door. He was slightly smaller than Frankie but looked fit; mid-forties, maybe, thinning sandy hair and a quizzical look in his hazel eyes. He had a book in his right hand, hanging by his side, and he wore brown corduroy trousers and an open-necked white shirt. 'Can I help?' he asked.

Frankie smiled and held out his hand. 'Frankie Houlihan, Jockey Club Security Department. Thought I'd save you a call as you were so busy.' Frankie could almost see the vet's brain whirring as he tried to force a smile and decide what to say. He masked things by raising the hand with the book in it, then apologizing and turning back inside to put the book on the table in the hall. When he came back to shake Frankie's hand, he looked a little more composed but the wideness in his eyes was still there.

'How do you do?' he asked. 'I'm so sorry I didn't get back to you. Had a problem with one of the private, non-racing clients I handle. Got his horse away in Ireland with him hunting and wanted some advice on the phone, so I've had my head buried in some reference books since you called. I do apologize. Please come in.'

Frankie followed him down the hall. 'No problem, I thought something must have cropped up and I didn't want to go ringing you again if you were still on the mobile.'

They went into the conservatory. Frankie said, 'I don't mind waiting, you know. Please finish what you were doing and I'll sit here a while and enjoy the peace and quiet.'

'Not at all. Crisis over. I was just double-checking something. Please sit down. Can I get you a drink?'

'No, thanks. I really don't want to keep you. It's no big deal. I just wanted to try and find out a few things about a horse I believe you treated.' Frankie sat in a deep, wicker-framed, well-padded floral chair.

Culling stayed on his feet, pacing slowly. 'Ah yes, you mentioned on the phone, it was Zuiderzie, wasn't it? Poor bugger. I always feel worse for the lad, you know, when we lose a horse. They're closer to them than anyone.'

'Indeed. It's a hard business.' Frankie was learning quickly that with nervy people like Culling it often paid to ask no questions and just let them babble on trying to fill the silence. He sat smiling at the vet.

Culling kept pacing. He said, 'I remember Martin's box-driver calling me. The horse was in a really bad state when I got there, shaking and shivering. Shocking sight. I got him here as soon as I could and opened him up. Thought it was a twisted gut. If you catch them quick enough, sometimes you can save them but I'm afraid it wasn't to be. Died on the table, poor bugger.'

Frankie nodded, looked like he shared the vet's care and concern. 'He'd won that day, as I remember.'

Culling looked straight ahead now and quickened his pacing. When he spoke, Frankie noticed the pitch of his voice had increased slightly. 'Yes, that's right, he did. Even more unfortunate.'

'What do you mean?'

'I mean for the connections. Just back to winning form, you know, then for that to happen. Most unlucky.'

'Would you have taken a blood sample before operating?'

'No. No time for that, I'm afraid.'

Frankie said nothing. The silence was broken only by Culling's footsteps on the stone floor.

Frankie said, 'So what happened next?'

'What do you mean?' He stopped now and looked at Frankie.

Frankie shrugged slightly. 'Did you call the knacker's man in?'

'Yes, of course. Of course.'

'And who do you use?'

'Forgive me, but may I ask what exactly it is that you're trying to establish?'

'I'm afraid I can't go into too much detail just now. It's to do with something completely separate that the department is working on. We thought there just might be a link somewhere.' Frankie sat forward, elbows on knees and lowered his voice slightly. 'To be perfectly honest, it's not a racing problem as such, it's to do with the illegal exporting of horse meat to Europe. Our friends in Whitehall have asked us to help out. As if we didn't have enough to do! '

Culling seemed to relax. He returned Frankie's smile. Frankie said, 'So who's your knacker's man?'

Culling suddenly looked troubled again. He backed slowly toward the chair opposite Frankie's and sat down. It was his turn now to lean forward, elbows on knees, expression pained as he shook his head. 'Look, this is really embarrassing for me. I'm, eh, I'm in a bit of a spot.'

Frankie nodded encouragingly, still smiling. 'If I can help you out, I will.'

'Well, you see, I don't call the knacker's man direct, I use one of his employees who'll turn out any time, day or night and, well, to be honest, he pays me a bit better than his boss does.'

'So he's moonlighting?'

'I suppose he is. Ask no questions, hear no lies.' He opened his hands in explanation or apology, Frankie wasn't sure which.

'So can you give me a name?'

The vet massaged his freckled cheeks. Frankie said, 'I'll make sure you are kept out of it if anything comes of this.'

Culling, head still bowed, raised his eyes toward Frankie. 'Can you guarantee that?'

'Yes, I can.'

'His name is Gerry Monroe.'

34

It was almost midnight when Frankie left Canary Wharf and the office of the *Racing Post* newspaper. He drove north much faster than he'd normally have done, unable to keep the adrenaline coursing through his body away from his accelerator foot. He'd had a good day. A bloody good day, even if he said so himself. He'd learned a lot about his job and about people and how to handle them, and it excited him. He felt more powerful than he'd ever done as a priest. Much more.

Back then, people believed he could grant them eternity in heaven through absolving sins. That suddenly seemed like nothing compared to what he felt he could do now. He'd been dead right about Culling; spot on. He knew the man was involved in something. OK, the vet wouldn't have made the best poker player in the world, but Frankie had got him on the hook and played him like an expert. Back in the car with Stonebanks, a triumphant Frankie had drummed on the dashboard and said with delight, 'Know when I knew I had him? When he didn't ask why I had asked about taking a blood test before the operation! Why on earth would I have asked that? Why didn't he question it?'

And Stonebanks had agreed and congratulated him, and asked where they went next. Well here was where they went next, corroboration. He'd called Maggie Cassidy and she'd promised to wait up although Graham was still bed-bound.

It was two-thirty in the morning and pitch-black on the final run to the Cassidy place. Through the trees and gaps in the hedges, he saw, as he drove, the light coming from the kitchen windows and the sight warmed him. Turning into the drive he thought he caught Maggie in his headlights as she stood at the window, arms folded, watching, waiting. Excited as he was at the news he had to give her, he decided it was best, at this stage, not to mention that he thought the horses might still be alive. Monroe was almost certainly the kidnapper; he had picked up Zuiderzie, Zuiderzie looked very like Ulysses, but it wasn't certain yet that his theory was correct. And if Zuiderzie was a fake Ulysses then which horse had Monroe used to stand in for the corpse of Angel Gabriel?

He cut the engine in the hundred yards or so before the door and coasted up, the steering wheel suddenly heavy in his hands as the power steering was lost. He didn't want to wake Graham or young Billy. As he got out of the car, Maggie was already in the open doorway of the house. She smiled as he closed the car door softly and put his finger to his lips as he mock-tiptoed across the drive to the house. She laughed quietly. 'You look like a drunk trying to creep in and not wake his wife.'

'I feel drunk, with power!' he said and Maggie was surprised when he hugged her warmly. They went inside. Embers in the grate still gave off a good heat, and Maggie took his jacket and hung it up as he sat by the fire.

'Whiskey?' she asked.

Checking his watch, he said, 'Don't know whether to say too late or too early.'

'Must be neither, then, which makes it just the right time.' She poured him a large whiskey with ice in a heavy cut-crystal glass. She already had a drink sitting on the hearth, and she settled on the rug as Frankie had seen her do so many times before. She raised her glass. He moved out of the seat toward her and they touched glasses gently. 'Here's to getting your money back.'

She smiled. 'Come on, then, don't keep me in suspense!'

He drank, and then went to where his jacket hung and took an envelope from the inside pocket. He took out two pictures and showed her one. She made a face which said, 'Maybe, maybe not.' He handed her the other print, which was of a man in a mask with just his vivid blue eyes showing. 'That's him,' she said immediately.

'That's what I told Stonebanks. That's corroboration. That's Gerry Monroe. And this is now a legitimate job for our friends in the police! I'll call them first thing in the morning.'

She looked straight at him, smiling admiringly. 'You're brilliant Frankie, well done!'

'All in a day's work! '

'Oh, I can't wait to tell Graham.' She hurried along the hall toward the bedroom but was back within a minute.

Frankie said, 'That was quick.'

'He's sound. I'll leave it. I'm dying to wake him, but the medication makes him so groggy. It'll be such brilliant news to give him in the morning, at the start of a brand-new day! '

'Should make a different man of him!' Frankie said and gulped down the last of his drink. 'Although we still need to catch Monroe.'

'Surely that wouldn't be too difficult, even for the police. They know who he is now, for God's sake. It should just be a matter of picking him up.'

'I hope so. Depends where he is.'

She moved to pick up his glass. 'One more?'

'Sure! Sure, if you're having one?'

'Why not? We're celebrating aren't we?'

'We are, we are.'

An hour later Frankie was on his fourth large whiskey. Maggie had already had two drinks before he arrived. She was on her sixth. Frankie too was on the rug now, legs outstretched, warming in front of the fresh logs, which crackled quietly. They'd talked about all that had happened since they'd first spoken on the phone, agreed they now felt like they'd known each other for years. They discussed plans for getting Gabby back and maybe the money, although Maggie said if this whole thing had taught her anything it was the value of love and family and normality, lack of upset, the beauty of a quiet life. xxx

They'd been silent for a while, sitting companionably, stockinged feet almost touching, staring into the fire, listening to the tick of the clock and the occasional hollow howl of the wind in the chimney. Maggie said, 'Tell me about your troubles.'

Slowly he turned his head away from the fire, smiling as he looked at her.

'You've helped so much with ours, with mine. I know you have some of your own.'

'Ahh, perceptive, you women!' He lowered his eyes but raised his eyebrows.

'Tell me, Frankie.'

He stared at the floor then into the fire again and seemed to gaze way beyond it. The yellow embers reflected in his eyes and Maggie couldn't be sure if tears were there. He said, 'I'll tell you about a girl called Kathy, who was all the stuff in the love poems and all the romantic books and movies and every pop-song lyric and, and… sentiment that was ever written all rolled into one… to me, she was. She was as much a part of me as the leg you see before you on the floor. When we were apart, her face was never out of my mind for a second. Not just her face but her person, her being. 'Twas with me in my mind as solid as though she herself was in my mind. She wasn't just a part of me, Kathy; she was a part that made me so much better than I was, so much more than I was, for she added all the things that I didn't have. She was beautiful, intelligent and brave, very brave… and honest and fair. She loved adventure and she loved coming home and she loved the weather and being outdoors, in the woods, in the rain, on horseback, on foot, with me, holding hands, feeding her life into me as surely as if she were giving me a transfusion. And I know that there are many who'll say this but I know without even having to think about it or analyse it or anything deep, any stuff like that, that there never was a couple anywhere that loved each other more than we did. There was no possibility that there could be. You'd be as well saying there were degrees of the speed of light as saying any couple loved like we did…' He drank.

'… anyway, couple's a poor expression for us, for the way we were. We were one, one person. Neither of us realized until we met that we'd each been only half a person. Then we clamped together… couldn't even see the join.' He smiled sadly.

Maggie watched him. 'How did she die?'

'She was thrown from her horse at Stratford after she won a race… She…' Frankie couldn't bring himself to say the words "killed outright". 'She never regained consciousness.'

Shocked, Maggie put her drink down and got to her knees, resting her bottom on her heels.

'My God, was that your wife? Frankie, that was only a few weeks ago! '

'October twelfth. Eleven weeks and six days ago.'

Tears came to her eyes as she watched him. The ironic smile, supported by alcohol, that had shown on his face from time to time had slipped slowly like a tired mask to leave him staring blankly into the fire, eyes cold and forlorn now. Maggie moved slowly toward him. She took his hand in both of hers. 'Frankie, I am so, so sorry. Here we are worrying about a horse and you've lost your wife. She was the one you left the priesthood for?'

He nodded but didn't look at her, eyes still blank. She said, 'If I could take her place and send her back to you, I would.'

He turned slowly toward her and looked into her eyes. 'Would you?'

His eyes slowly filled and the tears spilled over. She leant forward and put her left hand behind his neck, pulling his head down to cradle it on her bosom.

35

Hewitt left the big house once a week and travelled to Swindon to buy groceries. He had never gone into Lambourn since he'd arrived in the area, agreeing with Kelly Corell that it was best to keep away from the village, to protect his anonymity. He avoided Newbury for the same reason. Swindon was much less focused on racing, and he could shop there without too much fear of someone saying, 'Hey, aren't you the guy that moved into Kennedy's old place?'

Wheeling his supermarket trolley past the newsstand, Hewitt stopped dead. The face of Gerry Monroe stared at him from the front page of the *Racing Post*. The headline was EX-JOCKEY WANTED FOR KIDNAPPING: £50,000 REWARD. Hewitt bought a copy and pushed it into one of the shopping bags. He was nervous about being seen reading it. He now knew Monroe hadn't been kidding, and the two horses he'd been looking after for the slaughter man were probably the exact ones he'd said they were when he'd called the other day, Ulysses and Angel Gabriel.

Hewitt found himself by his car without realizing he'd walked there. He got in and opened the newspaper. The owners of Angel Gabriel were offering the reward for the capture of the kidnapper and the return of the stolen ransom money.

Hewitt's mind spun. He was in deep now. He was harbouring two kidnapped horses, two very popular horses. And he was holding ten thousand pounds in cash for Monroe in payment, waiting for the slaughter man to come and collect it. The only people likely to be coming now where the police. His hands shook as he loaded the shopping bags.

Back in the house, he called Corell and told him.

'And you still have the ten grand Pat Pusey brought you?'

'It's still here. It's in a cupboard in the lab. I don't want to be found with it, Mister Corell. And the horses, what will I do about them?'

'Don't be worryin', now, everythin'll be fine. Wasn't that exactly what we wanted, a couple of good horses to help you on a bit?'

'Mister Corell, I thought everything was going to be above board when I took this on. I was never willing to take any risks.'

'Sshhh now, will ye? There's no risk here. I'll sort any problems out. That's my side of the deal. Haven't I always got you just what you wanted when you wanted it?'

'Well, you have and I'm grateful, but I just feel this is getting out of control and I hate being involved in something that's out of control, I really do, Mister Corell. I can't stress that enough to you!'

'David, listen to me… you're not involved in anything, d'ye hear me? You're a good straight fella doin' a good straight job. Now if you have no more need for those horses, tell Monroe to get them to hell out of the place.'

'I don't know when he's coming back! I can't tell him anything!
'

Corell thought the scientist close to breaking point. He said quietly, 'Would you give me Mister Monroe's number and I'll contact him and ask him to get the horses out of there?'

'Hold on. Hold on a minute. I'll get it.'

While he was waiting for Hewitt to come back, Corell's desktop phone rang. He told the caller to hold. He took Monroe's number and promised Hewitt he'd call back soon. Pat Pusey was on the other phone sounding pleased with himself. He told Corell, 'Yer man's in jail in Limerick.'

'Who?'

'Brendan Gleeson.'

'Sure, that's sharp work by the guards in catching him for stealing my ten grand, and me not even reported it yet.'

Pusey laughed dutifully then said, 'I wish it was for that, boss, but it was drunk and disorderly. Want me to go and get him?'

'Get it done in twenty-four hours. I've got another job for you after that.'

Frankie and Stonebanks had spent forty-eight hours in Lambourn trying to trace Monroe. The man had few friends but Frankie had spoken to his former girlfriend who claimed she hadn't seen him for over a year. Stonebanks had spoken to his employer, the owner of the abattoir, who said it didn't surprise him to find that Monroe was a criminal, that he'd always seemed shifty, a bit of a loner who'd been resentful of most things, especially his fellow-workers. He also asked Stonebanks to add his missing horsebox to the list of lost property. Stonebanks took the registration.

The January night was cold, and Frankie and Stonebanks stood by the gas fire in Stonebanks's house drinking tea and eating lemon sponge cake. Stonebanks's police contact called. Frankie watched him smile for the first time in days as he made positive noises and jotted down notes. He hung up and turned to Frankie, still smiling. 'The horsebox left Holyhead on the Stena Line ferry for Dun Laoghaire on January fourth. It hasn't come back.'

Frankie smiled now. 'He's taken them to Ireland.'

'That's a fair conclusion, I think, Mister Houlihan.'

36

Sean and Jane hadn't missed a single evening doing the final rounds at Uncle Fergus's place. They'd help feed the horses and check them over, then bid them goodnight with a final pat on the shoulder or stroke of the nose. Afterwards they'd usually go back inside and tell Poppy how all the horses were and watch TV with her for a while or sit talking, sometimes long into the night. But Jane had sensed something different today with Sean, and she wasn't surprised when he asked her to come into the barn after evening stables.

She followed him as he climbed high on the hay up to the chair they'd made, just room enough between the sweet-smelling bales for them to sit comfortably side by side. This was the first time they'd been here after dark and although there was sufficient light from the dusty neon strips in the centre of the barn, it was colder than ever, and Jane shivered and moved closer to Sean as they settled down. He wouldn't look at her.

'What's wrong? She asked.

Sean stared at his feet. 'I don't know how to tell you…'

Jane swallowed a lump but tried to make a joke. 'You're not pregnant, are you?'

He barely smiled. She knew it must be bad. 'You're leaving,' she said quietly.

He nodded.

Now she stared at her feet, crossed her ankles and swung them slightly, linked her hands in her lap for a few seconds then crossed her arms and put her chin on her chest. The silence lasted a minute or more then Sean said, 'I'll come back.'

'You'll never come back if you leave. It'll never be the same.' There was anger in her voice. 'Stay!' It was a command.

He shook his head slowly. 'It's just for a few days. I'll be back.'

She jumped off the hay bale and stood, arms crossed defiantly. 'Right, I'm coming with you!'

'Yer kidding!'

'I'm not.'

'Uncle Fergus won't let you. Shit, it's worse than Chicago where I live! They have girls like you for breakfast. No - nobody eats breakfast where I come from. They'd have you for a late snack.'

'Oh, is that so, Sean Gleeson? Is that so? We'll see!'

Rather than meet, as usual, at Stonebanks's house, Frankie had asked that Stonebanks meet him in the George pub in Lambourn, the one most popular with the racing fraternity. Stonebanks had taken a bit of persuading that it would be a good idea for them to be seen to be concentrating on this case in public, but Frankie had made all the right decisions so far. Frankie was convinced that the reward would play a big part in someone coming forward with information, and he wanted to have the visual 'prompt' of seeing him and Stonebanks around as much as possible.

They sat drinking beer. It had been two days since they'd last spoken face to face. Stonebanks had been to Ireland with a CID officer to seek the help of the Irish police in tracing the horsebox. Frankie had been back to visit the vet, Peter Culling, to try and find out how much he knew about the private life of Gerry Monroe.

'How was good old Dublin?' Frankie asked.

'I didn't see that much of it - busy, I'd say. Your old home town, wasn't it?'

'Twas. Many years ago.'

'Do you miss it?'

'Sometimes I do. But it's changed now. Everywhere changes and it's kind of upsettin' when you've got such good memories of some of the places you knew as a kid, if you know what I mean.' Stonebanks smiled. 'There are still plenty of criminals there according to your Garda man.'

'No doubt. No doubt,' Frankie said, smiling too.

Stonebanks explained that the Garda had been very helpful and promised to do what they could, although they'd warned that

Monroe might have disappeared 'into the west' where there were still some very remote places. Frankie said, 'Let's give them a chance for a week or so then maybe we'll go over ourselves and have a look around.'

Stonebanks nodded slightly, and half-raised his eyebrows in a way Frankie had come to know as being non-committal. Stonebanks was a tough man to move from his home comforts for too long. He drank some beer and asked Frankie how he got on with Culling.

Frankie grinned. 'He's a strange character and I'd bet he knows a lot more than he's telling. I deliberately mentioned, again, the fact that Zuiderzie had won unexpectedly the day he died and yer man seemed to get extra nervous. He was working at Warwick that day which is where Zuiderzie won. I think there might be some connection between him and the horse winning.'

'Like what?'

Although he felt he was acting in some corny movie, Frankie had a good look around him to see if anyone might be able to hear before saying, 'Talk me through the dope testing procedure again.'

'You think he might have doped the horse? The sample was clean. You know that.'

'Take me through it anyway.'

Stonebanks put down his glass and started talking, using his hands a lot as Frankie had learned he was sometimes inclined to do. 'After every race, the stewards will nominate horses to be routinely dope-tested; the winner is almost always one of them. They're taken to a special box where a vet will take a sample of urine, split it into two smaller samples and label each. One is sent to the lab at Newmarket for analysis, the other is offered to the trainer to keep for reference, just in case.'

'In case a test proves positive and he wants to have it double checked?'

'That's right, but nobody takes that sample. They know that whatever comes back from the lab will be spot-on, and as no trainer in his right mind would dope his horse anyway, it's looked on as a pointless exercise.'

'Culling was the senior vet there that day,' Frankie said. 'Would it have been possible for him to insist on taking the urine sample from Zuiderzie himself?'

'Possible but highly improbable. It's the job generally given to the most junior vet, as I'm sure you can imagine. In fact even he, although he shouldn't, sometimes gets the stable manager to do it for him.'

'The stable manager?' Frankie sounded incredulous.

'Come on, Frankie, do you know how long you can wait around after a race for a horse to start pissing? Do you think these guys are going to be doing this six, eight, ten times a day?'

'Fair enough,' Frankie said. 'But Culling would have access to the dope box at any time?'

'That's right.'

'So he would have had access to the samples?'

'Yes.'

'So he could have switched the one for Zuiderzie?'

'Yes, I suppose he could have.'

Frankie sat smiling, trying not to look too triumphant. He picked up his glass and drank, still looking at Stonebanks over the rim.

'Come on, Frankie! Speculation, pure and simple! What motive could he have had?'

'Making money, by any chance?'

'Betting?'

'How else?'

'It would be much, much easier to dope the favourite to lose than an outsider to win.'

'Granted, but if you've got the knowledge and the opportunity and a good chance of getting away with it, how much better is it to dope an outsider to win? You're nobbling the favourite just as effectively and you can bet the winner too at a big price.'

Stonebanks shook his head slowly. Frankie sat forward across the low table, elbows on knees, hands clasped gently, head tilted, almost priestly again. 'Geoff, I was there that day. The horse looked very geed-up in the paddock, which was unlike him, he led from start to finish and was never in danger; his usual style was to be held up. He got back to the yard in a muck-sweat the likes of which the trainer had never seen before. Culling's called out and two hours later the horse is dead on the operating table, then on its way to the dog meat factory in Monroe's knacker's van. No chance of any further dope tests then, is there? The evidence has been destroyed. And if it has gone for dog meat there's going to be a few surprised dog walkers out there when their little Scottie whizzes past a couple of greyhounds after eating his dinner!'

Stonebanks smiled, shaking his head again. 'You and your blarney make a good-sounding case of it, Frankie, but in the end it really is nothing but speculation. You've had a couple of good results and you think you can suss everything now. No offence!' Stonebanks held out his hand, open, at arm's length in conciliatory gesture. 'I'm not having a go, Frankie, it's just that the confidence you get from being right once or twice can make you think you've got the whole world worked out. Believe me, I've done it.'

Frankie wasn't upset. 'OK, Geoff, fair comment but just keep an open mind yourself.'

Stonebanks held up his glass in a toast, smiling. 'Always do, Frankie boy. Always do!'

As Frankie pulled up outside Winterfold Cottage next morning his mobile rang; the screen told him it was Bobby Cranfield. 'Bobby, how are you?'

'I'm in great form, Frankie. Good to hear you sounding so well.'

'And you.'

'I just wanted to say how delighted I am personally at the progress you're making in this kidnapping case. You've been a bloody revelation! '

'Team effort, Bobby, team effort.'

'Ah, modesty forbids, as ever!'

They talked for a while about the case, then Bobbie invited Frankie to his box at Ascot the following Saturday. 'You must join me in the box, you cried off last time when that horse of mine got stuffed, remember Arctic Actor?'

'I do remember. You fancied him strongly that day.'

'Thought he couldn't get beat - but never mind, he runs again on Saturday and we're even more confident. You must come along, Frankie, have a day off, you bloody-well deserve one!'

'Bobby, it's very kind of you to ask. Can you just let me see how this week pans out? Can I give you a call maybe on Wednesday?'

'Sure, of course you can. You know where I am.'

'Good... Good.' Something was niggling at Frankie's mind, causing him to lose concentration.

'Fine then,' Cranfield said, 'I'll let you get on.'

'Yes... Bobby... what was the name of the horse that won the race yours got beat in, can you remember?'

He laughed. 'It's burned in my brain, old boy! Cost me a fortune that day. He was called Colonialize.'

'That's right, I remember now. Do you still think he was doped to win that race?'

'Why do you ask?'

'Something I'm working on. Could turn out to be nothing, but you just reminded me of that day you called me.'

Cranfield hesitated. 'I know it might have seemed a bit over the top at the time, Frankie, a bit sour grapes maybe, but I did do a lot of thinking before making that call. I know the dope test turned out negative and that sort of finished it in my mind, but if you're asking if it was a calm assessment at the time then the answer is yes.'

'OK. Thanks.'

'Can you say any more at the moment?'

'Not really. I'll call you when I can.'

'Well tell me about it when I see you on Saturday.'

'I'll do my best to make it, Bobby, thanks.'

'See you then.'

'Bye.'

Frankie sat staring through the windscreen. Colonialize had won that race in the exactly the same manner Zuiderzie had won his, bolting off from the start, leading all the way, and coming home unchallenged at a big price to upset a hot favourite. Frankie remembered walking through the ring that day and marvelling at the fat bookie Compton Breslin laying over the odds on Arctic Actor, taking fistfuls of money without flinching or shortening the price. Excitement grew in Frankie as he called Stonebanks's number.

'Geoff, get hold of one of your books and tell me who trains Colonialize.'

'What the hell are you up to now, Frankie?'

'Just tell me, Geoff!'

'I don't need a book. Tony Moffat trains him not three hundred yards away from where I'm standing.'

'Have you got Tony's number?'

'Hold on.'

Stonebanks came back with the number.

'Thanks. Call you back in a minute.'

Moffat's wife answered and it took a couple of minutes before the trainer came to the phone. Frankie introduced himself. Moffat said he'd heard about him. Frankie said, 'Sorry to be making a business call on a Sunday, but I wanted to ask you about that horse that won at Ascot for you, Colonialize. Have you anything else planned for him soon?'

'I'm afraid not, Mister Houlihan. The horse died on the operating table the night he won at Ascot.' The elation made it difficult for Frankie to find a tone of commiseration. 'Oh, I'm really sorry, what happened?'

'Horse arrived home shaking like he was sitting on a pneumatic drill, and sweating so bad there was a pool of water under him. I called the vet out right away and he did his best. Some form of aggravated colic apparently.'

'That's a real shame, I'm sorry. Who did the operation to try and save him?'

'Peter Culling.'

'Oh yes, I know him. Well I'm sorry, real bad luck.'

'Was it something in particular about the horse, Mister Houlihan?'

'No, not really. One of the big wigs has some hare-brained notion about establishing patterns for horses who win at grade one courses, load of nonsense. You know what they're like.'

'I do, er, yes, I know what you mean.'

'Anyway, I hope you have better luck for the rest of the season.'

'Me too. Thanks.'

When Frankie rang him back, Stonebanks wasn't that impressed. 'Frankie, who else would the guy call but his vet? The fact that it happens to be Culling could be purely coincidental.'

'How coincidental, Geoff, come on! The guy's a one-man practice; he works for the Jockey Club on course a hell of a lot. How many trainers can he realistically have on his books? A handful at most and now two of those, that we know of, maybe even more, have lost horses where he's been officiating at the course and also carried out the operations. Isn't there some rule that they must register dead horses?'

'They only need to let Weatherbys know for administration purposes so the horses can be scratched from future engagements.'

'Where can I get a list of those scratchings?'

'Call Charlie Cooke at Weatherbys tomorrow, he'll sort you out with those.'

'Only one problem; as I recall, Colonialize was too thin to be passed off as Angel Gabriel. Still, it doesn't blow any holes in my theory. Monroe would have lots of these horses through his hands, not just the ones he got from Culling.'

'True, but you're going to need some sort of solid evidence apart from the resemblance between Zuiderzie and Ulysses.'

'I know, I know, I'm working on it. Once I get this list of scratchings and make a few more calls, I'll go and see Culling again. Hey, you know the dope test sample from Zuiderzie; would that carry any sort of chemical ID for the horse himself?'

'Like a blood sample does? I don't know. It must have some sort of DNA imprint, I suppose. Even if it did, you'd need something to compare it with either from Ulysses or Zuiderzie and neither's around.'

'I was thinking that we might ask the forensic boys at Newmarket to go back to where we found the horse's body. Remember we had to drag him up the bank of that stream? There's bound to be pieces of loose flesh still around that these guys could find to analyse.'

'Could be. Could be, Frankie. It's been a few weeks but with the type of equipment they have, they may well be able to get something.

'Will you ask them?'

'Sure, but you're still going to need something else if the urine sample's no good. That sample might have been flushed away by now.'

'Geoff, will you stop saying you all the time? It's us, remember. We're in a team here. I'm not trying to win any prizes on my own.'

The pause was at Stonebanks's end this time. 'You're right. Or should that be we're right? I'll get on with my end of things, O Master.'

Frankie chuckled. 'Do that. I'll speak to you soon.'

Uncle Fergus dropped Jane and Sean off in Dublin at ten in the morning, promising to return and pick them up at five that afternoon. Jane had persuaded him to let them have the day out together so Sean could show her the sights. She'd badgered Sean into agreeing to go back with her after they'd spent the day trying to find news of his father. It was cold and clear, and as they made their way through the streets, Jane wished that it was sight-seeing they had come for. She wanted to spend time with Sean away from the farm. Being in the city together made her feel like they were a proper couple in a proper relationship.

She knew Sean hadn't been himself since last night. He was edgy and had gone quiet. Normally she couldn't shut him up. As they crossed the Liffey on O'Connell Bridge, she said, 'How far is it, Sean?'

'Not far.'

'How far's not far?'

'Fifteen minutes maybe.'

She took his hand and stretched her legs a bit to match his pace. She noticed a wariness in Sean that hadn't been there since the night they'd met. He was constantly looking around, scanning the faces of the people, especially those coming toward them. 'What's wrong?' she asked.

'I'm lookin' out for Pat Pusey and I don't want to see him.'

'The man at Dun Laoghaire?'

'The same.' Suddenly he turned left. 'Come on!' He pulled her along.

'What's up? Did you see him?'

'No. But there's more chance of it if we go all the way up O'Connell Street. We'll go the back way.' They turned left into Gardiner Street, which was busy but didn't seem to Jane as prosperous as O'Connell Street. She was nervous. After the tales of home Sean had told her, she expected the streets to be derelict with hollow-eyed men peering at them from doorways. She decided he must have exaggerated everything. They were so close to the centre of the city.

Sean hurried her across the road to Railway Street. The further along that street they went, the fewer people they saw. Graffiti marked the walls and pavement. Halfway along, Sean nodded toward a block of flats on the left, St Mary's Mansions. 'That's where Corell left his girlfriend after he cut her up.' Jane gripped his hand more tightly.

The flats on the right looked grim. Some houses were boarded up. Scruffy, snotty-nosed, coatless children played in the cold gutters. The day itself seemed to Jane to lose its sharpness, its brightness. She thought of how lucky she was. She was missing her family, even Billy. She'd rung home most days, lifting the phone each time with hope, desperate for good news about Angel Gabriel.

She knew that Sean, too, travelled in hope. She wished she hadn't said those nasty things about his father. Nobody could help what their parents were, and for all he'd been bad to Sean and his mother, Jane could understand how Sean still felt something for him and worried about him. She looked across at him and saw how tense he looked. He let go her hand, apparently to button his jacket, but Jane noted that he conveniently forgot to take it again.

At the next junction, they stopped. Sean pointed at the flats across the road in Killarney Street. 'Joseph's Mansions,' he said. She stared. It looked to her like some sort of prison building; metal sheets covered all the windows, graffiti was everywhere. The railings surrounding the block were rusted and dirty, and the strip of grass behind them was overgrown. In the bare branches of a tree was the twisted frame of an old bicycle.

Sean looked quickly around him then said, 'Come on!' He ran across the road. Jane followed. They hurried toward the arched entrance and went in, but Sean put a hand out to stop her before they left the cover of the arch and entered the quadrangle. He peeked out to the left; he didn't know who might be at the flat. It would be dead unlucky to find Pat Pusey or another one of Corell's men there at this time of day, but it was best not to just run right in.

The place was silent. He stepped cautiously into the quadrangle. Jane followed. She stood and looked around, feeling like she was in a deserted prison yard or one of those terrible concentration camps when the war had ended. Almost every door and window was blocked with thick metal sheeting. A huge puddle of dirty brown water held the wreck of a child's tricycle, a burst football and a flotilla of papers and polystyrene packaging. The only sign of human life was a string of washing running diagonally between the corners of the flats across to her. To her right, a few pigeons paced the dirty tarmac. Four huge rusty bins like vats stood in a row below the overhanging first-floor balcony. Signs fixed to the walls by Dublin Corporation disclaimed all responsibility for injury to any person venturing further.

Sean said, 'I think we're OK. Come on.' They moved toward a doorway in the centre of the row to their left and started up the stairs, the urine stench as offensive as Sean remembered it. Jane said, 'Ugh, that's horrible.' Turning the corner to go to his door, Sean met Kevin, the only other boy still living there.

'Shoggy! Where've you been?' Kevin said.

'On my holidays in Switzerland.'

'Have ye just come back 'cos yer da's dead or are ye stayin'?'

What was left of Brendan Gleeson lay on a slab in the morgue. His body, stretched out, took up just a few inches of vertical space. The bones and vital organs had been almost pulped. After throwing him screaming off the roof of a twenty-storey block of flats, Corell's men had gone back down for the body and had done the same thing twice more. The mashed corpse had lain there in full view for hours - the people knew better than to report anything. The man who stole from Kelly Corell had to be left on display until the police happened by.

37

Frankie and Stonebanks stood together in Stonebanks's study. They watched in silence as the fax machine slowly rolled out the list from Weatherbys of all horses that had been scratched from races in the past six months because they were dead. The machine beeped and stopped; Frankie carefully tore the sheet of paper and brought it to the table. There were fifty-seven horses on it. Frankie could have had the list an hour previously, but he'd asked Charlie at Weatherbys to place a tick beside each horse that died after a victory last time out. Apart from the two they knew of, there were four more. The name of one of them stopped Frankie's breathing. He froze completely, the paper in front of him at arm's length. Stonebanks watched him then reached for the list, taking it from Frankie's fingers. He looked at the six ticked horses, then, puzzled, at Frankie. 'What's wrong?'

Frankie stared at him. Stonebanks said, 'Jesus, you look like somebody just hit you with a hammer. What's up?'

'He killed Kathy,' Frankie said. 'Sauceboat. That was the horse she rode.' Shock had anaesthetized him. He spoke in monotone. Stonebanks looked again at the list. He reached for his formbook, skipping quickly through the pages to check the other horses that had been ticked. Each had won at a big price after leading all the way, the same as Zuiderzie and Colonialize had done, and like those two, were trained in Lambourn. Stonebanks looked across at Frankie. 'I know the trainers and I know the vet…'

Frankie waited.

Stonebanks said, 'Culling.'

Frankie linked his fingers, elbows askew on the table, and looked down. At least there was some reason to it now. His mother had been wrong, there'd been no punishment from God for what he'd done; no deliberate punishment at least, no grabbing back of a life in return for his desertion. Somebody had killed her. A man. Not God. Not his mother. Not Frankie. An evil, greedy man had killed his wife.

Frankie stood up. 'Let's go and see Culling now.' He spoke evenly although some emotion was back in his voice.

Stonebanks watched him. 'Not a good time, Frankie. We need to look at all the angles.'

Frankie pulled his jacket on. 'Won't take us that long to get there.'

'Frankie, sit down and think for a minute. Supposing Culling did operate on these two, supposing it was on the day they won, supposing Monroe picked up both corpses, it doesn't incriminate Culling. He could claim it was all simply coincidence.'

'Geoff, come on! This fella killed my wife and you're telling me to sit down and think! Get real! What is there to think about?' Frankie leant forward holding out his open hand, as though trying to make Stonebanks understand how simple this was.

'Frankie, whoah, slow down! You've just had a shock that would stop a bloody train and you want to go haring off. What kind of state is your mind in? Try and take a step back for a minute and look at the situation, will you? I'm sorry for you, I really am, but I can't just let you go after Culling right now. You've got a pretty personal interest now for a start, don't you think? Uh?'

Frankie stared at him silently.

Stonebanks said, 'Do you seriously think you're fit to do your job objectively right now? Because that's what you need to do. We've probably got enough to get the police in. Why don't we do that?'

'A minute ago you were saying it could all be coincidence, Geoff - make up your mind.'

Stonebanks looked flustered at that. 'If it is, let the police dig deeper.'

'If it is, or appears to be, the police won't bother digging deeper or they'll botch it the way they did with the kidnap! I'm not saying I, Geoff, not I, I, I! Don't you think I know inside myself how I'm reacting to this? I know when I'm calm and I know when I'm able to do my job. I'm saying us, let's you and me go to Culling's place. The betting is that these horses were doped to win, the dope sample switched by Culling on course, then the horses killed by him so they couldn't be tested again if anyone became suspicious in the few days after each race. For goodness sake, I told you that Bobby Cranfield called me the day after Colonialize beat his horse at Ascot, the day after, before all these suspicions blew up! He said then that he thought the winner had been doped! '

Stonebanks looked up at him. 'Frankie, I'm not saying you're wrong. Not in the least. I'm saying we can't prove it. It's a sound theory but we simply can't back it up.'

'Maybe Culling will confess!'

'Why should he? Why on earth should he? He's been a respected Jockey Club vet for years. His character is totally unblemished. There'll be bloody ructions if we go steaming in like the Sweeney trying to get a confession out of him. Can you imagine what they'd be saying about us? About the Jockey Club Security Department? About you, on your first assignment?'

The passion and impatience slowly drained from Frankie's face as he realized the logic of what Stonebanks was saying. He sat down again, slowly shaking his head. Looking at Stonebanks, he said quietly, 'He could be involved in the kidnappings too, you know. There's no telling how close his relationship with Monroe is.'

'Can't have been that close or he wouldn't have named him so quickly to you, would he?'

Frankie shrugged. 'Maybe.'

Stonebanks sighed. 'You could easily be right about Culling, Frankie, but there's nothing to really suggest he'd tied in with the kidnappings. At best we've got two different cases here and we need to make up our minds which one we're going to try and crack first.'

Frankie nodded.

'Now is it going to be Monroe or Culling? If we go for Culling with absolutely no solid evidence, we could lose him completely. He could up stakes and disappear. If we can get Monroe and tell him Culling dropped him in it originally, there's every chance Monroe will tell you all you want to know about Culling. At least then you have some evidence.'

Frankie knew he was right. He couldn't risk confronting Culling and losing him, couldn't have lived with that afterwards. 'You're right Geoff, I'm sorry.'

'Nothing to be sorry about, Frankie, nothing whatsoever. If it's Culling, we'll get him. I promise you.' He leant across the table and clasped Frankie's arm. Frankie smiled wearily.

Stonebanks said, 'Right, let's get to work. Let's try and nail this horse-switching theory of yours. I'll call the lab about the urine sample and speak to the forensic boys about a visit to the stream where we found the corpse.'

Frankie watched him, all business-like and confident, pick up the phone.

38

At the cemetery, Jane walked with Sean ahead of his mother and Aunt Phoebe, who had lent her sister the money to pay for this funeral. There was no one else except the priest. The undertaker's men, helped by the gravediggers, carried the coffin with little effort. Only Aunt Phoebe had seen what was left of Brendan Gleeson; she had formally identified the body to save Sean further distress. The Garda had found no evidence of crime. They had heard what had happened, but they knew there was no chance of convicting Corell. The officer in charge had put it down to suicide. Sean had been too shocked by the death and too afraid of the police to argue that it was murder. Jane had complained strongly on his behalf, marching into the police station and demanding to see the superintendent, but it had done no good. A cold-eyed man in plain clothes saw her and told her they had plenty to do without chasing their tails for years on this, and anyway, nobody would be rushing to commemorate the life of Mr Brendan Gleeson.

Except for Brendan's son, he was right. Nobody but Sean mourned the death. As Bridget Gleeson watched the coffin being lowered, she felt only the relief that she was finally free, that she didn't need to leave Ireland again if she didn't want to, that she could have her son back. The trouble was that Bridget wasn't sure now that she wanted him back. She'd had three relationships while she'd been away. All but the first man had treated her well. She was enjoying the freedom, having a good time. Watching Jane put her arm around Sean at the graveside, she thought that in little Miss

Pretty Face, he had quite enough. And he'd lived without his mother all this time. He had already mentioned going back to England with Jane for a while. Well, that would suit Bridget Gleeson just fine.

The priest finished as the rain started, heavy drops falling in the dark spots on the mound of earth by the grave. Aunt Phoebe stepped forward and picked up a handful of earth and threw it on the top of the coffin. Bridget did the same then bent and picked up some more. She turned and offered it to Sean. He looked up at her and shook his head. 'I'll not help bury me da,' he said with determination as the tears squeezed through again, stinging his eyes and the flesh just below, which was raw from rubbing. Jane squeezed his hand tighter, then put her other arm around his shoulder and led him away toward the car as the dark clouds finally burst and the freezing rain cascaded down.

Two researchers from the horseracing forensic laboratory in Newmarket found shreds of skin and hair at the site where the horse said to be Ulysses had been dumped. But no comparable samples were available from any lab or from his ex-trainer, who had, as part of his training regime, had his horses blood-tested regularly but retained none of the samples. The same applied to Zuiderzie, whose urine sample had also been disposed of by the lab after proving negative for dope.

Frankie needed a break. For all Stonebanks had said that the potential doping of these horses and the kidnappings were two separate cases, proof that Ulysses' carcass had actually been that of Zuiderzie would at least have told him that Ulysses and Angel Gabriel were probably still alive or, at least, had not been killed by Monroe at the time he claimed. As far as Ulysses was concerned, although he hoped for the horse's sake that it hadn't been slaughtered, making his arrogant, spiteful owner feel better didn't matter to him. But it would mean an awful lot to Frankie to be able to return Gabby to the Cassidys - which reminded him, again, he really should call Maggie.

He'd been avoiding it since that night when he'd told her all about Kathy, that drunken night when he'd been so hyped up with the good news about Monroe that he'd let himself go too far. He had never drunk that much before in his life, never talked like that to anyone about Kathy. He blushed as he recalled it. He had always wanted to tell Maggie about Kathy, but not in that way. It made him feel somehow that he'd given away some of their secrets. And when Maggie had said she wished she could take Kathy's place, bring her back to him, well, he thought that was so like Kathy herself to have offered that. Kathy would have done the same.

Kathy. Kathy. Kathy. What a burden had been lifted since finding out about Sauceboat. It was a feeling he couldn't understand; if he was right about the horse having been doped by Culling, surely it was a terrible thing? It might not have been murder but it was manslaughter. An awful crime. And yet, his heart was lighter. A large part of the guilt he'd felt at her death had gone. There was an earthly reason for that death. And now, probably above all this, he had something to hang it all on, someone to blame, a way of finalizing this wretchedness he had thought was going to be with him all his days.

Frankie wanted to spend some more time sitting in the George in Lambourn, jogging memories, reminding people that there was a fifty-thousand-pound reward waiting for the person who nailed Gerry Monroe. He was due to meet Stonebanks in the pub and, as he pulled up in the car park, Maggie Cassidy called him. He saw her name on-screen and immediately felt guilty for not ringing her.

She seemed nervous when she heard his voice, almost upset. She said, 'Frankie, I'm really sorry to bother you.'

'Don't be daft; it's me who should be sorry. I've been meaning to call.'

'No, no, you've got a million things to do. Look, it's just that Jane's coming home tomorrow. I want to try and plan how best to tell her about Gabby, and I just wondered if there was any news about him.'

Frankie closed his eyes and reproached himself. 'Maggie, I'm sorry, I've just been trying to sort things out with Joe Ansell. Joe thinks he might need another week or so.'

There was a silence for a few seconds then she said, 'Will he, you know, keep for that long?'

'Yes, Joe's confident he will be OK. You'll have him home in a week. That gives you a bit of leeway to let Jane settle back in. You can delay the news for another week if you want to.' Frankie wanted so much to tell her what had happened, the temptation was almost irresistible.

'I could do with a week's grace,' Maggie said. 'She's upset enough. Her boyfriend's father was killed in an accident. Sean's coming back with her.'

'Oh that's terrible, Maggie, I'm sorry to hear that. You must be at the end of your tether. Is Graham any better?'

She hesitated. 'I'm afraid not. He's still in bed, still very, very down.'

Frankie drew a long breath and sighed. What to do? He believed completely in his theory that Ulysses and Gabby had not been killed by Monroe and he knew that telling Maggie about it so she could tell Graham would give him so much hope... but if he turned out to be wrong and Graham was plunged back again into the thoughts of the savaging his horse had undergone, it might well be worse in the long run.

She said, 'Are you OK?'

He knew she meant was he alright after all the emotions of the other night, but he let it pass. 'I'm fine, Maggie. I'm fine. I just wish everything would come together so you can all get your own lives back to normal. I'm just about to go into the busiest pub in Lambourn. I'm meeting Stonebanks here. We're really hopeful of picking up something on Monroe very soon.'

'I'll say a prayer.'

'It's a deal. I'd better get in here. I'll call you as soon as I have something.'

It was Friday evening. The pub was busy, smoky, noisy with music and chatter. The talk was as it had been in this pub on Friday nights since it had opened in the thirties, of hopes for tomorrow, the big racing day of the week. Half-drunk lads boasted of how far their horse would win next day, placed side bets with doubters, mocked others making similar claims. At the bar and in corners, tips were whispered and gossip exchanged. Frankie and Stonebanks moved around, chatting to lads, to girls, trying to pick up any scrap that might lead them to Monroe.

The pub grew warmer as it became busier, and a young blonde girl playing pool hauled off the heavy yellow sweater she wore, pulling up the skimpy blue T-shirt underneath to reveal her black bra. The lads around the pool table made various noises and one of the girls shouted loudly, 'Ooohh, Belinda!'

Frankie was close by, and he smiled with the others as Belinda pulled her T-shirt down again and leant forward to make a shot.

Frankie noticed a heavy locket dangling from her throat. He moved closer. The locket was swinging slightly. It was a gold case with a clear front. Inside it was a lock of dark hair. Belinda played her shot. Frankie went up to her and nodded toward her locket. 'You looked after Zuiderzie?'

She smiled widely at being recognized. That's right.'

'If you let me borrow what's in your locket for twenty-four hours I think I'll be able to tell you exactly how he died.'

Late afternoon, the next day, the call came which told them that the DNA analysis on the horsehair from Belinda's locket matched that taken from the flesh and hair found at the place where the supposed Ulysses' carcass had been left. Stonebanks smiled at Frankie. 'Well done! You were absolutely right!' Frankie shook the outstretched hand, smiling widely and feeling a strange satisfaction, a contentment he'd never experienced.

'It was Zuiderzie, not Ulysses,' he said to no one in particular.

Stonebanks pumped his hand. 'Ulysses may well still be on his travels, my friend!'

Frankie picked up his jacket. 'And I'm on mine. The Cassidys deserve to get this news face to face.'

'You just want to see them smile, and take the plaudits! ' Stonebanks said.

'You'll get your fair share of credit, don't worry!' Frankie laughed.

Stonebanks put an arm on his shoulder. 'Only kidding, Frankie. You deserve it all.'

Frankie was halfway out of the door when he turned. 'You sure you don't mind me going to Shropshire? Don't mind carrying on ferreting around down here for some news on Monroe?'

'I don't mind at all. Stay a few days if you want. We can keep in touch by phone.'

'No. I mean, thanks Geoff, but no. There's too much to be done down here. Somebody must know something about Monroe's whereabouts. If the horses are still alive, somebody must know where they are. They need looking after, vets, shoes and all the other stuff. Somebody must know something. I'll be back tomorrow.'

Stonebanks held his hands up. 'Fine, fine. It's your call, Frankie boy. If you change your mind, just let me know.'

39

On the drive north, Frankie decided to call Maggie and give her advance warning of the news he was bringing. The decision on telling Graham that the Cheltenham body was not Gabby was one she'd have to make. If Frankie arrived unannounced, it might be much more difficult to pull Maggie aside and tell her. It would be easier to do it this way.

When she put the phone down, Maggie was elated, but she had already decided not to tell Graham about Ulysses. Although it was certain that the carcass Graham had seen at Cheltenham had not been that of Gabby, Frankie had told her to think long and hard before telling him right now. Both horses could have been killed by Monroe since then if he had panicked, and Maggie was terribly afraid that Graham wouldn't be able to withstand another let-down if she built his hopes up now. She'd asked Frankie if he'd have dinner with them and went to the kitchen now with a spring in her step, but trying not to raise her hopes too high.

Jane and Sean arrived home that afternoon. She'd told them that the police and Frankie and his colleagues were doing everything they could to find Gabby, but she was sure that Sean had other things on his mind. She'd taken to him immediately and told him he could stay as long as he wanted. She went now to tell them that Frankie was on his way and would be having dinner with them.

Frankie was talking to Maggie as she filled the dinner plates with roast pork, potatoes and vegetables. Billy came running in giggling, with a smiling Jane hot on his heels and Sean just behind them. 'Settle down, please!' Maggie ordered, carrying the plates to the table.

'I'll get you later!' Jane promised Billy who pulled a face. 'Hi Frankie.'

'Hello. Did you have a good break in Ireland?'

'Yes, thanks.'

'I see you captured one of the natives,' Frankie said, nodding toward Sean who stood awkwardly in the middle of the kitchen.

'That's Sean. He's my boyfriend.'

Frankie walked over to Sean and held out his hand. 'Pleased to meet you, Sean.'

Sean shook Frankie's hand. 'Hello, Father.'

Everyone looked at Sean. Jane said, 'He's not a priest anymore, Sean.'

Sean blushed pink. 'Sorry.'

Frankie chuckled. 'Nothing to be sorry about, Sean. Call me Frankie.'

Sean nodded. Maggie said, 'Shall we sit down?'

Billy watched where Frankie made for, and quickly moved to be alongside him. Jane, Sean and Maggie sat opposite. Frankie spent time gently coaxing Sean into conversation, talking about Dublin and the parts of it they knew. But Frankie made sure he included Billy in the chat. He liked Billy and knew the boy looked up to him for some reason. Maggie had told Frankie how worried Billy was about his father.

'How's the inventing going?'

'I'm working on, well, trying to think up a device for protecting horses against getting kidnapped.'

Maggie and Frankie glanced at each other. Maggie had told Frankie she'd been hoping they could avoid talking too much about the kidnap. Sean had done a lot to take Jane's mind off it but Billy seemed, understandably, obsessed by it. Maggie knew that Billy's motives were centred on his father, not the horse. Getting the horse back, for Billy, was just a means to getting his father back.

Now Sean joined in. 'Maybe they could put those microchips into horses. That's what they've started doing with the ponies in Dublin. Then you'd know where they were all the time.'

Billy nodded. 'That's a good idea, but I thought that any criminals might just cut the horse open and take it out. They put the chips just under the skin so they'd probably be easy to cut out. But it is a good idea.'

Maggie looked at her son with pride. She thought it very kind of him to handle the rejection of Sean's idea so well.

'Maybe they could bury them deeper in the horses,' Jane said protectively.

Billy nodded. 'Maybe.'

Jane looked at Frankie. 'Mum said you're making progress, Frankie. Do you really think we'll get Gabby back?'

Frankie looked at Maggie who shrugged slightly and half-smiled as though to say, "We're into it now, might as well go with the flow." Frankie said, 'We've a very strong suspect, a man called Gerry Monroe. Your mum and dad have identified him as the fella who stole the money and we're almost certain he has Gabby and at least one other horse. The police are looking for him here and in Ireland.'

'In Ireland?' Jane asked.

'We know he took a horsebox there, one he stole from his employers. He went there not long after kidnapping Gabby.'

'So Gabby might be in Ireland and we've just left there,' Jane said.

'All we know for sure is that the horsebox went there. We're kind of assuming Monroe was driving it and that the horses were inside. There's a big reward for anyone who can tell us where Monroe is. Your mum put up the money.'

Jane turned to her mother. 'How much, Mum?'

'Fifty thousand pounds. But only if Monroe's caught and the money he stole is returned.'

Jane nodded. 'That's good.'

'Mum,' Billy said, 'couldn't we have another reward just for getting the horse back? That's what Dad needs. It doesn't really matter about this Monroe guy.'

Maggie looked at him tenderly as she realized how thoughtless she'd been. 'Yes, Billy, we could. And we should. Shouldn't we, Frankie?'

'Sure. Of course. I'll talk to the police about it.' He glanced at Maggie and she suddenly realized the spot she'd put him in. Only a few people knew that the dead horses were not Ulysses and Angel Gabriel. The press certainly didn't know.

Jane said, 'But we want to catch this man, too, Monroe, don't we?'

'Without a doubt,' Frankie said.

There were a few seconds of silence then Sean said, 'I have a piece of paper that says Gerry Monroe on it with a phone number… and some directions to a house… near Lambourn.'

Everyone looked at Sean, and his brow furrowed in a frown and he sat quite still. Frankie said, 'Can I ask where you got it, this paper?'

Sean looked at him silently for a moment then said, 'I took it out of me da's pocket when he was drunk one night. I… I thought it might be money. He never ever gave me any money and I needed to buy things for the house.'

'It's OK, Sean. You've done nothing wrong. When was this that you took the paper?'

'Twould be a while back, a long while. 'Twas after me da had been to England on a message for Kelly Corell.'

Frankie opened his mouth to speak then stopped, as though pondering, seeking the best words. 'Kelly Corell from Dublin?'

'That's right. The gangster fella. I was–' He stopped as Jane jabbed his thigh with the butt of her fork.

'Your da worked for Mister Corell?' Frankie asked.

'He did. He's his chauffeur mostly, but he does a lot of things for him.' Sean didn't seem to realize he'd lapsed into the present tense. Jane sat staring straight ahead as though conscious of her mother's ever-widening eyes on her, as Sean's background began taking shape.

Frankie said, 'And you still say you have this paper, Sean?'

'Tis in me room at home. On top o' the chest o' drawers. At least it was when I was last in there for I threw it there and haven't tidied up since.'

Frankie and Maggie smiled at his honesty. Sean said, 'D'ye think it might be the same fella, the one yer after?'

'It might and it might not, but I wouldn't mind seeing the paper. How would you feel about flying over with me tomorrow?'

Sean looked at Jane. She nodded vigorously. Sean said, 'Will it be OK to come back with you too?' Frankie laughed. 'Of course it will!'

In a corner of the departure lounge at Dublin Airport, Frankie waited while Stonebanks ran through in his mind the directions Frankie had just read to him from the paper. 'I think it might be Kennedy's old place. I'd heard someone bought it last year.'

'Do you know who?' Frankie asked.

'I don't, but I could try and find out.'

'My car's at Liverpool Airport, but I'm going to fly back to London and come straight to your place if that's OK.'

'Of course. I'll see what I can dig up by the time you get here.'

Frankie put his phone away and turned to Sean. 'Hungry?'

'I'm fine thanks.'

'Want a drink, then?'

Sean nodded. 'Yes, please.'

They sat at the table, Frankie with a mug of cappuccino and Sean with a glass of Coke. Frankie said, 'Are you sure you don't mind going back via London?'

Sean shook his head. 'I don't mind.'

'I can put you on a train to Crewe. Jane and her ma will come and pick you up there.'

Sean nodded. Frankie smiled and said, 'You'll not be away from her too long then. I'm sure you'd rather have Jane's company than mine.'

Sean shrugged and drank some Coke. Frankie wondered what was going through his mind. The kid must be totally bewildered by all that had happened in the last few days. 'I was sorry to hear about your da,' Frankie said. 'It couldn't have been easy for you going back there today.'

'D'ye think Kelly Corell is involved with kidnapping the horses?'

'I don't know. I hope in a way he isn't, for I hear he's not a very nice man at all.'

'He killed me da.'

Frankie stared at him. 'He killed your da?'

Sean, grim-faced, nodded and sucked Coke through his straw. 'Jane said I wasn't to tell her ma right away until she gets to know me better, so would you please not tell her?'

'I won't tell her without your permission.'

Sean nodded again and said, 'Me da's supposed to have stole ten grand off him, but I don't believe he did.'

Frankie, taken aback at the cool way Sean was talking about the murder of his father, said, 'Have you been to the police?'

'They said it was suicide and that they wouldn't want to be wasting time on it but everybody knows it wasn't suicide, for Pat Pusey and the rest of Corell's men had been lookin for me da for a while. That's how me and Jane met. Pat Pusey had me by the throat down at the ferry terminal tryin' to get out of me where me da was and me not havin' seen him for ages. I couldn't tell him and wouldn't've even if I knew.'

'I'm sure you wouldn't. Did you tell the police this?'

'Jane told them but they paid no heed.'

Frankie shook his head. 'Let's see what comes out of all this kidnapping business. See if Corell is involved and then we'll go back to the police. I have some friends in England who know some people pretty high up in the Garda.'

'They'll not do anything about Kelly Corell for he has the guards in his pocket, so he has. He pays them bribes and has stuff to blackmail a few of them.'

'Well, let's just see.'

'So d'ye think me da might have had somethin' to do with the kidnappin' with him havin' that paper with Monroe's name on it?'

'I don't know, Sean. Maybe not. I think Mister Monroe was into more than just kidnapping. It could have been something else completely. The ten grand your da's supposed to have stolen, what was the story behind that, do you know?'

'He was supposed to take the money to a man in England and he never turned up is what they say, but I don't know for I hadn't seen him for a while and he never said much to me anyway.' Frankie nodded, watching Sean's face, trying to imagine the life he'd had, the relationship with his father. 'Do ye think those directions mean somethin'?' Sean asked.

'Might do. Might be something. Might be nothing.'

'What will you do when ye get back, will ye be goin' to that place?'

'I think we probably will.'

'Can I come?'

Frankie hesitated. Sean said, 'Me da must've been there, or he wouldn't have had those directions in his pocket. I'd like to come with you and see where he'd been when he was over in England.'

'Can we wait and see how the land lies when we get to London?'

'OK. It's just that if all this has anythin' to do with why me da was killed, I'd like to try and help.' Their flight was announced on the PA system. Frankie stood and smiled at Sean. 'That's fair enough. We just need to see how best you can do that. Ready to go?'

Sean got up. As they walked toward the departure gate Sean looked up at Frankie and said, 'Was it hard bein' a priest? Is that why ye left?'

Frankie smiled and put his hand on Sean's shoulder. 'I'll tell you about it on the flight.'

40

It was late evening when they got to Stonebanks' house. Frankie had spoken to Maggie, and Sean to Jane; he was staying with Frankie at least until tomorrow. Sean watched Stonebanks and Frankie sitting side by side at the kitchen table. The piece of paper with the directions and phone number lay in front of them. He'd liked Stonebanks when Frankie introduced him and he liked Frankie too, and wondered why couldn't he have had one of them for his da? He felt guilty for thinking that and apologized silently to his father.

Stonebanks tapped at the paper with a pen and said, 'The number is Monroe's mobile, I checked it with his ex-employer.'

'What about the house?' Frankie asked. The man who owns it, did you manage to find anything on him?'

'It was bought almost a year ago by a company called One Point Four Limited based in Jersey. I'm trying to find out more about the directors and stuff but it's hard work. Anyway, the word is that somebody is definitely living there.'

Frankie nodded. 'Want to go and have a look?'

Stonebanks grimaced. 'We just need to be careful here, Frankie. It's not a licensed premises. We've got no jurisdiction.'

'So we're out driving, we take a wrong turn and stop at a house for directions.'

Sean was all for this idea, but he saw Stonebanks shake his head. 'It's not that kind of place, Frankie. It's remote. Sits in the middle of the woods at the end of an old track. Anyone taking a wrong turn off that road, anyone with any sense, would turn round again before he got anywhere near the house.'

'It's dark, Geoff,' Frankie pointed out. 'We can drive so far and walk the rest.'

'And how are we supposed to see where we're going?'

'Take a torch,' Sean suggested.

Frankie smiled. 'There y'are. That's the answer.'

Sean said, 'If anybody comes out youse can say I got lost and youse were out lookin' for me.' Frankie said, 'That's a good idea, Geoff. At least, if we do meet anyone and Sean's with us, it'll make it look less suspicious on our side. It's not as if you'd take a boy with you if you were up to anything, is it? No offence to you, Sean.'

Stonebanks sighed and stood up.

The flashlight stayed unlit as they walked down the track toward the house. The full moon gave sufficient light through the leafless trees, bright enough, at times, to cast shadows. The sound of their shoes on the gritty track seemed loud to a nervous Stonebanks. He said quietly, 'I think the house is just around this bend.'

The house was in view from around the bend but still two hundred yards away. Lights showed through three ground-floor windows. They moved forward cautiously and were still a hundred yards away when Sean whispered, 'I think there's a camera on top of the gate.'

They stopped. Frankie and Stonebanks tried to focus on the gates. Frankie said, 'I think you're right, Sean.'

'We'd best go back,' Stonebanks decided. 'We can get the police here in the morning.'

'Geoff,' Frankie said, 'whoever's in there could be gone in the morning.'

Stonebanks turned to face him. 'Frankie, this is getting a bit out of our league now. We should go back.' Frankie stood silent. Stonebanks said, 'Can you picture the tape off that camera getting played in court or on TV or something with us creeping around a private citizen's house, two Jockey Club Security Department officials with a teenage kid? No offence, Sean.'

Sean said, 'I could climb up there and cover up the camera.'

'You could Sean,' Frankie agreed, 'but I think we can maybe find another way in.'

'Frankie, come on, for God's sake!' Stonebanks said in frustration.

'No, Geoff, I don't want to let this go. You've got to admit I've been patient. I took your advice in not going straight for Culling, in trying to get Monroe first. As soon as we get Monroe, I can get the man who was responsible for killing my wife. Monroe might be in that house now. I can't just turn around now and go and sleep easily tonight. Do you think you could if you were me?'

'I don't know Frankie. I just don't know!' He seemed rattled.

Frankie reached to grasp his arm. 'Why don't you go back to the car and wait?'

'What are you actually going to do?' Stonebanks asked.

'Just have a little wander around the back. There must be another way in.'

'Then what?'

'I'm going to try and look through those windows. If I see Monroe, you can call the police then. I won't go any further than that.'

Stonebanks rubbed his face with both hands. 'Promise?'

'Promise.'

They stepped off the track into the woods and continued toward the house. Twenty minutes later, after skirting the perimeter, they stood touching the eight-foot-high railings, which they now knew surrounded the whole property. Stonebanks said, 'This must have cost a fortune.'

'Whatever they're doing in there,' Frankie said, 'They're not taking many chances, are they?'

'I could climb that easy,' Sean offered.

'No!' Stonebanks said.

Frankie said, 'I could climb it pretty easily myself, I reckon.'

Stonebanks sighed heavily and said resignedly, 'I'll wait here.'

'Give us a boost then!' Sean said. Frankie helped Sean over and Stonebanks helped Frankie. Where Sean had scrambled easily down the other side, Frankie jumped, landing awkwardly and rolling in the wet grass. 'Ye alright?' Sean whispered.

'I am.'

They moved toward the windows, picking their way across the gravel driveway. Frankie was aware of the sudden heightening of his senses as the adrenaline kicked in. He thought of Kathy. The fact that she would have loved this and that he was doing it for her helped him feel close to her again. He glanced across at Sean, light from the windows on his face now. He looked alert but very calm, and Frankie recalled the scrapes he used to get into as a boy and realized that Sean would probably see this as tame compared to some of the things he'd done.

They reached the first window, Frankie at one side, Sean at the other, Frankie moved just enough to squint through the glass. Sean, watching, copied him. They saw no one inside. Frankie crouched and crept toward Sean. Sean followed him around the corner to the next window. The pane was frosted. They stood listening. The clink of glass on glass could be heard from inside.

The final rectangle of light was cast on dark, soft earth. Frankie reckoned it was a flowerbed. Their feet sank almost to the ankles as they crossed it and came alongside the window. Sean ducked this time and went to the other side. Carefully, Frankie moved his head until he could look inside. A man sat in an easy chair, his right profile clearly visible. Beside him on a small circular table was a can of Guinness. He was smoking a cigarette and laughing. The sounds of a TV quiz show were audible. Frankie didn't recognize him.

Sean was looking in too. Then Frankie became aware of Sean turning to stare at him. He glanced across and realized from his face that the boy knew something. Frankie quickly put his finger to his lips and signalled Sean to crouch again and come toward him. When he was by his side, Frankie took his arm and pulled him a few yards further away from the window. 'Do you know him?' he whispered.

'It's Pat Pusey. I think he might be the one who killed me da.'

Frankie leant forward until his face was close to Sean's. 'Are you OK?' he asked.

Sean nodded. Frankie thought he looked shocked. 'Are you sure?'

He nodded again. Frankie took his hand and led him away, crouching past the first two windows they'd looked in. Staying close to the walls, they made their way round to the front of the house. Frankie wanted to stop there and take stock but the moon shone directly on them, and he kept moving until they'd rounded the corner back into deep shadow. He stopped and turned, squatted and pulled Sean to hunker down too. 'Are you alright? Did that spook you, seeing Pusey?'

'A bit, but I'm grand now.'

Frankie smiled and patted his shoulder. 'Good man! Are you fit to have a look round the back of the house with me before we leave?'

'Sure.'

Frankie led again. This side of the house was in darkness. He stopped at the corner and peered round it. He saw some faint lights on a square building, above what looked like stable doors. Shoulder still touching the wall, he crept toward the building, stopping opposite it about twenty feet away. Stables. Both half-doors closed. Frankie and Sean stood silent for a few moments. There was the sound of a shod hoof on concrete. Frankie looked down at Sean. The boy's eyes were wide again, as they'd been when he'd seen Pusey through the window. 'Let's go,' Frankie whispered, and they went across to the box doors. There were five of them, all with the bolt across but none padlocked.

Frankie gently took hold of the galvanized steel bolt and worked it to the left. It squeaked. He stopped. He leant on the upper door to take the pressure off the hasp. The bolt slid smoothly all the way across, and the door opened. He heard movement inside the box, then a head loomed out of the darkness toward him and he stepped back in fright. The head came across the door and the big horse looked at him inquisitively, ears pricked. Frankie had seen many pictures of Angel Gabriel in the Cassidy house; quite a few were head and neck shots as the horse had that distinctive 'Look of Eagles' about him, as Graham Cassidy had said. He reached to stroke the long nose. He couldn't be dead certain but he'd have had a decent wager that this was the horse. There was a strong temptation to use the flashlight, just for a few seconds, to shine it inside and see if the rest of him looked like Angel Gabriel.

He decided not to. Instead, he whispered, 'Gabby!' The horse's ears flicked toward him, but he couldn't be sure if it was a reaction to the name or just the sound. But it made him smile. He looked at Sean and he smiled too, slowly in a way that endeared him to Frankie.

Frankie loosed the bolt on the door to the horse's left; the box was empty. He looked in the one in the right, had to lean over and it took a while for his eyes to adjust to the almost complete darkness. There was a horse there, against the back wall. He opened two remaining boxes. Empty. He shut them all again, having to push gently at the big horse's nose to move his head back into the box.

They went behind the boxes, kept walking until they reached the perimeter fence, then followed it round to where Stonebanks waited. He was holding on to the railings. 'Where've you been?' he asked.

'We took the scenic route, didn't we Sean?'

'We did.'

'Any the wiser?' Stonebanks asked.

Frankie said, 'One of Corell's men is in there with, we think, at least one other person. There are two horses in a stable block at the back. One of them, or should I say the head of one of them, looks very like Angel Gabriel.'

Stonebanks nodded. 'Did you see the other person?'

Frankie shook his head. 'Heard glasses clink in a room. Couldn't see through the window.'

'It could be Monroe,' Stonebanks suggested.

'I think that's not unlikely.'

Frowning, Stonebanks stared at the moon. 'We need a reason to get the police in.'

'How about a positive identification of Angel Gabriel?'

'That would help. How are you going to do it?'

'I'll call Maggie and ask her to drive down now.'

'And shin over the fence?'

'She could bring Jane,' Sean said. 'Jane can climb.'

'Good thinking.' Frankie reached for his mobile.

41

Maggie sped south. Jane was beside her, one minute unable to stop talking, the next silent, biting her nails, which she hadn't done since she'd turned seven. Maggie felt guilty for giving Graham two of those pills upon which he'd become so reliant, but she'd had to ensure he'd sleep soundly until she returned, which might not be until the early hours.

Stonebanks met them as agreed outside the George in Lambourn. He introduced himself and they got into his car. The moon was high as they trekked through the woods, all three in dark clothing. Stonebanks lost his bearings, but Jane put them back on track when she saw the faint light from the house. Frankie and Sean had been back to the house twice. Little had changed. Pusey was still in his chair, although he was asleep. Vague sounds came from the room behind the frosted glass but no one had emerged.

Frankie smiled at Maggie through the railings and Sean did the same at Jane. They received two very strained smiles in return.

Stonebanks helped Jane up on his side and Frankie let her put her feet on his shoulders on the other. When she was safely on the ground, Sean reached to touch her arm, then her hair. Her gaze fixed on Frankie as her hand searched for Sean's hand. He took it. Frankie said, 'You'll be in no danger, Jane. I won't let anything happen to you.'

She nodded. 'You'll be fine, Jane,' Sean said.

Frankie led them along the fence to the back of the house. When the stables came in view, he stopped and turned to the teenagers. 'Just a thought - if it is Gabby, is he likely to make much noise when he sees you?'

Jane shrugged. 'He could. He might,' she whispered nervously.

Frankie thought about it. 'If you stayed ten yards away to the side and I got him to stick his neck out of the box, would that be enough for you to tell?'

'Definitely.'

'Good. Let's do that.'

Two minutes later Frankie was again easing back the bolt on the middle door. The horse was waiting this time and his head came out as Frankie opened it, going all the way, so Jane could see him against the weak lights and get what help she could from the moon overhead. She squinted through the darkness then turned to Sean. 'I need to get a bit closer.'

'Get behind me then, crouch down so he doesn't see you,' he whispered.

Jane crouched behind his shoulder, peeking over when she was five yards away. Frankie watched her; he could see only her right eye and forehead in the moonshine, and he saw a tear rise as she nodded her head. Gabby seemed to sense her, to smell her; he turned and whickered softly. Frankie stroked his nose then pushed slowly, Gabby's hooves scraping the floor as he reluctantly backed away.

Jane took a lot of persuading to get back in the car and return home without the horse. It was only when Sean agreed to leave and travel with her that Maggie was able to head north again in the hope they'd get back before Graham woke.

The police were at Hewitt's before midnight, but the plan was to try and do it peacefully, to wait until someone came out to feed the horses next morning. If they were being properly looked after, this should happen quite early, probably while it was still dark.

By six a.m., there were six men inside the grounds; four were armed police, one was a special negotiator, the other was Frankie Houlihan. Concealed in the woods nearby were another dozen armed police. Frankie concluded that if Monroe was still carrying the rifle he'd used to threaten the Cassidys, he was going to be heavily outgunned.

David Hewitt rose within minutes of his alarm clock beeping at six-thirty. He switched on the bedroom light and went to the toilet, then the bathroom. Under the shower, he was planning the day with some excitement. He'd been working long hours this past week and was close to a breakthrough in the project. It had taken a while for him to adjust to the presence of the Irishman in the house, but Pusey had treated it as a holiday, boozing and watching TV. Hewitt admitted to himself that Pusey's overall laid-back approach had helped him calm down and refocus on the project. The threat of Monroe's return, the demands he might make about the two horses, the possibility of the police suddenly turning up - these no longer dominated Hewitt's thinking.

He'd still have preferred not to have the horses there. Apart from the risk of sheltering kidnapped animals, they were too much trouble to look after. He knew Pusey had been told by his boss to make sure the horses stayed there. Hewitt concluded they had their own plans for making money out of them, but Pusey hadn't laid a brush on either of them nor filled a water bucket.

Dressed now, he hurried downstairs. Still, he thought, there was a good chance he was going to make a breakthrough in the next forty-eight hours. Then he could get away from them, away from this house, these woods, back to Marcia, to civilization.

He went outside, pulling on a thick fleece jacket, leaving the door open behind him. The gravel rattled under his boots as he hurried toward the back of the house and the feed room. He stopped, remembering it was always best to get the empty water buckets out of their boxes first. As he reached for the bolt on Ulysses' door, he heard someone speak behind him and his mind registered the slight tension in the voice. This is the police. We are armed. Stand completely still.'

Hewitt had a sensation of this not happening, of watching a movie. He didn't stand still; he turned around with a silly smile on his face. Two policemen in flak jackets and helmets had rifles pointed at his face. The taller one, his voice a higher note now, said, 'Stand still! Don't move!'

A look of horror quickly replaced the smile on Hewitt's face. His legs gave way and he slumped softly to the ground.

Frankie came out from behind the stable block and hurried across to Hewitt. He said to the police, 'It's not Monroe.' Both officers moved closer, their weapons still pointing at the unconscious Hewitt. From his position on one knee, Frankie raised a hand. 'I think you better ease up, fellas. If he opens his eyes now he might die of shock.'

'He might be faking,' the taller one said.

Frankie looked up at him. The big cop crouched quickly and frisked Hewitt, turning him roughly on his stomach to complete the job. Hewitt stirred at this and Frankie signalled to the police to back off a bit. 'You OK?' he asked Hewitt, making sure he filled the man's vision as he turned again on his back and opened his eyes. Hewitt looked bemused. 'I think you just fainted,' Frankie told him. Hewitt blinked and sat up, his face level now with Frankie's. 'I'm a Jockey Club Security Department intelligence officer. Do you feel like talking?'

Hewitt looked stunned and blurted out, 'I didn't steal the horses or the money!'

'I know you didn't. Do you know who did?'

'Monroe.'

'Where is he?'

'I don't know. He brought the horses here on Christmas Day. I haven't seen him since.'

'Has he contacted you in any way?'

'No. Not at all. Honestly.'

'Who else is here with you?'

'A man called Pat Pusey.'

'What's your relationship with him?'

Hewitt rubbed his eyes, tried to gather his thoughts. 'None... none really. He's here to... to sort of help his boss.'

'To help him do what?'

To look after me, I suppose. I'm doing some work for Mister Corell, that's his boss, some important research work. I was getting worried about the behaviour of Gerry Monroe and Mister Corell sent Pusey to... to guard me, '

Frankie looked round then turned again to Hewitt. 'Where is Pusey now?'

'In bed, I think.'

'What time does he normally get up?'

'Between nine and ten, depending on how he's feeling.'

Frankie smiled warmly at Hewitt. 'You look very uncomfortable there and I need to ask you more questions. Is there somewhere we can go where Pusey won't hear us?'

Hewitt thought for a few moments. 'We could go into the cellar. It's just a few yards that way.' Hewitt pointed to the centre of the house wall.

'OK. Would you mind just sitting for a minute or two more while I brief my colleagues?' Hewitt nodded. Frankie clasped his arm and smiled again. 'Good man!' Frankie straightened and walked back toward the house wall, motioning the tall cop to follow him. Frankie spoke quietly to him then went across to the perimeter fence.

Ten minutes later, he was inside the damp cellar with Hewitt. Frankie sat on the corner of a heavy table littered with various pieces of rusting metal and old tools. A vice was fixed to the end opposite Frankie, cobwebs laced between its opened jaws. Hewitt stood a few feet in front of him, shivering every few seconds. A striplight cast a greenish glow on them. The tall cop stood by the inside of the door cradling his weapon.

Frankie wasn't making the headway he'd hoped to. After almost five minutes of questioning, Hewitt too was becoming frustrated. He said, 'Look, Mister Houlihan, I cannot tell you what the project is! It's a professional matter. I'm a scientist. I'm retained by Mister Corell to see the project through and confidentiality is a prerequisite to the success of it. I'm doing nothing illegal.'

'You're harbouring two horses that were kidnapped and a man who is a known criminal in Dublin. The man you admit is your paymaster is one of Europe's biggest gangsters. You admit to paying money regularly to Monroe to bring live animals here for research purposes. Mister Hewitt, even if your project isn't criminal in itself, all the other stuff is making you look very unlikely to be awarded the Upstanding Citizen of the Year medal. You may well find that the Crown Prosecution Service takes a more serious view of your behaviour than you seem to.'

'But—'

'And, even if the police don't prosecute you, Mister Corell is not going to be at all pleased with you when all this gets out. You may have seen the indulgent side of him so far. I know a child who can tell you of Mister Corell's other projects, like the reaction of the sphincter when its owner is fixed to a snooker table with a hammer and six-inch nails. The project to test elasticity of the human body when dropped from two hundred feet onto concrete.'

Hewitt stared at him, unblinking, as though in a trance. Frankie said, 'I'm not kidding you, Mister Hewitt.' Hewitt slowly shook his head. Frankie sighed and continued, 'Look, I'm not too troubled about your project. And I believe you when you say you don't know where Monroe is. But we really need your help in getting evidence on Corell. You tell me you've met him, that he's happy to come here and talk to you. All you need to do is wear a little tiny bug and ask him the right questions.' Hewitt buried his face in his hands and seemed to sag again. Frankie moved forward in support and helped him across to sit on an old wooden chest with steel bands on its lid and rope handles. 'Are you alright?' Frankie asked, softening his voice now. Hewitt hung his head, elbows on knees, hands still hiding his face.

'Jesus God in heaven, what have I got myself into?' he groaned.

'You can get yourself out of it,' Frankie said.

Hewitt looked up. 'I'm a scientist, man! And I'm a coward. I've never been in a fight in my life. Jesus, you saw me faint out there at the sight of a couple of guns. I thought Corell was a straightforward businessman. I thought I was being headhunted from the place I used to work. Do you think I'd be sitting here if I'd known how all this would turn out? My God, I won't even be able to talk if I ever see Mister Corell again, won't even be able to bloody breathe without shitting myself. You might as well ask me to fly in the air as try and deceive this man. Can't you see that? Can't you understand it?' His arms were open in a pleading gesture; his expression was one of despair, of desperation.

Frankie nodded. 'I do see. I'm sorry.' Frankie walked back and leant against the table again, rubbed his tired, gritty eyes and stood thinking for a while. He looked across at Hewitt and asked, 'Has Pat Pusey ever met Gerry Monroe?'

Hewitt shook his head wearily. 'No.'

'Are you sure?'

'He asked me a lot of questions about Monroe, what he was like, what his background was, did I think he was dangerous. He's never met him.'

Frankie was silent again for a few moments, then said, 'What do you want to do?'

Hewitt looked up and Frankie saw hope mixed with fear. 'I want to go home. I want to get my project stuff from the lab and go home.' His voice was weak, like a child's.

Frankie stood up straight. 'Come on then. Your project stuff will have to wait. You can come back for it, but if you want out of here now, I can fix that.'

'Home?'

'Police interview first, I think, but I can see no real reason, if you've been telling me the truth and I think you have, that you won't be home soon. 'Where is home?'

'Norwich.'

'Not that far.' He reached for Hewitt's arm and helped him up.

'Seems a million miles. A lifetime away.'

Frankie led him out of the cellar. The policeman followed, closing the door gently behind him. The first tinge of daybreak showed through. Frankie walked Hewitt toward the fence. 'How are you at climbing railings?' he asked.

42

Back at Stonebanks's house, Frankie relished the mug of tea and bacon roll the big man put in front of him. The two other men in the kitchen were police officers; Trevor Prentice, who was in charge of the squad that had moved in to Hewitt's place, and Kevin Wildman, the negotiator.

Frankie had been impressed by Wildman when he'd been introduced in the early hours of the morning. The man had an air of quiet capability about him, confidence untainted by cockiness. In his mid-thirties, he was compact and fit looking. During the briefing that morning in Stonebanks's house, Frankie grew more certain that they could pull off what they hoped. He knew that to do his job properly, Wildman would need to be cool, unflappable, a good actor. He seemed intelligent. He listened to the brief, asked only pertinent questions, made some notes.

By the time Wildman climbed into the horsebox Stonebanks had arranged, Frankie told his two remaining companions that all they needed was a bit of luck.

Wildman pulled up at the gates, lowered his window, stared aggressively up at the lens of the CCTV camera and leant heavily on his horn. Within two minutes, he saw Pat Pusey walking purposefully toward the gates. When he reached them, Wildman glared at him through the windscreen and stayed on the horn a few seconds longer, before jumping to the ground and walking cockily forward to face Pusey through the bars.

'You Pusey?' Wildman asked.

'Who are you?' Pusey was staring just as aggressively as Wildman. They were like boxers in a nose-to-nose. Wildman said, 'I'm Gerry Monroe and you've got ten grand of mine and two horses.' Pusey seemed confused for a moment then hardened his eyes again. 'Piss off, Monroe. You're a day late and a dollar short.'

'Open the gates, bog man, or your boss doesn't get his project finished.'

'Says who?'

'Says me. I've got Hewitt in the back. You ought to tell him not to go shopping so early in the mornings before his bodyguard's up and about. Or maybe you should get your arse out of bed a bit quicker. Cut down on the old Guinness at night.'

The slightly dazed look was back on Pusey's face as he tried to figure out how to handle this. He said, 'Let me see Hewitt.'

'Let me see my ten grand. And let me in so I can pick up my horses.'

'Your horses, is it? My arse! The horses you stole you mean! The horses you will not now be gettin' back! '

'Oh, I'll be getting them back or you can explain to Corell how you managed to bugger up a year's worth of work and an awful lot of investment.'

Wildman saw the uncertainty begin to deepen in the Irishman. Pusey said, 'Is Hewitt in the back of that horsebox?'

'How do you think I knew you were here? Does anybody else know apart from Hewitt and Corell? D'you think Corell told me? Who else but Hewitt would know you fill yourself with Guinness every night and that you're never out of bed before nine in the morning? Hewitt's in the back with this week's shopping including your two dozen cans of beer. Maybe that'll make you open the gates.'

Pusey looked angry. He moved closer to the gates and said, 'Listen you cocky bastard, just 'cos you nicked a couple of horses from some dopey trainer, don't think you're anywhere near my league. I've put bullet holes in fellas ten times tougher than you.'

Wildman mimicked his accent. 'Ahh now, don't be givin' me all that old bollox your mate Gleeson did. Sure he was full of threats too. But at least he looked the part.' He sneered as he spoke the last sentence.

Pusey reddened quickly. 'Ye think so? Well where d'ye think Brendan Gleeson is now? Gleeson did your ten grand in at cards on the boat - correction, Mister Corell's ten grand. What d'ye think happened to him?'

'What? He had to wash Corell's dishes three nights running?'

'He's dead! I threw him off a twenty-storey block of flats. Three times.'

Wildman sneered again. 'Why? Did you miss the ground with the first two throws?'

Pusey took a step back, put his hands on his hips and stood shaking his head. 'You have got a death wish, Monroe.'

'I've got a wish for my money and my horses, Mister Pusey. Now open the gates and go get the cash and I'll give you back your scientist and ride into the sunset.'

'No. I'll tell you what we'll do. You'll let Hewitt out of the van in the next two minutes then you'll piss off and not come back. Have you got any idea in yer stupid head about how dangerous a man Kelly Corell is? This is a man who doesn't really need people like me to handle people like you. Mister Corell will take great pleasure in doing it himself. He specializes in nailing men to snooker tables and I mean proper men, not boys like you. He cut open his own girlfriend from neck to crotch... these were people who just said something wrong to him. Can you imagine what you're going to get for fecking up this project?'

Wildman put up his hands in mock horror then slowly held them out so Pusey could see them. They were still and steady. 'See how much I'm shaking? Listen to me, Pusey. I'm going to get back into that cab and start the engine. I'm going to reverse a hundred yards then come back as fast as I can. If you want to have gates that actually work, you better make sure they're open. And if I hit them, you can take responsibility for what happens to Hewitt as he bounces around in the back.' Wildman looked coldly through the gates then strode toward the cab and climbed in.

He reversed quickly and changed gear. Pusey moved to the side and punched a code into the control panel. The gates swung silently open as Wildman accelerated. He went through and carried on to the stable block. Pusey followed, reaching in his jacket as he went and producing a pistol. Wildman jumped from the cab and went quickly toward the stable doors. 'Hey, Monroe!' Pusey called. Wildman turned to see Pusey pointing the pistol at his head. He stopped and slowly raised his arms.

'That's more like it, Mister Monroe. That's more respectful. Actions speak louder than words sure enough.' Smiling, he walked toward Wildman, stopping six feet in front of him. 'I'm not hearing so much of yer lip now, big man?' Pusey said.

'I don't talk so well with guns pointing at me. You should have let me see it back there and saved us a lot of time.'

'Yer right, I should have. Now you are goin' to open the back of that van and let Hewitt out.'

'Or?'

'Or I'm going to blow your bollocks off.'

Wildman shrugged. Pusey signalled him round, turning with him. 'Open it.'

He walked wide of Wildman to the rear of the box and watched him reach to undo the door mechanism. They swung open. Wildman hit the button to start the ramp lowering, then moved to the side. Pusey half-turned away to keep the gun trained on Wildman. As the ramp edge reached the gravel, Pusey glanced into the back of the box to see four police marksmen with rifles aimed at him. On the floor was a monitoring and recording machine.

43

Stonebanks had the pleasure of ringing the obnoxious Christopher Benjamin to tell him that Ulysses wasn't dead after all and that the Jockey Club Security Department had retrieved his horse. When the owner recovered from the surprise, he told Stonebanks that his department had failed in its duty by not finding the horse within twenty-four hours of it being stolen, and he warned that Ulysses better be unharmed.

Frankie set off north in the horsebox Wildman had been driving to deliver Angel Gabriel to the Cassidys. They knew he was on his way. Graham Cassidy, out of bed, shaved and fully dressed for the first time in weeks, stood at the window watching the road. After a short time, he had to ask Maggie to bring a stool from the breakfast bar. He eased himself onto it. 'I can't believe how weak my legs are,' he said.

'You haven't used those muscles for a long time.'

He went back to his vigil and his thoughts. He knew that Maggie sensed his wish to sit quietly, his need to try and find his way back into normal life. When the depression finally lifted, he knew the guilt would try hard to bring it back. He had to confront the fact that he'd failed Maggie, failed the family, the horses, the business just when he was needed most. He knew nothing of this would ever be cast in his face, but it didn't ease the ache. Then there was the debt, the huge debt he owed Frankie Houlihan, a man with enough pain of his own, real pain and no family to support him, to see him through it. Frankie had not only held his own life together but Graham's too, the whole family's. There was a proper man. And here was he, a mental wreck, waiting for the real man to bring home his horse. His dream. His life.

The children were outside scanning the road, listening for the horsebox. It was their shouts and screams that brought him off the stool. With Maggie at his side, he went out. Maggie told the children to come away from the entrance so the box could turn in. Jane, Sean and Billy all moved reluctantly, each walking backwards as the roof of the box came along the hedge tops.

It turned in. Frankie straightened the wheel and smiled and waved. When he stopped, the children ran to the back of the box. Graham and Maggie stayed to greet Frankie as he jumped down from the cab and came toward them. Maggie stepped back, and Frankie realized she was putting her husband first. To Frankie, Graham's face looked sad although he was working hard at a smile. He looked gaunt, pale, old. But he managed to open his arms as Frankie reached him and they embraced warmly, Frankie turning him as though in a dance. Neither spoke. Maggie watched as Frankie patted Graham's shoulder gently.

After a minute, Frankie stepped back, holding Graham by the arms. His eyes shone with happiness as he said, 'Let's get him out.' Graham nodded. 'Will you do it?' Frankie said. 'I'll get the ramp down. You go up and lead your horse out, back where he belongs.'

Maggie moved forward and hugged Frankie, briefly but warmly. 'Thank you.' She said quietly.

Frankie squeezed her then broke away. 'Let's get Gabby.'

The children helped with the doors and the ramp. Maggie stopped them from rushing up it. Graham stood at the bottom. Angel Gabriel's head protruded from a stall set at right angles to the rear. The big horse glanced at his trainer, then turned his head away as though he'd fallen out with him. Graham smiled properly for the first time since Christmas Eve. He walked up the ramp. 'Come on, you old bugger,' he said, 'we've got work to do.'

44

Two Garda officers flew over to interview Pat Pusey. They asked him if he would testify against Kelly Corell if they arrested him for the murder of his girlfriend. Pusey refused. They told him if he didn't they'd make sure Corell got a copy of the tape of his conversation with Wildman. They added a plea- bargain offer in his own prosecution for the murder of Brendan Gleeson. Pusey accepted. Corell was arrested that night and charged with the murder of Mary Heaps.

Twenty-three tissue samples from racehorses were found in Hewitt's freezer. Each was labelled with the horse's name and the date the sample had been taken. The six winners Culling had pronounced dead on his operating table were tested, and showed significant amounts of a 'go-faster' drug. After being charged with unauthorized experimentation on animals, and being shown a newspaper report on the arrest for murder of Kelly Corell, Hewitt gave the police details of his project.

He'd been trying to become the first scientist to clone a racehorse. Corell had agreed to fund the research in the belief that clones of top-class horses would allow him to make a fortune in betting and that their subsequent careers at stud would bring in millions of pounds.

Under the most severe pressure, Hewitt continued to insist that he had no knowledge of the whereabouts of Gerry Monroe.

Frankie needed Monroe to get Culling fully on the hook. But despite national publicity about the return of Ulysses and Angel

Gabriel, with frequent mentions of the reward and publication of Monroe's picture, no one had come forward. Frankie had delivered what everyone else wanted out of this mess. He knew he was in serious danger of running out of time in getting what he wanted. All he had to go on was Hewitt's evidence and the doped samples from horses Culling had treated.

Stonebanks stuck to the cautious line he'd taken all along. 'Frankie, what we know is that these horses were doped by someone when they won. They then took seriously ill back at the stables and Culling operated on them. They died on the operating table.'

'Wrong, Geoff,' countered Frankie. 'Hewitt said they were alive when Monroe brought them in. He delivered them and took them away again the same day. So that's one thing we do have Culling on.'

'What we have his word against Hewitt's. Whose would you take?'

'I'd take Hewitt's.'

'Would a jury?'

'I don't know.'

'Even if they were alive when they left Culling's place, I'm not quite sure what he could be charged with. What you really need to prove is that he doped them and I think that is going to be very, very difficult!'

'OK, OK! If he doped them, where does he keep the stuff? If it's at home then let's try and get the police in with a warrant.'

'I used up all my favours getting them to turn out at Hewitt's place in the middle of the night armed to the teeth. We're going to need a lot more evidence to get a warrant authorized for Culling's place.' Frankie shook his head and thought for a while. An idea came to him and he was just about to blurt it out then thought better of it. He said, 'Look, why don't I just pay Culling another visit on my own and see what he says? He's a pretty nervous fella and he might just own up to it.'

'Yes, or he might inject you with some of the stuff he gave the horses! '

'I'll take my chances, Geoff.'

They staked out the entrance to Culling's place. The vet had been on duty at Wincanton. Stonebanks spent the time trying to talk Frankie out of going on his own. They reached a compromise -

to allow Frankie an agreed amount of time in the house. After that, Stonebanks would be coming in to find him.

It was dark when Culling's car nosed through the pillars and along the short drive. 'Give me twenty minutes maximum, then come to the door.' Frankie said. Stonebanks nodded in agreement. Frankie checked the micro-recorder in his inside jacket pocket was switched on.

Culling was undoing his tie when he opened the door; the light shining from behind him on Frankie's smiling face. The vet was in silhouette and Frankie couldn't be sure if he looked shocked. 'Sorry to call unannounced, Mister Culling. My boss and I have been waiting for you to come home.'

Culling looked back out toward the road. Frankie said, 'He stayed in the car. I'll tell you why if you can spare five minutes.'

The vet stared at him, cold-eyed, apprehensive. 'I'm tired, Mister Houlihan. It's been a long day.'

'Been a long season. For everybody.' Frankie returned his cold stare.

'What do you want?' Culling asked.

'I've got a proposal for you.'

'On what?'

'On keeping you out of prison.'

Culling started closing the door. 'Goodnight Mister Houlihan.'

Frankie shrugged. 'Goodnight. I was told to try the easy way and I did. I'll go and get my boss now and the police. See you again shortly.' Frankie turned and started back across the gravel drive.

'OK,' Culling said. 'Come in.'

Frankie turned. 'No thanks. It wasn't me who wanted to give you the chance. My boss told me to do it and I did. You didn't take it.' Frankie started toward the gate again. He heard the vet hurrying after him, felt a hand on his arm. He stopped. Culling stepped in front of him, barring his way. Lights from the porch let Frankie see the film of sweat on the vet's brow. He looked worried.

'I'm sorry,' Culling said. 'Please come in and tell me what your proposal is.'

Frankie stared at him, pursed his lips, looked toward the gate again then turned slowly to walk back to the house.

Culling lead him into the conservatory. 'Would you like a drink?' His voice was shaky.

'No thanks. I just want to pitch this then I'll have done what I've been told to do and I can get out of here.'

Culling's worried look deepened. He joined his fingers, steepled them in front of his still-buttoned jacket. 'Please go on.'

Keeping a note of distaste in his voice, Frankie said, 'Sauceboat. Zuiderzie. Colonialize. Gallopagos. Kilkenny Lass. Broadford Bay.'

Frankie watched Culling's face grow paler. He continued, 'You doped all of them to win. The drug you gave them had side effects, which suited you fine because you knew you'd be the very man the trainer would call. You brought them back here, pretended to operate, then told the trainers they'd died on the table. Monroe picked them up the next day, still alive. Unfortunately for you, he didn't kill them right away. He traded them on to a scientist for experimental purposes. We have the tissue samples the scientist took. They're pumped with dope.'

The vet was pacing, his chin raised as though he was studying the glass roof. Frankie was becoming convinced now that he was confronting Kathy's killer. He paused, knew he needed to concentrate on seeing this through before his emotions overcame him. He focused on keeping his voice cold, that note of distaste in it that was important to the plan. 'Why aren't you looking at me? Because you don't need to, do you? You know the story, Mister Culling. You're just waiting to see the order I'm going to tell it in.' The vet didn't reply. He kept walking. Frankie said, 'Now we come to the bit that really makes me sick. I want you to know that before I tell you it. Despite what you've read about Monroe still being missing, we know where he is. Gerry Monroe's holed up in a little village in the west of Ireland. Somebody higher up than me decided to do a deal with him. That's how we got the two horses back. He's repaid most of the money he stole too and he's put you in the frame. That was the deal.'

'Why would you let him go?' Culling asked.

Frankie stared at him, battling hard with his emotions now, trying to maintain an air of detachment. 'I wouldn't knock it until you've heard the proposal for you.'

Culling cleared his throat and kept walking. Frankie said, 'It wasn't my decision to let Monroe go. He's a thief and a bringer of misery. I can tell you the thinking behind it from higher up... Monroe stole a couple of horses and some money. He's given them back. No big damage done to racing. But we know we have a vet out there doping horses. Major damage to racing if he carries on and gets caught. Damage can be minimized by Jockey Club Security catching him, keeping it in-house, saving the reputation of racing and therefore the industry. All very gallant, Mister Culling, don't you think?' Culling looked more thoughtful now. Frankie went on. 'All just absolutely hunky-dory so long as the poor punters out there never find out what's really been going on. If they did, they'd lose all faith in the product they spend five billion pounds a year on. No betting revenue, no levy payment to racecourses. No racecourses, no industry. So what do we do, Mister Culling? What do we defenders of justice at the Jockey Club do?' He paused. Culling waited. Frankie went on. 'We let criminals walk. Criminals like Monroe. Like you, Mister Culling.'

Culling paced another two lengths of the floor then stopped. He turned to Frankie. 'I think I grasp your proposal, Mister Houlihan, but please dot the i's and cross the t's.'

Frankie didn't find it difficult to put the necessary edge of anger in his voice. 'Not *my* proposal, I want you to remember that!' Culling nodded. 'You write and sign a confession and a resignation letter. You serve out a month's notice during which you will be watched at all times on a racecourse by one of my colleagues. At the end of that month, you disappear from racing forever. If you try to come back at any point, the confession will be used against you.'

Culling sat down in the chair opposite Frankie. 'If all these things had happened and I signed a confession, how do I know you won't take it straight to the police?'

'For the reasons I've just told you. A call to the police from my boss and they'd be in this room now with me ready to charge you formally. We have a tape Monroe made of a conversation with you. We have his written evidence. The bottom line is we don't need your confession. And I personally, as you might have picked up, do not give a toss if you don't sign the confession. I'm all for doing it the hard way.'

Culling joined his hands under his chin. He took a long unblinking look at Frankie, the said, 'How much time do I have to decide?'

Frankie looked at his watch. 'Three minutes. No - how long would it take you to write a confession, maybe two minutes? That means you have one minute to decide, two to write.'

Culling slowly bowed his head, rubbed his face. He stayed that way for a while then said, 'If you knew why I did it, Mister Houlihan… '

There it was. Here he sat. The man who had taken away the most precious thing Frankie had ever had, would ever have in a hundred lifetimes. And he was offering to explain why he did it. Again, Frankie forced himself to concentrate. He needed a signed confession. 'I know why you did it - for money. Same as the rest of them'

Culling bowed his head again. 'No, it wasn't like that! I'm dying, Mister Houlihan! I have a year or two to live, at most…' He went on to tell Frankie of his terror of dying, of suffering the same fate as the last three generations of his family. He told him about the Everlasting Life Company, about the plans he'd had. Told him about 'a bookmaker' (not naming Breslin) and his payments. And Frankie's anger grew. He thought it was all some intricately planned lie that Culling had concocted in advance in case he was ever found out.

The vet looked at him pleadingly. Frankie shook his head slowly. Culling got up. 'Look, look, I'll let you see something…' He went out and came back quickly with a briefcase. He opened it and showed Frankie all the literature from the Everlasting Life Company, gave him the letter accepting him, the certificate guaranteeing a place in their cryogenics capsule. 'Why do you think I live alone?' Culling asked. 'Do you think I don't want a wife and a family like any other man? But why should I indulge myself? How selfish would it have been to marry, to leave a grieving wife behind? How selfish to have children? To afflict another generation? All I ever wanted to do was to have another chance. I haven't spent a penny of that money on myself, on material things. I just wanted a chance to live again, to live like you live, Mister Houlihan! I did what I did so I can live again after death, to bring children into the world who have the same chance as you of seeing seventy or eighty years of life!'

Frankie looked into his eyes, convinced now that Culling hadn't made this up but unsure whether he was seeing madness at work or desperation. He said, 'And you believe these… these charlatans can give you this?'

'The principle is sound! Look at the progress there has been in medicine in the past fifty years. It is virtually certain that someday, disease will be completely eliminated. It might be a hundred or two hundred years but it will happen! '

'And you think they can bring you back to life too, to benefit from it.'

'Yes, I think they'll have advanced that far.'

'To be able to play God?'

Culling nodded vigorously and Frankie saw that he truly believed this, and the rage that had been building in him began to fade. He lowered his head, shaking it slowly in disbelief that Kathy had died not because someone had wanted a yacht or a New York penthouse; she'd been taken away from him because this poor, deluded man wanted to live forever.

Raising his head, he looked at the pathetic, wild-eyed, sweating figure sitting opposite and all he felt was a welling sadness at the pointlessness of it all, at the terrible waste. He needed to leave, to get away from this man. Slowly he rose to his feet. 'Are you going to write a confession or not?'

Culling stood up. 'I'm going to write it. I just wanted you to know why I did it. You seem to despise me. You obviously disagree one hundred per cent with what your bosses have asked you to do. Not your idea, you said, you needed me to know that. Well I need you to know that I didn't do it out of greed or for personal gain.'

'Sure, sure.' Frankie was wearily dismissive. He looked at his watch and said, 'I'm leaving in exactly two minutes.' The vet sighed and left the room. Frankie heard a door bang down the hall. A few minutes later Culling returned and handed him a folded piece of headed paper. Frankie opened it and read it.

'Satisfied?'

Frankie looked into his eyes for a long moment then said, 'Bad question to ask, Mister Culling. Bad question.' And he turned away down the hall and out through the door.

Culling sank into the soft chair in the conservatory, put his head in his hands and wept with relief. Less than an hour later, he heard another knock on the door and recognized Frankie's outline through the glass. When he opened it he saw two uniformed policemen flanking Frankie, and he recognized Stonebanks but not the other man in the long dark coat. Frankie said, 'Mister Culling. This is Detective Sergeant Saunders of Newbury CID. He has your confession and the tape I made.' Frankie sounded exhausted. There was no note of triumph in his voice.

Culling looked terrified. 'You lied!' he said.

'I did.' Frankie took two steps forward and looked straight into Culling's eyes. 'Remember Kathy Houlihan? The girl who died on Sauceboat? I was married to her. You killed my wife. Your foolish, crazy, selfish scheme killed my wife.'

Culling looked horrified. He held his breath as Frankie stared at him for what seemed a long time. Then Frankie turned, head low, shoulders sagging, and walked away, back through the gate and down the road.

45

Throughout February and March, Frankie spent every weekend with the Cassidys. They made sure he was involved as closely as possible with the training of Gabby for the Grand National. And he relished it, loved it. Fridays couldn't come soon enough so that he could travel north. He'd traded off all these winter Saturdays with his colleagues, promising to cover for them in the summer. He just didn't want to miss a minute more than necessary of the of the big horse's preparation for the great race.

His relationship with the whole family developed, bonds strengthened, especially between him and Graham. Maggie said she'd never known her husband talk so much as he talked to Frankie. And Graham steadily began finding himself again, gradually winning back his mental strength in tiny victories. Frankie helped nurture this. He'd seen the damage that had been done to Graham, recognized it, and had wanted to help repair it.

Sean benefited too from Frankie's company, as did Billy, who blossomed and grew in confidence with the praise Frankie gave him, the respect he showed. Jane and Maggie, still strong and whole, watched it all from the sidelines and marvelled at how sensitive and soft and insecure men could be. They saw Frankie begin to heal his own wounds through the way he was ministering again, helping others. Frankie too realized this and found that the steady fading of grief brought no weakening of his relationship with Kathy. It improved it. He thought about her just as often but the thoughts were bringing more and more smiles and fewer tears.

As they moved into Grand National week and Angel Gabriel was flying on the gallops at his best ever, Graham said, Frankie found the anticipation around the yard almost unbearably intense and finally he truly understood the seduction of the training life - the powerful addiction to hope. Three days before the race, he hit the downward slope on the racing roller coaster; Angel Gabriel stood on a stone, bruised his foot and was declared by Graham to be unfit to run in the big race.

The adrenaline they'd all been buzzing on for weeks evaporated in a minute and plunged everyone but Graham into despair. As he led the badly lame Gabby into his box, he stopped to comfort a distraught Frankie with a smile and a slap on the back. That's racing. There's always next year.' And they all knew that Graham was hurting even more than the rest of them, but they took strength from it for they realized he was back to his old self.

In early April, after talking with Sean, Maggie wrote to Sean's mother in London offering her a job and a small cottage. It took Bridget Gleeson three weeks to write back and say no, she was happy in London, but would maybe try and see Sean every Christmas if she could afford the fare.

Culling went for trial in April, as did Corell in Dublin. Culling got five years for the manslaughter of Kathy Houlihan and three years for defrauding punters by doping racehorses. His lawyer managed to get the sentences to run concurrently. Culling named Breslin, and the bookie was charged with conspiracy to defraud and jailed for two years.

After the first day of Corell's trial, somebody with a high-powered rifle shot Pat Pusey dead as he left the courthouse. He had never taken the witness stand. Corell's defence team successfully argued that the tapes of Pusey's conversation with Wildman were inadmissible, that they were the rantings of a small-time crook trying to make himself look bigger by concocting tales of violence and murder. Corell walked free.

On the last day of April, a heat wave drifted slowly across Europe and settled over the British Isles. It was to be the longest since UK weather records began. Maggie and Graham watched their daughter and Sean build their loving relationship in the heat of the summer. After a family discussion, including Sean, they wrote to Bridget Gleeson asking if they could become Sean's legal guardians. She replied quickly this time, saying she'd be more than happy to agree.

Frankie spent much of the summer house hunting. By mid-August, he'd chosen a modern flat in an exclusive complex on the outskirts of Newbury; close enough to Lambourn to keep his eye on the hub and far enough away to avoid the back-stabbing and politics.

By early September, the experts were forecasting the end of the heat wave. There had been little more than a few millimetres of rain since June. Hosepipe bans had long been in force across all populated areas of the country, forest and moorland fires had taken animal and human lives.

At Keshcarrigan in Ireland, the water level at Laura Lake was lower than even the oldest fisherman could remember. Late one Saturday afternoon, the local police took a call from a walker saying he thought that a vehicle was in the lough, a big lorry probably, he could just see the roof. An hour later, divers recovered the bloated, fish-bitten remains of Gerry Monroe. Identification proved difficult, but the registration plate on the horsebox matched the kidnap and cash theft report they'd had on file since the beginning of the year. It was also possible to link the abandoned Kawasaki motorcycle with the false number plates that lay rusting behind the police station.

The divers brought out the expensive suitcase Monroe had stored the money in. The quality of the seals had kept the half-million pounds completely dry.

The Cassidys took Frankie's advice and managed to gain the agreement of the Irish police not to make public the recovery of the cash until a date mutually agreed. It was November when all the papers for their adoption of Sean Gleeson were finally signed and sealed. The Irish police had not contacted them again, so they decided to say nothing publicly about getting their money back. In keeping with their promise of a reward, they deposited fifty thousand pounds in an account for Sean, to which he'd be given access on his eighteenth birthday.

By Christmas, Sean still hadn't got over the shock of it. Often his mind would go back to the night he'd rifled his father's pockets in the hope of finding a fiver. Instead, he'd cursed when he'd pulled out the 'oul' piece of paper the paper that had lain for months in his bedroom because he'd been too lazy to tidy up.

Sometimes he'd wander out at night to talk to Pegasus, who had a warm box now and was properly groomed and fed but no better behaved. 'Fifty grand, Peg, for an oul' piece of paper! Would ye credit it?' And he'd move in close to stroke the grey nose and the pony, disdainful as ever, would nudge him hard back the way he came. 'Oi! Don't push yer luck! There's some real horses here, ye know! Any more of that and ye'll be back tied to yer clothes pole in Joseph's Mansions!'

Dear Reader,

Thank you for buying For Your Sins. We have a number of other titles for sale, and we plan to release three or four new titles a year.

If you would like advance notification of publication, please join our mailing list, which you can find at this website: http://eepurl.com/DytaD

Best wishes
Richard and Joe